THE OTHER BROTHER

KRISTEN GRANATA

DEDICATION

To Kelsi & Addison:
My girls, may you find love that sets your souls on fire, and propels you toward
being even better
versions of yourselves.

PROLOGUE

harlotte

"ARE YOU COMING?" I ASKED.

"Not yet." Dad stuck his head through the kitchen doorway and smiled. "I'll be home in a bit."

I waved and turned around to give the empty bakery a last once-over. The registers had been closed out; the thermostat was set to seventy-eight; the countertops were wiped clean. I jingled my car keys as I strode to the front door and switched off the lights. I jumped when I heard a loud clanging come from the kitchen. I ran to the back of the store and pushed the kitchen door open.

"Dad! Are you—" My feet froze when I saw two large men in black suits standing over my father, lying on his back on the tile floor. Several pots and pans had landed next to him. He wore an expression that I had never seen on him before: terror.

Some say that when you are faced with possible death, your whole life flashes before your eyes. I expected to see a montage of clips in my mind, playing like an old family movie spinning on a reel. I thought I would see my mother when she was alive, or a birthday party in my backyard when I was a child. I did not experience any of that, though.

In those mere seconds we all stared at one another—as if someone had pressed a pause button—all I could focus on was the quiet. I will never forget that silence. It was the sound of my life changing, forever.

The older, rounder, of the two men pointed at me. "Grab her."

"Run!" my father yelled.

My track legs took me all the way to the front of the store before the younger man caught up to me.

"Gotcha!" He grabbed hold of my arm.

I pulled back and tried to shake myself free. I did not want to leave my father with these men, but if I could get out of the bakery, I could get help.

"Stop squirming!" The oaf kicked the kitchen door open with his large, shiny black shoe. "Where do you want her, John?"

John's soulless eyes swept around the room. "Grab that stool and put her next to her father."

Dad was now zip-tied to the handle on the oven door, sitting on a rolling stool. I used to roll around the kitchen on that stool as a kid. Now, a new memory would be attached to it.

Dad could not bring himself to make eye contact with me. I was forced to sit beside him while my wrists were tightly bound to the same handle on the oven.

"Introduce us to your daughter, Frank," John said with a sly smile. "She's very pretty."

I cringed as he made a show of surveying my body. I turned to my father, a mixture of fear and confusion churning in my stomach. "Dad ...?"

"Shut up and listen, blondie," John growled. "Your father here owes us money. We had a deal. Isn't that right, Frank?"

"I told you boys—you will get your money. I just need some extra time. Please, just leave her out of this."

This. What was *this*?

"We already gave you extra time. What the fuck do you think we are—a bill you can make late payments on whenever you need to? That ain't how this works, and you know it."

"How much money do you owe them?"

The younger, still-nameless man stroked my cheek with the back of his hand. "You don't have the kind of money we need, princess."

I jerked my face away from his touch. "Don't touch me."

The two men chuckled. "I like her, Frank," John said. "She's got spunk."

"My father is a man of his word. If he says he's going to pay you back, he will get the money. Why can't you give him more time?" I knew it wouldn't work, but I had to try. I'd seen movies like this, and they did not end well for the people who were tied up.

"Charlotte, stay out of this," my father warned.

"Stay out of this? I'm tied to the oven, Dad!"

My father hung his head. "Please, John. Just let her go, and you can do what you want with me."

John laughed again. "Oh, we're not going to kill you, Frank. You owe us money. You're no good to me dead."

I wanted to heave a sigh of relief, but I could sense a catch coming. If they weren't planning on killing us, what were they going to do? Death might be the better option with these thugs. Dozens of equally horrifying scenarios played in my mind.

"What do you want, then? I can have the money to you by Friday. I swear!" Dad sounded frantic.

John grinned, showing all of his yellowed teeth. "We came to get some insurance."

Dad's eyebrows furrowed.

John pointed to me.

My heart pounded in my throat as the younger man stepped toward me with a pocket-knife in hand and cut one of my wrists free, holding it tightly in his hands. Tears flooded my vision. I tried as hard as I could not to let them escape. I did not want to give these goons the satisfaction of seeing me cry.

"John, Tommy, please," Dad begged. "Please don't do this. I will have your money by Friday. You have my word."

"Oh, we're going to make sure of that," John said in a low voice. His eyes darted to Tommy. "Do it."

Without hesitation, Tommy snapped my wrist like a twig.

A scream forced it way out of me, and the tears came out with it. I had tried to be tough, but the pain in my wrist was too much to bear. I lifted my leg and kicked Tommy's shin as hard as I could from my seated position.

Tommy lurched forward, grabbing his shin. "Ow, you bitch!" He swung his arm and backhanded me across my cheek.

"Stop!" Dad screamed. "Please, stop!"

John cackled. "Fifty-thousand dollars, blondie. That's how much money your old man owes us. Take that wrist as a warning. If we don't get our money by Friday, your other wrist is next."

Tommy cut my right arm loose, and then Dad's.

Dad wrapped his arms around me, tears streaming down his face. "Charlotte, I am so sorry. I'm so sorry!"

I backed away from him, cradling my wrist. My protector, the man I once sought comfort from, was now a stranger.

John and Tommy were halfway out the door at the far end of the kitchen when John looked back and grinned evilly. "You should get that wrist checked out. It looks broken."

I grabbed a ladle, the closest thing within reach, and hurled it at him with all my might. The spoon barely missed his shoulder, bouncing off the door frame. He threw his head back and laughed as he closed the door behind him.

"Come on, honey. I'll take you to the hospital." Dad wiped his tears with the back of his hand.

"How are you going to get $50,000 by Friday?"

"Don't worry about that. Let's go. When we get to the hospital, we'll say that you fell and landed on your wrist."

The lies rolled off his tongue so easily. How had I not known? How had I not seen it? A tornado of questions swirled in my head. I leaned against the counter to steady myself. "Those guys are coming back in seven days, Dad. I don't want my other wrist broken, too. How are you getting that money?"

He sighed, rubbing the stubble on top of his head. "Can we talk about it on the way to the hospital?"

The sooner I get to the hospital, the sooner I'll get pain meds. I turned without a word and exited the kitchen.

Outside, I scanned the empty parking lot while Dad locked the shop door. I knew John and Tommy were gone, but they had left me with a frightened feeling in addition to my purple, swollen wrist. The pain was so bad I wanted to vomit, but the pain of my father's secret hurt worse than any broken bone ever could.

As my father drove to the hospital, I studied him out of the corner of my eye. With his round face and brown eyes, we did not look alike, though we shared the same nose. I was the spitting image of my mother. Did Mom see what just happened? What would she say in this situation, if she were still here?

"I'm still your dad, you know. I'm the same person you've known your whole life."

I shook my head. "The man I know would never get involved with people like that."

"It's complicated."

"Well, you need to figure out how to un-complicate things before those guys come back."

It was silent for the remainder of the car ride, and I was relieved. Anger mounted inside me, and I needed to regain my composure before we got to the hospital. My wrist and I were now part of Dad's lie, and I needed a story that would be both believable and easy enough to remember when I retold it.

When he parked, Dad unclipped his seatbelt and turned to face me. "I really am sorry about this, Charlotte. I never wanted to drag you into my mess."

I pulled on the door handle and stepped out of the car. I wanted to reassure Dad that everything was okay ... but it wasn't. I had a habit of holding grudges against those who betrayed me. I never thought I would have a grudge to hold against my own father. After my mother died, it was just the two of us. We were inseparable. We told each other everything, or so I thought. What had happened along the way?

I insisted that he stay in the waiting room while I had my wrist x-rayed. I needed to think of a plan, and I could not do it with his guilt-filled eyes on me. He wore the same expression when he told me Mom was going to die. And I would now do the same thing I did then: try to make it all better.

As expected, my wrist was broken and needed to be casted. I had just graduated high school, and now instead of spending my summer in the pool, I'd be spending it in a bright pink cast.

I raised my arm when I returned to my father in the waiting room. "My consolation prize after our fun night."

He put his arms around me, but I remained stiff.

On the ride home, I gazed out the window at the palm trees as we passed by. Apalachicola, Florida had always been my home. I had friends. I was on the track team. I'd had a normal life. Until tonight.

When I told Dad my plan, he remained quiet. I knew he was trying to think of another way out of this mess.

He pulled into our driveway, killed the engine, and sighed heavily. "That bakery has been in our family since before you were born. Your mother loved that place. It's all we have left of her."

I nodded.

"You can say it. I know what you're thinking."

"What am I thinking?"

"You're thinking, if it meant that much to me, then I would not have gotten involved with those guys in the first place. I wouldn't have put my business and my daughter in jeopardy."

I nodded again. I could not deny it. Not even for him.

"It's hard to explain. Sometimes you think you're making the right choices in life, but those choices can turn out to be the wrong ones, and you just didn't foresee how badly it could go."

I looked down at my cast. "Every choice has a consequence. Now we both have to deal with the consequence of your choice."

"I don't know what to do."

I took a deep breath. "My plan is the only way."

Chapter One

CHARLOTTE

"Oh my God. There she is," Mallory whispered.

I followed the direction of her less-than-discreet pointer finger. Two girls walked through the cafeteria. One had coppery red hair and she bounced when she walked. The brunette she was with had thick curls cascading down her back, and her left arm was cradled in a sling. Everyone's animated conversations suddenly turned into hushed murmurs as the two friends made their way across the room.

"Should I know who that is?"

"Don't you watch the news?" Mallory hissed.

"I don't like to watch the news."

"The girl with the curly hair—that's Merritt. She was just in a coma for two weeks. She was in an awful car accident."

"What happened?"

"Her father killed himself. She showed up to his funeral completely wasted, and on the way home she crashed her car right into a tree. Head-on collision. The whole thing burst into flames. Someone pulled her out and saved her life, but no one knows who it was."

I now felt guilty for gawking at the poor girl and shifted my attention to my half-eaten slice of pizza. "This is exactly why I don't watch the news."

Mallory waved her hand, her voice returning to its normal volume of three hundred. "Please. This isn't your small town in East Bumble-fuck. Bad shit happens. All. The. Time."

I took a sip of soda. "Bad shit happens in East Bumble, too." Little did Mallory know, her new friend was well aware of the bad things that could happen—and the bad things one had to do in order to escape it all. My chest tightened as the memories slithered out of the dark corners I locked them in. *No. Not here.* I inhaled deeply, forcing myself to remain in the present.

"Holy balls!"

I jumped, startled out of my thoughts. "What?"

"Chase Brooks is talking to Merritt! First, she gets rescued from certain death, and now this. That is one lucky bitch."

"Her father committed suicide, and she was in a horrible accident. I wouldn't exactly call her lucky."

"If you knew who Chase was, you'd understand how lucky she is. Look."

I looked over my shoulder, trying not to be obvious. Chase was tall, muscular, and blond. He looked like a model from California, chiseled jaw and all.

"Gorgeous, right?"

I shrugged as I turned back around. "He's not bad."

She blinked several times. "Are you a lesbian?"

"No!"

"I'd still be your friend if you were."

"I am not a lesbian, Mal."

"Okay. Point out someone in here that you find attractive." She crossed her arms over her chest, and leaned back in her seat.

"You can't tell if you like someone just by looking at him. It's so much deeper than that. Who cares if he's good-looking if he's not a good person?"

"Your vagina cares."

I cringed at her crudeness. Sensing I had to play along, my eyes swept around the campus cafeteria.

"Come on, Char. You're not picking out your future husband.

You're just looking for someone who is visually appealing to you. That's it."

Across the room, a group of boisterous boys were tossing a football back and forth. They hooted, hollered, and hit on just about every girl who walked through the doors. I continued scanning until I settled on a boy at the far end of their table. With thick dark hair and olive skin, he stared at his phone while he ate lunch. He stood out amongst the crew of rowdy frat boys he was sitting with. Visually appealing was an understatement.

I nodded in his direction. "Him."

"Well, now I know why you don't like Chase."

"Why?"

"Because you like the bad boys."

I stole a second look at him. "How is he a bad boy? He seems so calm and quiet."

"That's not calm and quiet—that's troubled and brooding. That is Tanner Brooks."

"Brooks? Is he related to Chase?"

"Yup. That's Chase's brother. Chase is the sexy, charismatic rock star, and Tanner is ... well, he's just the *other* brother."

"You asked me to find someone good-looking." I shoved a piece of pizza crust into my mouth.

"He is, but I wouldn't touch that one with a ten-foot pole."

"What makes him such a bad guy?"

"I grew up with those boys." She gestured to the group with her fork. "They're typical eighteen-year-olds, for the most part. They're impulsive; they do and say dumb shit; and they'll stick their dicks in any available holes they can find. But Tanner has got major anger issues. He always had a bit of a temper, but it has gotten so much worse over the past couple years. Last year, he punched Jimmy Panico so hard that he had to get homeschooled for the rest of the year." She shook her head. "Honestly, I don't think Jimmy's been right ever since."

"Why the change?"

"No one knows. Chase is nothing like him, and their parents are so nice. Tanner was just born with a chip on his shoulder. Maybe it's steroids."

"People are not born hating the world. Those people usually feel like the world hates *them*."

Her eyebrows lifted. "Wow. That's some insightful shit, Dr. Phil." She stood with her tray in her hands. "Come on. We've got about five minutes, and I need to pee like a racehorse."

I smiled and shook my head as I lifted myself out of my chair. One thing I'd learned living on Staten Island for the past few months was that New Yorkers overdramatized everything. Mallory was loud and proud as she liked to put it. That's how she introduced herself, and I liked her instantly. Everything Mallory said was filled with passion and conviction. She could make a conversation about a dish towel sound interesting. We decided to become friends when we realized we were in three of the same classes this semester. Though we were different in most ways, she was a good friend. I needed that, now more than ever.

College was much different from high school, as was Staten Island from my small town back in Florida. Nobody cared who I was or where I came from. Nobody asked questions. Nobody even noticed me. I went to class, and then I left. I kept to myself. That was it. Despite being one of the few girls here with blond hair and blue eyes, my plan to blend in was off to a great start.

I followed Mallory across the cafeteria to the garbage cans. Like magnets, my eyes found their way to Tanner again. He joined in the conversation with his friends now and then, but he never smiled. His irises were as dark as his hair, and his facial features were set in a natural scowl. *What had happened to him?* Something must have. I tried to picture him punching someone, angry and red-faced, but I couldn't. He looked too calm. Reserved. Stoic.

"Charlotte! Watch out!"

One of the football-playing boys jumped backwards to reach for his friend's overthrown pass and crashed into my tray. My soda spilled all over my shirt, soaking the ends of my hair. Sauce from the pizza remnants on my plate smeared against my chest. All the boys shouted in unison, as if they were at a live football game, making me feel all the more horrified. *So much for blending in.*

The boy who knocked into me turned just as red as I knew I was. He picked up my tray from the floor and set it on top of the trash area. "I am so sorry. Are you okay?" Worry flashed in his bright green eyes as they lowered to my cast.

He was cute. *Why hadn't I noticed him earlier?*

"I'm fine. Just suddenly regretting the decision to add extra ice to my soda."

He smiled and outstretched his hand. "I'm Gabe."

"Charlotte." I shook his hand and mustered up a sheepish smile.

"Nice throw, dipshit!" Mallory screeched to the boy who had thrown the football. "Come on. We're going to be late."

I picked up the empty cup from the floor and tossed it into the trash as I walked toward the exit.

"You're leaving already?" Gabe asked.

I waved as I walked backwards. "I have to get to class."

Gabe pulled a black Sharpie out of his back pocket. "Wait." He closed the distance between us and gestured to my cast. "May I?"

I held my wrist out, watching as he scribbled something onto my cast.

"Call me later."

Mallory tugged on my elbow before I could respond. "Let's go, girl!"

I took the door Mallory was holding open for me and walked outside. "Alright, how dumb do I look?"

"Dumb, no. Wet rat, yes."

Great. We walked briskly down the path, attempting to make it to our building before Professor Ballard started calling attendance. Everyone would already stare at us for walking in after the lecture began; my soaked and sauce-stained shirt would only cause them to stare longer.

Just then, I heard the sound of footsteps hitting the sidewalk behind me. Clutching my purse, I spun around. Both confusion and curiosity collided in my mind.

Tanner Brooks was chasing after me.

. . .

TANNER

MALLORY LEANED IN TO CHARLOTTE'S EAR. "KEEP WALKING."

What the fuck did I ever do to Mal? I slowed to a walk beside Charlotte. She stiffened, keeping her gaze fixed straight ahead. "Gabe's a nice guy, but he's not exactly a gentleman."

"What?" She turned her striking blue eyes toward me.

I tore my shirt over my head and held it out to her. "You're going to be cold sitting in class with a wet shirt."

Her eyes traveled down my torso. Now I had her attention. Girls were so easy. Flash a six-pack at them, and they start drooling.

"Uh ... n-no. No thanks."

No?

"That must be such a foreign word to you." Mallory snickered.

"Fuck off, Mal." I looked back at Charlotte, whose eyes were still glued to my body. Good. She was interested. "Charlotte, I'm Tanner." I draped my shirt over her shoulder and offered her the slight smirk I knew girls loved. "It's nice to meet you."

I turned around before she could reject me again and strutted back in the direction of the cafeteria. Let her get a look at my ass as I walk away. It's a fan favorite.

Who was this girl, and where did she come from? I would have seen her before if she lived on the island. I definitely would've tried to get between her legs. She was eating lunch in the cafeteria, so she must go to school here. Then again, so was I, and I didn't go here. No, I didn't have the luxury of college.

At my car, I swung my work shirt around my shoulders and buttoned it. *Back to reality.*

CHARLOTTE

MY MOUTH FELL OPEN AND I STOOD THERE, BLINKING, AS I watched Tanner walk away. I didn't know if it was from the sheer shock of him giving me the literal shirt off his back, or because I was mesmerized by the way his ass looked in his jeans. That was a good ass to have.

Mallory rolled her eyes. "Reel your tongue in. I'll go find us seats."

I changed in the bathroom and ducked into class. Tanner's shirt smelled like delicious, manly cologne. It was five sizes too big on me, but I was grateful that I did not have to sit in wet embarrassment for the next hour. The air conditioning was cranking in every building in the late-August heat, and I would have been cold. For someone who was preceded by such a scary reputation, Tanner's gesture was thoughtful and kind.

Ten minutes later, in the middle of Professor Ballard's lecture, Mallory passed me a note. I had to stifle a laugh when I unfolded it:

Wipe that dreamy look off your face ... I know what you're thinking.

I QUICKLY SCRIBBLED MY RESPONSE:

Gabe was cute. What's his deal?

MALLORY HUFFED AS SHE WROTE AND THEN TOSSED THE PAPER ONTO my desk the next time Ballard turned to the white board again:

Don't pretend to be sitting there in Tanner's shirt thinking about Gabe.

I GLARED AT HER AND CRUMPLED THE NOTE. IF TANNER WAS

trouble, then I needed to steer clear of him. I had barely escaped my father's drama back in Florida, and all I wanted was a quiet, normal life here in my new residence. I focused on the professor for the remainder of class. However, I did allow myself to inhale the scent of Tanner's shirt several more times before the lecture was over.

When class let out, Mallory and I walked toward the parking lot together. "Don't walk home today. I'll give you a ride. It's sweaty balls out here."

"I'm going straight to the bakery. I can walk."

"Shut up and let me give you a ride."

As grateful as I was, I took my life into my hands every time I got in the car with Mallory. Riding with a New York driver was like a scene out of the movie *Speed*, except there was no bomb aboard the vehicle, and therefore no reason to drive like a maniac.

The shopping plaza was crowded when we arrived. A white Escalade cut in front of us, and Mallory slammed on the brakes for the third time since we'd gotten in the car. She flipped her middle finger and held down her horn as the driver sped past us.

"Jeez, Mal."

"You're in New York now. The people here are crazy. You're going to have to toughen up if you want to survive."

"That's not tough. That's just aggressive driving."

"Beeping your horn is hardly considered aggressive driving. They put the horn here for a reason."

"I highly doubt they put the horn there to accompany your middle finger."

She laughed. "You bet your ass they did! Oh, look! There it is!"

I leaned forward to see out the windshield as she signaled to turn into a parking spot. The name painted on the glass door of Dad's new bakery read *La Dolce Vita* in puffy teal letters. I was admiring the storefront when a silver car quickly turned in front of us, taking the spot we'd been waiting for. Mallory hit the brakes, again, and I braced myself with my hand on the dashboard.

Mallory rolled down her window. "Fuck you, asshole! I'll find where you live and kill your whole family!"

"Jesus Christ, Mallory!"

She opened her mouth and placed her hand on her chest. "We will find another spot. No need to take the Lord's name in vain, Charlotte."

I giggled and sat back in my seat. "You're nuts!"

Mallory whipped into another spot. As I stepped out of the car, I was hit with a foul stench. "What is that smell?" I pinched my nose. "It smells like hot garbage."

Mallory smiled as she puffed out her chest. "That's the smell of Staten Island. Home of 'The Dump.'"

"I heard they closed that down years ago."

"They did. Imagine what it smelled like while it was open."

I grimaced as I pushed my sunglasses to the top of my head. We stepped inside the bakery, and a silver bell knocked against the glass as the door closed behind us. The smell of fresh paint wafted up my nostrils. Everything looked shiny and new. The glass display cases were bare, waiting to be filled with dozens of cookies and cakes. It paled in comparison to our old bakery in Florida, but it was untainted by bad memories of frightening men who snapped bones in half for fun. This was all we had now. It was a good enough place to start over.

Dad emerged from the kitchen. "Hi, girls. What do you think?"

"It looks great in here, Mr. Thompson."

I motioned to the wide storefront window. "You should get some tables and chairs to put by the window here. Maybe a couple outside, too."

"Yeah. This way, people can enjoy the lovely aroma of pollution with their morning croissants," Mallory quipped.

Dad chuckled. "All right. I'll let you pick out the tables if you want."

I ignored his offer. "The teal paint looks great."

"Mom's favorite color. Are you ready to be my main cashier?"

I shook my head fervently. "No, thanks."

"Can I work here, too?" Mallory asked.

Dad smiled. "Of course."

"We're not working here," I said.

"Come on, Charlotte. I could use the extra money, and we would have so much fun working together!"

Dad took a step toward me. "You always loved working in our bakery."

I shot him a *that was before I had my wrist snapped in half by two gangsters because of you* look.

"Please?" Mallory whined.

I let out a defeated sigh. She wouldn't take no for an answer. Not without an explanation, and I knew I didn't have one. "Fine."

Dad and Mallory exchanged triumphant grins.

I knew my friend couldn't understand why I did not want to work with my father. After seeing only a handful of interactions between the two of us, she'd decided that I was "mean" to him. I hated hearing that. Dad and I had always been close, and we'd often dreamed about what it would be like to run the family business together once I was old enough. Now, I wanted nothing to do with the bakery—or him. It was difficult being cold toward him. But it was even harder pretending everything was okay.

Though I was relieved to be twelve hundred miles away from John and Tommy, I still looked over my shoulder everywhere I went. I'd been traumatized, and I carried the constant reminder around on my arm in the form of a cast. I hoped the paranoia would go away in time.

And I hoped it would take the resentment toward my father with it.

Chapter Two

TANNER

Another shitty lunch in this shitty cafeteria of this shitty school. But I needed to get away. Away from my job. Away from my family. Working at my parents' auto body shop had its perks, but those perks were diminishing right along with my father's health. Being here with friends was something that could take my mind off everything for a while, even if they acted like jackasses. I used to find them funny. I didn't find anything funny anymore.

Out of the corner of my eye, I spotted Charlotte. Her blond hair, like strands of gold, caught my attention when she walked through the door. It was rare for anybody to have blonde hair on Staten Island. It was also rare for anyone to have a face like hers. Beautiful. Flawless. *Oh, shit.* She's walking toward me. I put my phone down and my back straightened in my seat.

"Thank you." She held my neatly folded shirt out in front of her. "I washed it. I hope you don't mind. I followed the proper care instructions on the tag."

I raised an eyebrow. *Did she seriously think I gave a shit if she washed it?* "You didn't have to return it."

"Well, I wasn't going to keep it."

"Why not? Probably looks better on you." The image of Charlotte in my shirt and nothing else flashed through my mind.

"I don't need it. I have lots of shirts. I mean, not from other guys. I just mean that I have ... my own ... shirts ... like, in a closet. I bought them ... with my own money."

She's nervous. What was it about me that made her nervous? I hoped it was because she found me attractive, and not because she'd heard what I did to Jimmy Panico. Mostly everybody has been scared of me since that day. I don't want this girl to be scared of me.

"Good. I'm glad you have lots of shirts. I like the one you're wearing." I lowered my gaze to her perky tits sticking out of the top of her neckline. They weren't big, but they were perfectly shaped and bouncy. I'd been thinking about how they would feel in my hands since I saw them outlined through her wet shirt yesterday. Clearly it had been too long since I'd been with a chick if that's all it took to get me going.

She looked down at her tank top, and her cheeks flushed. I'd embarrassed her. She was definitely not like any of the girls I had known. Most of them wanted their tits to be stared at.

"Okay, bye." She turned and walked away.

I could feel the corners of my mouth tugging upward. It had been so long, I almost forgot what it felt like to smile. I wanted to run after her. I wanted to ask how she broke her arm. I wanted to ask why her eyes looked so sad. I wanted to know everything and anything I could about her.

Then, I heard Gabe call her name. Her face brightened when he spoke to her. Her face didn't do that while she was talking to me. It was probably best that I didn't try to pursue things any further with her. I was a piece of shit, and she was an angel. Gabe wasn't good enough for her either—I wasn't sure who would be—but at least he wasn't fucked up like me.

I dumped my tray and headed back to work. My brother was on me as soon as I walked through the garage door of the shop ten minutes later.

"You're late," Chase called from his side of the garage.

"Yeah, well, you were gone for two fucking years. I'm allowed an extra five minutes for lunch."

"When are you going to let that go?"

"When are you going to get off my ass?"

Silence.

My self-righteous older brother had returned from California not too long ago. I wish he hadn't. He was a pain in my fucking ass. I was angry at him for leaving to pursue his dream while I was stuck here. Now, I'm even angrier he returned. Chase being home is yet another reminder of our depressing reality: Dad is dying.

I needed to drown out my thoughts. I reached into my toolbox for my earbuds and stuffed them into my ears. Turning up the music on my iPod, I shoved it into my pocket and got back to work. Burying myself in work was just about the only thing I could do at this point.

Later that afternoon, Mom left to take Dad to another doctor's appointment. Chase went home for the night. I liked being here alone. I preferred solitude. I was in the front office getting ready to close out the register when the door opened. *Fuck me.* I forgot to flip the sign to Closed.

To my surprise, Charlotte walked through the door.

"Charlotte. What are you doing here?" *Did she know I worked here? Was she looking for me?* Judging by the shock on her face, she wasn't.

"I, uh ... I saw the car sitting in the lot out front. It's for sale?"

"You want *that* car?"

"How much are you selling it for?"

"Eight thousand."

Her eyebrows shot up. "That piece of junk is $8,000?"

"That is a 1969 GTO! That is not a piece of junk!"

"It's completely scratched and dented."

"Sure, it needs some body-work and a fresh coat of paint. I know the numbers aren't matching, but it's still a classic."

"Numbers aren't matching?" she echoed.

"You have no idea what I'm talking about, do you?"

"Not in the slightest."

I slid the register drawer closed and dangled a set of keys in front of her face. "Let's go for a drive." I walked around the counter and held the door open with my foot, hoping she would follow.

She walked past me out the door, and I was relieved. Every little inch she gave, I would take. "Do you know how to drive stick?" I asked, knowing damn well that she didn't. Most girls didn't. Especially on this godforsaken island.

She groaned. "It has a stick shift? Forget it."

"That's okay. I'll drive so you can see how it runs."

"There's no point. I can't buy it if I can't drive a stick."

I swung open the passenger door for her. "Just get in the car." I wasn't ready for her to leave.

I sensed her reluctance, but she got inside. Once we were buckled in, I roared the engine to life. I felt Charlotte's gaze as I moved the different levers, maneuvering the vehicle out of the parking lot. I was good with my hands. I wanted her to know that.

I turned down a side street, about to show her what this car was really capable of. Once we were nowhere near the main road, I changed gears and the car took off. At the end, I quickly spun the steering wheel to the left, sending us into a complete 360. Chicks loved this *Fast and Furious* shit.

"Tanner!" she squealed, squeezing her eyelids shut.

Was she scared or excited? I couldn't tell. I thundered back down the road from which we came, skidded around the corner, and finally slowed to a stop when we returned to the shop's parking lot.

Charlotte flung her seat belt off and smacked my shoulder. "What the hell is wrong with you?"

"I wanted to give you a proper test drive."

"Well, you should've warned me that you were going to pull a NASCAR stunt like that!"

"You wouldn't have gotten in the car if I'd told you."

"Exactly."

She looked so adorable with her furrowed eyebrows and her scrunched nose. I had the sudden urge to grab her and kiss her, but I didn't think that would go over so well. "Ah, you're fine," I said, waving my hand. "So, do you want to buy it or not?"

"Like I said: I don't know how to drive stick."

"I can teach you."

She shook her head and stepped out of the car. "No, thanks. I'll find something else."

That's when I noticed black numbers written on her cast that weren't there earlier today. "What's that?"

"My cast?"

"No. The numbers on your cast."

"Oh. Gabe wrote his number on it. After I saw you in the cafeteria. He said he would show me around Staten Island. You know, since I'm new here."

Fucking Gabe. Heat spread throughout my chest. I didn't want her spending time with that guy. I didn't want his hands on her. "Have fun with that creep."

"Creep? Just yesterday you said he was a nice guy."

"He just got dumped by his girlfriend not too long ago, so he's on the rebound and looking to get laid. I'm just saying, I'd be careful if I were you."

"Every guy is looking to get laid. I'm sure you're no different."

"I don't have to look to get laid."

Her face twisted in disgust. "Thanks for the test drive." She swung the passenger door shut and walked away.

I shouldn't have said that about Gabe. I didn't have any right to feel this way about someone who isn't mine. Still, I wanted to show her that I was different. I wanted to show her—to show myself—that I could be the man she deserved.

But I knew better. I'm not worthy of someone like Charlotte. I can't have her. I had to let her go. So, I watched her ass move in her denim shorts as she walked away from me.

CHARLOTTE

I GRIPPED MY CAN OF PEPPER SPRAY IN MY HAND AND STIFFENED every time I heard a car drive past on my daily walk home from school. I had applied for a gun permit my first week in New York. Once I received it, my cast would be off and I would be purchasing a gun. The night John and Tommy came to the bakery, I hadn't been prepared. I was defenseless. I swore I would never feel like that again. If Tommy ever found where I was hiding, I'd be ready.

Ever since we'd left Florida, I'd been suffering with what could only be described as panic attacks. At least, that's what Google told me when I researched my symptoms. *Post-traumatic stress disorder.* Something would trigger a memory and I was instantly back in that bakery, filled with fear. Most of the time, I was able to control the episodes. Other times, I was forced onto the floor gasping for air while I cried.

I breathed a sigh of relief as I approached my apartment complex. Tucking my pepper spray back into my purse, I trudged up five flights of stairs. Though the stairwell was poorly lit, I preferred it to the rickety elevator. Before, I'd never had an issue with confined spaces. Now, I avoided anything that made me feel trapped.

I made a beeline for the shower after locking the front door behind me. Tanner's comment regarding Gabe echoed in my mind. Had Gabe asked me out for sex, or was Tanner lying? Why would Tanner feel the need to lie about something like that? I didn't know what to believe. If Gabe was trouble, Mallory would've told me. Instead, she warned me about Tanner.

Yet, Tanner was the one who'd lent me his shirt, and offered to take the time to teach me how to drive a stick shift. Neither of those gestures seemed to fit with the information I'd heard about him. *What was his deal?* I wanted to know more.

Curiosity killed the cat, Charlotte. I towel-dried my hair and plopped onto my bed. If I wanted to create a new life here, I needed to play it safe. Tanner was *not* safe.

I took out my phone and dialed the numbers inked across my cast.

"Hello?"

"Hi, Gabe. It's Charlotte."

"Hey! Glad you called. I was beginning to think you wouldn't call."

"Nope. I was looking at a car that I wanted to buy."

"Did you buy it?"

"No. I don't know how to drive stick."

"I don't know how, either. I'm sure you'll find something else," he said. "So ... do you wanna hang out?"

"Sure."

"Great. Text me your address. I'll come get you."

As soon as I ended the call, I texted Gabe my address. I got dressed and sat on the barely-there balcony that overlooked the parking lot. *What a view.* If I were in Florida right now, I'd be night swimming with my best friend, Carla, amongst the peaceful chirping of crickets. We'd be belting out Backstreet Boys lyrics, or quoting lines from *Gilmore Girls*, and we'd definitely be discussing the details of Carla's unplanned future wedding to her boyfriend.

Carla had always been there for me ... until I couldn't allow her to be. I disappeared without a call, text, or explanation. For all Carla knows, I was abducted by aliens. Every night, I wished I could call her, even just to let her know I'm okay. I couldn't make a careless mistake though. No one could know where I was. It was safer this way.

Life was so different here. The houses on Staten Island were all crammed on top of each other, without any land or space to separate people from their neighbors. Rap music, wailing sirens, and beeping horns could be heard at all hours of the night. Worst part? I was alone. Sure, I had Mallory, but our friendship was new, and our talks were mostly school-related. I didn't even know if she watched *Gilmore Girls*.

When Gabe arrived, I pushed the memories from my mind with practiced ease and put on a smile. *I live here now, and I have to get used to it.*

Gabe's light brown hair was neatly styled, and his boyish grin spread across his face when he saw me. He wore khaki-colored cargo shorts and a yellow T-shirt. His arms were not as muscular as Tanner's, but he was lean and toned nonetheless. *Why are you comparing him to Tanner, you idiot?* I shook my head, as if that would knock him out of my brain like a coconut from a tree. He shouldn't be in there, no matter how good he looked without a shirt on. *Don't think of him shirtless! Bad, Charlotte. Bad.*

"Are you ready for your tour, miss?" Gabe walked to the passenger door of his black Jeep and swung it open.

"Yes, sir."

"Please remember to keep your hands and feet inside the vehicle at all times, and whatever you do—don't feed the animals."

I giggled as I climbed inside.

"Our first stop is the Woodrow Diner. I ordered us cheeseburgers with fries, to go. I figured we could eat in here while we drive around. Is that okay with you?"

"Sure. Dinner and a show. I can give you the money for my burger." I rummaged through my purse for my wallet.

Gabe took my purse and placed it on the floor by my feet. "Stop. It's my treat."

"Oh." *Was this a date?* "Thank you."

"So, how did you break your wrist?"

"I fell. I was at my dad's bakery. There was some flour on the floor and it was slippery. I landed on my arm, and boom. Broken." I'd rehearsed the lie enough times that it sounded natural when it came out. I hated lying, but it's not like I could admit what really happened.

"Ouch. When do you get it off?"

"Next week. I can't wait."

"I broke my ankle playing soccer when I was a kid. Hurt so bad."

I cringed remembering the pain I'd experienced when Tommy snapped my bone in his bare hands. The memory of the sickening crunch sounded in my ears, turning my stomach.

"Where are you from?"

"Florida."

"Do you miss it?"

"I miss my friends and my pool. I miss seeing the palm trees everywhere. I miss the familiarity of it all."

"In time, this will feel like home, too."

I sure hope so.

After Gabe picked up our food, we ate while he drove us to our next destination. He pointed out random, meaningless places along the way, and I pretended to be interested. Then, he turned the Jeep down a narrow road with trees on either side of us. I did not know such a heavily wooded place existed within the city streets. I would've thought it was beautiful if I wasn't so leery about where he was taking me. I glanced at my purse down by my feet, wondering how quickly I could grab the pepper spray if I needed to.

"I know it looks like I'm taking you down here to kill you," he said, as if reading my mind. "But I promise I'm not."

"What is this place?"

The road we were on opened into a giant parking lot. There were several paths surrounding the parked cars; people were jogging, riding bikes, and walking dogs. The setting sun made for a beautiful backdrop against the thick trees.

"This is Clove Lakes Park. Down that path right there," he said, pointing out his window, "are benches where we can sit by the water and feed the ducks. I figured you'd like it. It's the closest thing we have to Florida."

"Wow. This is so nice."

Gabe parked and jogged around the front of the car to open my door. He reached behind my seat for a bag of birdseed and held out his other hand for me to take as I hopped down. We walked along one of the paths until we reached a clearing by the lake. The sun cast a mixture of pink and orange swirls into the sky. I inhaled deeply as I looked out at the still water. The sour garbage smell did not reach this far north on the island.

We sat on an empty bench near the water's edge. Gabe tossed a handful of seeds to the ducks and they quacked as they waddled over to us.

"I can't believe how calm it is here. It's like we're not even in New York anymore."

Gabe smiled. "I'm glad you like it. I come here for a run almost every day. It's a nice place to get your mind off everything."

I miss running. Why did I stop once I got to New York? "What are you trying to get your mind off of?"

He looked down at the bag of birdseed. "My girlfriend and I broke up last month. We were together for a long time, so it was tough. Running makes me feel at peace." His bright eyes met mine. "It's better now, though."

"How long were you guys together?"

"Most of high school. She said since we're in college now, she wants to do her own thing, and that I should, too."

"Maybe she's right. Now is your chance to go out and experience life, without being attached to someone."

"I'm here with you, so I look at it like she did me a favor."

I smiled, tossing another piece of bread toward the ducks. Was he being sincere, or was he just a smooth talker?

"What about you?"

"What about me?"

"Did you leave behind any broken hearts in Florida?"

I laughed once, looking down at my lap. "No."

Gabe brushed a strand of hair away from my cheek and tucked it behind my ear. His fingertips lingered on my face as he leaned in a bit closer. "I'm glad you called me tonight."

Uh-oh. "Me, too. It's nice to have another friend to hang out with."

Gabe retracted his hand upon my use of the six-letter F-word, and we returned to making small- talk as we fed the ducks.

Tanner had told the truth about Gabe's recent breakup. Was the rest of what he said true, too? Gabe didn't seem like he was trying to get into my pants. If he was, this was a pretty elaborate scheme just for that. Then again, the wool had been pulled over my eyes before. I was not ready to trust anyone at this point. I didn't know if I ever would be.

Chapter Three

TANNER

I looked out the window for the third time in ten minutes. Now that I knew Charlotte walked home every day after school, I tried to catch a glimpse of her passing by. That was all I could have. A glimpse of something I couldn't have.

I shoved another folder into the filing cabinet and glanced up just in time to see Charlotte. Clutching something in her hand, her head tilted toward the ominous sky. The forecast for this afternoon called for heavy rain. *Why didn't she have a car?*

A clap of thunder boomed overhead, and then it down poured. Charlotte was going to get drenched. I snatched my car keys off the nail on the pegboard and grabbed a clean towel from the garage. I sprinted to my car and peeled out of the parking lot.

The poor girl was soaked to the bone when I pulled behind her. She turned around as she heard my hollow exhaust following her and squinted through the deluge to see who I was.

"Get in!" I shouted out the open passenger window.

"I can't! I'm soaked!"

She was worried about my car. *I think I'm in love.* "I have leather seats. It's fine. Just get in!"

She swung open the door and got inside. I lowered the air conditioning and wrapped the towel around her shoulders.

"I'd offer you my shirt again, but you look like you would need my whole outfit." I paused, smirking. "I mean, I'll take my pants off if you want me to."

She ignored my comment and squeezed the water out of her hair with the towel. "Thank you so much for the ride. Where were you headed?"

"Nowhere. I saw you walking past the shop and figured you could use a lift."

"Oh." She looked surprised. People were always surprised when I did something nice. I guess it didn't happen very often. "I'm sorry you had to leave work just for me."

"I'm not." Her wet top, yet again, clung to her tits, and I wanted to peel it off her. It took all the restraint I had not to. She wasn't the kind of girl who got fucked in a car. *Think about something else before you pitch a damn tent in your pants and embarrass yourself.* Car. Tree. Tits. *Fuck.*

"Where to?"

"My apartment is down Rossville."

"Do you have anything going on right now, or can we make a pit stop?"

"No, please. You're doing me the favor, so I'll go wherever you need to go."

Turning down a side street, I pulled the car over and unclipped my seat belt. "Switch seats with me."

"What?"

"I'm going to slide over into your seat. I want you to sit here."

"No way. I know what you're doing. I can't drive this thing."

"Yes, you can. Just switch." Without waiting for her to move or respond, I climbed into her seat.

"Ow!" She grunted as she tried to climb over my legs. "You're too big to do this."

"Yeah, I hear that a lot." I chuckled to myself.

"You're an idiot."

"I hear that a lot, too."

"I can see why."

I didn't want to be a dick, but I enjoyed irritating her.

She sank into the driver's seat and helped me swing my legs onto the passenger side of the car. She had to pull my seat all the way forward to reach the pedals. *Damn.* She looks good in my Mustang.

"All right. The most important thing you need to remember is: If you crash my car, I will have to kill you."

Her eyes widened, and I smirked. "Kidding. Well, sort of."

"We shouldn't be using your car. I don't think I'll be very good at this."

"You'll be fine. Trust me. You've had sex before, right?"

She cocked an eyebrow. "Excuse me?"

"Think of it this way: Driving a stick is like having sex. You have to know your car very well—how it works, what it needs from you, what each noise means. You can't force it. You have to use your whole body and mind to get the vehicle to do what you want it to do."

Her lips parted slightly and then she shook her head. "So, what do I do first?"

"These are your gears. Whenever you want to change a gear, you have to use the clutch." I reached over and pointed to the pedal on the left. "You have to use your left foot to operate the clutch."

"Clutch on the left. Got it."

"The brake pedal is in the middle, and the gas pedal is on the right—just like in a regular car. The trickiest part is changing gears. If you don't get it in the correct spot, it makes a really loud noise." I moved the shifter, and an unpleasant sound screeched throughout the car.

She cringed. "That's terrible."

"We'll take it slow, and I'll help you change gears."

She nodded, squaring herself in the seat, placing her left hand on the steering wheel and her right hand on the shifter. I'd never seen anything sexier.

"If you pop the clutch too quickly, you'll stall the car. Most people do this, so I'm just preparing you ahead of time."

"Do you ever stall the car?"

"I did when I first learned how to drive a stick."

"Who taught you?"

"My dad. He had so much patience with me. I tend to get frustrated very easily."

She nodded as if she already knew this about me.

"The car is in neutral while we're stopped right now. You're going to push the clutch in and shift the gear into first. Then, come off the clutch slowly while pressing on the gas at the same time."

She did as I instructed, but stalled the car on the first try.

"Oh, no."

"That's okay. Try it again."

She exhaled and tried again. This time, the car accelerated.

"Awesome! Now, you'll need to shift into second when you see the needle on the tachometer point to the three."

"I'm going to stall again, aren't I?"

"Probably." I didn't mind. She could burn my transmission up for all I cared. I just needed her to stay with me.

Carefully, she executed each step in the order I told her. She braced herself for the ear-piercing noise, but it never came. The car did not stall and we accelerated down the road.

"I did it!"

I applauded. "That was great. Let's practice slowing down."

She glanced at me out of the corner of her eye. "Can we go up one more gear?"

My eyebrows lifted. "You want to go faster?"

"Maybe one day, you'll teach me how to do a doughnut or pop a wheelie or something."

I threw my head back with laughter. "If you pop a wheelie in anything but a motorcycle, that's not a good thing." *I am going to marry this girl.*

She shrugged. "Okay. I step on the clutch, and then I move this into the number three," she said as she performed each action. "Then, I come off the clutch and step on the gas."

The car lurched forward even faster.

"You're a natural."

"Okay, okay. Help me slow this thing down. I'm getting nervous."

I showed Charlotte how to downshift and she pulled the car off to the side of the road until we came to a stop. I made sure to put the car into Neutral and reached over to turn off the engine.

"What do you think?"

"I think it's going to take me a while to learn how to drive a stick without you in the passenger seat helping me."

"Guess you'll have to take me with you wherever you go."

"Yeah, right."

I wasn't joking. "You can buy the GTO, and I'll help you learn how to drive it."

I could see the wheels turning in her mind as she considered me, holding me captive with her penetrating gaze. I'd remain until she looked away. She always looks away, as if trying to conceal something she didn't want me to see.

"I'd like to buy the car. I just need to go home and get the cash."

"You're going to pay me in cash?"

"Is that a problem?"

"No, cash is fine. Just wondering why you have $8,000 in cash lying around your house."

"My dad is old school. He hides his money under his mattress."

She was lying to me. *But why?* "You should get him a safe. God forbid there is ever a fire, his money is gone."

"Good idea." She pulled the keys out of the ignition and handed them to me.

"Why are you giving me the keys?"

"I have to go home to get the money."

"You don't seriously think I am going to let you walk all the way home, and all the way back here, do you?"

She shrugged.

"You're going to practice driving home."

"Oh, no. I can't do that. I can't drive with real cars on the main road."

"Yes, you can. I am going to help you."

She groaned as I stuck the keys back into the ignition. She was able to shift successfully into first gear as she pulled onto the main road. Her hands were at ten and two, and she sat stiffly in her seat.

I rolled my lips together and suppressed a smile. "You do know the speed limit is forty here, right?"

She shot me a look that made me want to strip her down until she was naked. She had a fire inside her, beneath her good-girl exterior. *Why was she trying to hide it?*

"Yes, I am aware."

"You're not from around here, are you?"

"Nope. Just moved here a few months ago."

"Let me guess. You're from somewhere down south."

"Why? Because I'm not screaming obscenities out my window and honking my horn like a maniac? Just because I moved to New York doesn't mean I have to act like the heathens who live here. I have no problem doing the speed limit and obeying traffic laws."

"You know, you're sexy when you give me attitude."

Her cheeks flushed, and I grinned. I liked watching her reactions from the passenger seat.

"You're right, though. You shouldn't have to change who you are just because you moved to a new town."

"I really just want to blend in."

"Why? Everyone here sucks."

"How do you know I don't suck, too?"

"You're a good person. I can tell."

Her face fell, and she paused before answering. "You don't know me."

"You made sure to follow the wash instructions on my shirt. How terrible could you be?"

She bit back a smile. "That doesn't prove anything."

"Sure, it does. It shows you care."

She pulled up to a red light and turned to face me. "Maybe I'm just very particular about laundry."

"You could be. Still, something tells me you're a good egg. I can feel it." Her eyes lingered on mine, and this time, she didn't look away.

"You should smile more often." Her voice was so soft, I almost didn't catch it.

"Then you should hang around me more often." I'd smile every damn day if she was by my side. She was fucking perfect, and she had no idea. I wanted to show her.

The light turned green, but I wasn't going to tell her that. The longer she remained focused on me, the more I was convinced that she wanted me as much as I wanted her.

The car behind us beeped. Fucker ruined my moment. I could get out and beat him with his own arms.

Charlotte snapped back to reality. Flustered, she didn't remember to press the clutch. The car stalled, but not before making that horrendous grinding metal sound.

"Oh, God! I'm sorry!" Her hands flapped as she tried to figure out where to put them.

"Relax. It's okay. Go through the steps again."

"People are beeping at me! I'm blocking traffic!"

I placed my hand over hers on the shifter. "Take a deep breath and relax. Ignore everyone else. Just go over the steps again. Clutch, gear, clutch, gas."

I helped her guide the shifter into first gear; she released the clutch and stepped on the gas. Within seconds, she was able to accelerate and continue driving. My hand remained on hers to help her until we arrived at her apartment.

"You need to stay here. I'll be right back."

"You not ready for your parents to meet me yet?"

She muttered something as she got out of the car, and a smile tugged at my lips as I watched her disappear into her apartment building. Maybe I'd ask her to dinner when she got back. *Is it too soon?* I'd never asked a girl out on a proper date before.

My phone beeped with a text. My stomach twisted as I read it:

MOM: THE DOCTOR ADVISED US TO STOP THE TREATMENTS. IT ISN'T working, and it's exhausting Dad. The cancer is too aggressive. He said we just have to make Dad comfortable now.

MAKE HIM COMFORTABLE. HOW DO YOU MAKE SOMEONE

comfortable for death? All that time I'd spent trying to be hopeful ... a fucking waste. Dad was the strongest one out of all of us. How could he not beat cancer? So many other people did. It wasn't fair. Why did it have to pick him? Why couldn't it be me? I'd make the switch in a heartbeat if I could. What were we going to do without him?

CHARLOTTE

I RAN UP THE APARTMENT STAIRS BY TWOS AND CLOSED THE FRONT door behind me. "Dad?"

"In the bedroom, sweetie."

I stood in the doorway of his room. He shoved his feet into his slippers, signaling that he was in for the night.

"Remember when you said I could buy a car with some of the left-over money?"

"Yes, of course. Did you find one?"

"I stopped by the auto body shop on my way home. There was a car for sale, so I asked about it. I test drove it and everything. I just need the cash."

"It's in the safe. How much is it?"

"Eight."

"It runs well?"

"Yep." I punched the numbers on the keypad of the safe in his closet.

"Do you want me to take a look at it before you buy it?"

"No, thanks," I murmured as I counted the money and stuffed it into an envelope.

"I'm ordering Chinese for dinner. Do you want your usual?"

"No. I won't be home for dinner tonight."

"Okay." He sounded disappointed, but I pretended not to notice.

I sealed the envelope and walked to the door.

"Char?"

"Yeah?"

"I love you."

I paused to look at him long enough to feel the guilt gnaw at me. "Love you, too, Dad." I closed the door and trotted back downstairs.

Tanner didn't look up from his phone as I swung myself into his car. Though I was only gone for a few minutes, his whole demeanor had changed. I could actually feel it inside the car. Something was off.

I held out the envelope of cash. "You can count it, make sure it's all there."

He nodded as he took it, though his focus remained glued to his phone. *Who was he talking to?*

It was silent and awkward on the ride back to his shop. I didn't stall the car once, but Tanner didn't cheer for me. His hand didn't guide mine on the shifter. He sat beside me, stiff and cold. What was worse, I felt disappointed.

Back inside the shop, I signed paperwork for the car in continued silence. What happened during the time I'd gone in to my apartment? Maybe Mallory was right—maybe he wasn't stable if this is how quickly his mood could change.

When I finished signing each page, I slid the papers across the counter to Tanner. I remained where I stood, waiting for some sort of response from him.

"We're done here. You can go. I have a lot of shit to do."

My jaw nearly hit the floor.

He turned around to face the filing cabinet behind him, shoving my paperwork inside a folder.

I walked toward the door, wanting to run in embarrassment, but I turned back around and took a breath. "What happened to the nice guy who taught me how to drive a stick ten minutes ago?"

He pinned me with a look over his shoulder, his irises now twice as dark. "I never said I was a nice guy."

"Well, you sure as hell fooled me!" I pushed the door open and let it slam behind me as I stomped to my car in the parking lot. I fumbled with the key, my breaths short and quick.

Tanner had struck a nerve.

I started the car but hesitated before putting it into reverse. I glanced at the shop, tempted to go back inside.

Why do I care if Tanner's nothing more than a dick?

Because he isn't, that's why.

I should march inside and demand to know what his problem is.

No.

Tanner was no good for me, and I knew it. Instead of wasting any more time on him, I drove out of the parking lot.

Chapter Four

CHARLOTTE

Walking with Mallory to class the next day, my phone rang in my purse. I turned it over and saw a number I didn't recognize.

"It is Gabe?" she asked in a singsong voice.

"No. I don't know this number." I rejected the call and shoved my phone back into my bag. A minute later, the number called again.

"It's probably a telemarketer. Answer it and curse them out."

"I'm not cursing anybody out."

"Why not? I do it all the time. Tell them you'll hunt them down and kill them in their sleep. They'll never call back again."

"You are seriously disturbed." I clicked the green button on my screen. "Hello?"

"Hey, Charlotte. It's Tanner."

My stomach flopped.

"See? You should've cursed him out," Mallory whispered.

I waved her away from the phone. "How did you get my number?"

"It was on your paperwork. I hope you don't mind."

"Oh, you hope I don't mind? You're back to being nice now?"

He sighed. "I'm sorry about the way I spoke to you yesterday. I shouldn't have treated you like that."

"Why did you?" I didn't want him to think I cared, but I'd never seen someone's mood turn so quickly before. I wanted to know why.

"I can explain later. Are you free tonight? Come by the shop."

"I'm not free."

"Got a date with pencil dick?"

"That's none of your business, and don't call him that."

"Stop being difficult. Just come by the shop later."

"I am not being difficult! You're lucky I'm even entertaining this conversation after the way you acted yesterday!" I paused, awaiting his response. "Hello?"

Mallory chuckled as we walked through the doors of our building.

"He hung up on me!"

"I heard."

"What arrogance! He thinks he can just summon me to the shop after being rude to me. Did I tell you how rude he was yesterday?"

"You did. Several times."

"So rude! He's got another thing coming if he thinks I'm going to see him later." We took our seats. "Why are you looking at me like that?"

"If he's rude and arrogant, then don't go by the shop later."

"Oh, I won't."

"Good. Forget about him."

"Already forgotten." I opened my spiral notebook and wrote the date on top of the blank paper, preparing for the next hour. My heart beat rapidly, and I tried to slow my breaths. I took a swig of water from my bottle, hoping the cool liquid would soothe the heat inside me. I had to stop letting Tanner get under my skin.

Still, I couldn't shake the feeling in my gut as I drove past Tanner's shop later that evening. At the corner of the street, I stopped at a red light and stared at the shop in my rearview mirror. *When this light turns green, you are going to continue driving straight.*

The light turned green. I took a deep breath and quickly jerked the car to the right, turning down a side street. I drove around the block and pulled in when I came back around to the front of the shop. Tanner's Mustang was the only car left in the lot.

Tanner was behind the counter when I walked inside. His raised brows and open mouth told me he didn't expect me to show. *Why did that make me feel bad?*

I propped my hand on my hip. "Well, let's hear it."

"Hello to you, too."

I glared at him, refusing to let him break me.

He stood and walked past me to the door I had just entered through. "Come on."

"Where are we going?"

"For a drive." He held the door open, waiting for me to follow.

"I don't want to go for a drive. You told me to come by the shop, and I did."

"Why did you?"

Because I'm an idiot. "I want an explanation for yesterday. Then I'm leaving."

His large hand wrapped around mine, and he gently tugged until I was standing outside. "Just get in the car, please." He gestured to his Mustang. "I'll drive."

I let out a sigh as I opened the passenger door and sat. We were on the road for several minutes before either of us spoke. I watched the turns Tanner made until we arrived at a playground outside an elementary school building. Tanner swung open his car door and motioned for me to follow.

I followed him onto the empty playground. He sat on a swing and waited for me to take the one beside him.

"I was being genuine with you when we were driving around yesterday," he said. "But when you went inside to get your money, my mom texted me. My dad is ... he's sick. They were on their way home from the doctor, and they didn't exactly get good news. It put me in a mood."

"What's wrong with your dad?"

"He has cancer. The doctor said treatments aren't working."

My heart wrenched. "I am so sorry."

"Yeah. Everybody's sorry." He rolled his eyes, and I somehow knew it wasn't directed at me.

"When did you find out?"

"About two years ago. Right after my brother left for California." He laughed once. "Chase thought he would be a rock star or something. The next Bon-fucking-Jovi. My parents kept the cancer a secret from him so he could keep his golden head up his ass. Then, the cancer got more aggressive, whatever the fuck that means. Mom told Chase to come home. We're not sure how much longer Dad has."

The mystery surrounding Tanner became clear. Mallory said Tanner's anger spiraled out of control a couple of years ago. That was when he'd first found out about the cancer. He wasn't a bad person, or a crazed lunatic. He was in pain. This was something he could not control. This was something I completely understood.

"My mom had cancer." The words left my mouth before I could stop them.

"Had?"

I nodded. "She died when I was five."

"Shit. I'm sorry."

One corner of my mouth lifted. "Everyone always is, right?"

His slight smile mirrored mine, and a butterfly fluttered in my chest. His irises, dark and deep, were framed by his dark brows and chiseled cheekbones. Many times, I'd heard the expression about eyes being windows to our souls, but I never truly understood it—until now. Tanner held all of his pain, his worries, and his emotions inside. I could see it all churning like a brewing storm. There was good inside him, too. I saw it when he smiled. What was more, something in me wanted to make him happy just so I could see that smile more often.

I tried to ignore the delicate wings flapping around my heart. I attempted to get the angry feeling back, but it had already dissipated. How could I be angry with someone who was going through something as painful as losing a parent? He needed someone. A friend. I did, too.

"I'm sorry I was a dick yesterday. I get like that sometimes."

"You know, just because you're going through something doesn't mean you get a free pass to act like that toward people."

"I know."

We swung in silence and after several minutes, I lost our staring contest. "Why do you care what I do with Gabe?"

"I don't want to see you get hurt."

"Why do you care if I get hurt?"

"Because you're a good person."

"Why do you think I'm such a good person?"

"Why do you have so many questions?"

"Because I'm trying to figure you out."

"Good luck with that," he said. "I can't figure myself out half the time."

I bit my tongue.

"How did you break your wrist?"

"I fell. I was at my dad's bakery in Florida, and I slipped on some flour."

"Okay. Now tell me the truth."

My stomach twisted. "What are you talking about? I fell."

"I can tell when you're lying."

"How?"

"You don't look me in the eyes when you lie. Just like when you told me your dad hides money under his mattress. Also, your voice changes, like when you said you weren't free tonight on the phone."

"What are you, CIA or something?"

"If I told you, I'd have to kill you." He wiggled his eyebrows until I cracked a smile.

"You're an idiot."

"And you're a liar. Tell me how you broke your wrist."

I looked into his eyes so he'd know I was telling the truth. "I can't. There're things about me better left unsaid. It's safer that way."

"Safer? Now look who's in the CIA."

I grinned.

"What are you doing tomorrow night?"

I tried to think of a lie but thought better of it. He already knew my tells. "I don't know. Nothing, I guess."

"You should come out. We're all going to Big Nose Kate's."

Was that really someone's nickname? Poor girl. "I don't know who Kate is. Would she mind if I came to her party?"

Tanner laughed so hard, his eyelids closed and crinkled in the corners. "Big Nose Kate's is the name of a bar. I'm going there with some friends for Shawn's birthday. You should come. Bring Mallory."

How would I explain this to her? I could hear her judgement already.

"My brother will be playing there with his band."

"You mean," I touched my chest, "I get to meet Bon Jovi?"

He smirked and pushed my swing with his foot, sending me sideways into the air. "Smart-ass."

I giggled, allowing my swing to crash into him. I now understood Tanner's choice to bring me here. A playground felt innocent and care-free—two things I'm sure he hadn't felt in a long time. I hadn't either.

Tanner slowed his swing and stood, signaling that it was time to head back. "Say you'll come tomorrow."

I rose from my seat. "I'll talk to Mal."

He took my hand and drew me closer. His fingers laced with mine and goosebumps shot up my arm. "Say you'll come tomorrow."

My gaze landed on his lips before I could stop myself. They were close enough for me to touch, and I could smell his cinnamon gum on his breath. The butterfly trapped in my chest multiplied as I imagined what it would be like to be kissed by those lips. Silky-smooth, plump lips. Would he give light teasing kisses, or would he be fire and passion? Something told me he'd be both.

Tanner caught me looking, and a pleased smirk formed on said lips.

I took a few steps back, for fear he would hear the sound of the kick drum inside me. "I'll talk to Mal," were the only words I could form.

TANNER

I SAW HER AS SOON AS SHE STEPPED FOOT INTO THE BAR. YOU couldn't miss her. Maybe it was because she was a goldenrod in a field of weeds. Maybe her skin seemed so pale in contrast with the fake tans surrounding her. It definitely had something to do with her pouty pink lips that I wanted to suck on.

But for me, it was her eyes. Charlotte had a pair that could hypnotize you. Luminous blue spheres with sunbursts streaking through them. Electric orbs that brightened even your darkest day. A lot went on behind those eyes, but she only let a small fraction of it show. There wasn't much I wouldn't do to keep them on me.

"Quit staring so hard, bro," Derek shouted into my ear. "You need to play it cool."

I arched an eyebrow without taking my focus off Charlotte. "Like you know anything about playing it cool."

"I bag plenty of girls because I know how to play their fucked-up games."

"There's the difference between you and me, fuckhole. I don't need to play any games to get girls."

"Ah." He waved his hand. "Maybe the old Tanner Brooks didn't have to play games. This pathetic excuse for a man you've turned into —you've lost your touch. I can't even remember the last time you bagged a girl." He tipped his beer bottle in Chase's direction. "Even your brother's gone soft, man!"

I controlled the urge to punch my best friend in his dumb mouth and averted my attention to my brother as he talked to Merritt Adams across the room. He had been in love with her since kindergarten. I was glad to see them together. If she hadn't woken up from the coma after her accident, Chase would have been devastated.

"Incoming. Here comes your girl."

Charlotte wore a yellow halter top and the tiniest pair of white shorts. Girls knew exactly what they were doing when they put on white shorts—they knew it drove men wild. She looked less plain than usual, and that excited me. She was dressed for me. My mouth spread into a wide grin as her eyes locked on mine.

Mallory whispered something in her ear, and Charlotte bit her lip to keep from laughing. I would have to ask her about that later. She didn't smile much, and I wanted to learn how to make it happen more often.

I wrapped my arms around her in a bear hug. Anything to touch her. "You came."

"I told you I would talk to Mallory."

Mallory smirked. "You're welcome."

I held out my closed hand and fist-bumped her. "Mal, have you met my single friend, Derek?" I patted Derek's arm. I didn't know if he was interested in Mallory, but I didn't give a shit. He needed to be my wingman. Mal was fiercely protective over her friend, and I wanted Charlotte to myself tonight.

Charlotte pushed Mallory closer to Derek. "This is my single friend, Mallory."

Mallory took his hand with a confident smile and led him to the dance floor without saying a word. Apparently, she was a designated wingman, too.

I held out my hand to Charlotte. "Ready to dance?"

She shook her head. "No."

Seriously? "Do you not like dancing?"

"I do. I just can't dance with you."

"Why the fuck not?"

She crinkled her nose and closed her eyes as if it hurt her to say the words. "If I dance with you, I will owe Mallory twenty bucks."

My eyebrows could not have lifted any higher. "You bet her that you wouldn't dance with me tonight?"

"I did."

Fuck that. I set my beer on the windowsill and dug into my back pocket, pulling out my wallet. I leaned in just inches from her face. "Don't ever bet against me, baby." I took her hand and pulled her through the crowd. Tapping Mallory on the shoulder, I handed her a folded twenty-dollar bill.

She took it with a knowing smile and winked before returning her attention to Derek.

I drew Charlotte in close, and we began to dance. She felt rigid at first—hesitant. I wanted her to relax. I placed her hand on the back of my neck and carefully sandwiched her casted arm in between us.

"Is your wrist okay?"

She nodded, looking everywhere except at me.

My hands traveled to her waist, and I brushed my fingertips against her slightly bare midriff. *Behave. You don't want to scare her away.* Our bodies moved in rhythm with the music, and Charlotte relaxed against me a little more with each passing song. She even turned around at one point and pressed her ass onto my dick. *Let's hope she takes the stiffness as a compliment.*

As much as I enjoyed being behind her, I twirled her around and pulled her close against my body. My chest was pressed against hers. I had the perfect view down into her cleavage, but that wasn't where I wanted to look. I needed her to look at me.

As if she heard my thoughts, her eyes flicked up at me. Blue eyes always seemed cold. They lacked depth. But not hers. Charlotte's were a limitless ocean, and I was sinking under. When she looked at me, I was on top of the world. I was invincible. All the pain inside me dissipated.

"You look incredible," I spoke into her ear, resisting the insatiable desire to nibble it.

"So do you."

With her arms draped around my neck, her fingers ever so gently stroked the hair on the back of my head. It calmed me and tortured me at the same time. I imagined her gripping handfuls of my hair with her legs wrapped around my waist. I kept my hands planted firmly on her hips, but I could feel them twitching, dying to roam all over her body.

I grinned. "Best fucking twenty dollars I ever spent."

CHARLOTTE

I NOTICED HIS EYES WERE ABSENT OF PAIN TONIGHT, THOUGH I knew it was not gone for good. I felt lucky. I was aware that most people did not get the chance to see him like this. What a sight it was to see him happy. Tonight, he was not the hot-head with the bad reputation. Tonight, he was gentle and kind ... and sexy as hell.

It became more and more difficult to control myself being so close to him. He smelled like cologne and sweat. It was an intoxicating combination, though I'd never thought so on anyone else. The image of his bare upper body, burned into my memory from the moment we'd met, only made matters worse. My hands wanted to slip under his shirt to feel if his skin was as smooth as it looked. And those lips. *Ugh, those lips.* They were so close to mine, taunting me. I'd only have to tilt my chin a fraction of an inch. *No. Look away. Get it together, girl.*

We danced until Chase took the stage for his last set. As much as I didn't want to let go of Tanner, I was thankful for the break. Derek and Mallory walked to the bar with us. Tanner ordered me a water, and I contemplated dousing myself with it instead of drinking it. I needed something to snap me out of the trance I was in.

Tanner tapped his bottle against Derek's and Mallory's before chugging almost half of it. All three of them were definitely feeling the effects of the alcohol, and I was prepared to drive everyone home.

"Has anyone seen the birthday boy?" Derek asked.

Mallory's top lip lifted in a snarl. "He's probably rubbing his junk against some poor girl on the dance floor." She pointed Shawn out to me. "He's such a skeeze."

"Speaking of, where's pencil dick tonight?" Tanner asked.

I lifted my chin slightly. "I don't know anybody by that name."

"Why do you keep calling him that?" Mallory asked. "How do you even know what his dick looks like?"

"His name is Gabe, and he has an early morning tomorrow, for your information."

"We all have early mornings." Tanner threw back the rest of his beer and set it atop the bar. He took my hand, twirled me in a circle, and dipped me backwards. "His loss is my gain," he said with a wink. When he set me upright, he turned toward the bar to order one last round.

I leaned closer to Mallory's ear. "Why does he keep mentioning Gabe like that?"

"He knows Gabe likes you. He's jealous." She paused. "Shit. That's a first."

The band packed away their equipment, and the crowded bar emptied into the parking lot. I held onto Mallory's arm to guide her as we shuffled out the door. Someone bumped into me, and I dropped my car keys. I let go of Mallory to bend down and grab them. Then, I felt a firm slap on my ass.

"Hey!" I spun around to glare at Tanner. *I know he's drunk, but that was uncalled for.*

I looked up to see Tanner holding birthday boy Shawn in the air by his throat. Veins bulged out of Tanner's neck, his cheeks flushed, and he had a menacing look in his eyes.

"Tanner, let him go!" I pulled on his arm, but he had a solid grip around Shawn's throat.

Shawn's face turned several shades of purple.

"He can't breathe!" Mallory shrieked.

"Tanner!" My voice sounded strained as panic set in. "You're going to kill him! Stop!"

He loosened his grip and dropped Shawn onto the ground. Shawn rolled over onto his side, gasping for air. Another guy in the crowd extended his hand to help him to his feet.

"Don't you ever lay a fucking finger on her again," Tanner growled. He turned and stormed off into the parking lot.

"Where are you going?" Mallory shouted. "Where is he going?"

"I don't know." I matched his long stride with two of my own to keep up with him. "Tanner, you can't drive like this. Where are you going?"

"I need to get the fuck away."

"What was that back there? Why did you attack him like that?"

"He put his hands on you! I just taught him a lesson."

"He's drunk. You didn't teach him anything!"

"I was trying to defend you!"

"I don't want you to defend me by strangling someone to death!"

"He's fine."

"I didn't even recognize you. That was terrifying!"

"Stop being so dramatic."

Lava pooled in my stomach. *Dramatic?* I dug into my purse and pulled out two ten-dollar bills. I crumpled them in my fist and tossed them at him. "Here's your money back. Worst fucking twenty dollars I've ever spent!"

I whirled around and marched to my car.

"Did you just curse?" Mallory asked, sounding amused.

I swung open the door. "Go get him so we can leave." I couldn't let him drive drunk, but I was too mad to even look at him.

Mallory sighed. "I am too drunk for this." Then she shuffled across the parking lot.

Chapter Five

CHARLOTTE

anner tried to contact me the remainder of the weekend, so much that I had to shut off my phone. By Monday morning, I had thirty-seven combined missed calls and texts from him. I deleted without reading or listening to any of them and rolled out of bed. Today was the grand opening of the new bakery.

I stepped into my black yoga pants and pulled the white T-shirt over my head. I stared at the shirt's teal lettering in the mirror, and then at the picture of my mother framed on my dresser. I looked at her every morning and made a wish that she were still here. I knew it was silly, and would never come true—but I did it, anyway. It was like making a wish on your birthday candles. Pointless, yet somehow necessary. I pulled my pony tail through the back of the matching white hat and walked out of my bedroom.

Mallory beat me to the bakery. She bounced over to me, entirely too chipper for my dreadful mood. "I love that I get to wear a T-shirt and a hat to work!"

I forced a smile. "Are you ready for your first day?"

"I am. Have you spoken to Tanner?"

"Who?"

"Oh, that's cold, girl." She giggled as we walked inside.

I inhaled deeply. The air was filled with the familiar sugary aroma of delicious baked treats—a sign that my father had been here since the break of dawn.

"Wow. Your father made all of these?" Mallory knelt down, peering into the glass display case.

"He did. He'll give you a doggy bag to take home at the end of the night." I handed Mallory an apron, and tied mine around my waist.

"What should I do first?"

"Start making coffee. Then, I'll show you how to use the computer for the register."

She angled her phone overhead and scooted next to me. "Let's take a selfie on our first day at work!"

I backed away, waving my hands. "No. I don't want any pictures of me floating around social media."

"My page is private, you freak. Come on! We look so cute!"

"You swear your page is private?"

"Yes, duh."

I reluctantly leaned in and smiled for at least seven pictures, none of which satisfied Mallory.

"This is the last one, and then we're getting to work," I warned. "If you don't like it, slap a filter on it and get over it."

"You're grumpy in the morning."

"Morning, ladies!" Dad burst through the kitchen door carrying a tray of fresh doughnuts.

"Everything looks great, Dad."

"Smells great, too," Mallory chimed in.

"Thank you. We open in ten minutes!" He arranged the doughnuts onto a glass serving dish and covered them with a lid. He whistled as he headed back into the kitchen.

Once I flipped the sign on the door to Open, the day flew by. We were understaffed, and I was grateful when two women came by to fill out applications. We survived the morning and lunchtime rushes, finally able to sit for a minute when the constant flow of customers died down in the evening.

"My feet," Mallory exclaimed as she hopped onto the counter next to the register.

"My back." I clutched my lower back as I eased onto the counter beside her. I slid my phone out of my apron to check the time, and saw a text from Gabe:

GABE: HAVEN'T HEARD BACK FROM YOU ALL WEEKEND. SHOULD I take the hint and leave you alone?
Me: Had phone trouble this weekend. I'm sorry.

"LET ME SEE TANNER'S TEXTS. I BET HE TEXTED YOU A BUNCH OF times." Mallory leaned over my shoulder.

"I deleted them." I hopped down and turned my back to her, pretending to wipe down the counter.

"All of them?"

"Yup. No sense keeping them." I couldn't allow myself to trust that Tanner could control his anger. Hearing the rumors was one thing. Seeing him in action was another. I had been hurt by the hands of a sadistic brute who took pleasure in causing pain to innocent people. I wanted nothing to do with anyone who was capable of doing something like that to another human being.

TANNER

I TRIED TO CONTACT HER THE ENTIRE WEEKEND. CHARLOTTE SENT my calls straight to voicemail and left my texts on Read—all thirty-seven of them. All I wanted was for her to answer with something. Anything. Curse me out. I didn't care. I just needed her to know that I was sorry for the way I'd acted. I needed her to forgive me.

Today was the grand opening of her dad's bakery, and I knew she would be there. This was my Hail Mary pass. If she saw me in person, she wouldn't be able to ignore me. I walked into the bakery, but she didn't turn around when the bell smacked against the door. She was in the middle of talking to Mallory. Mallory's eyes grew wide when she saw me.

"No sense keeping them," Charlotte was saying. "I don't want to be involved with somebody who has that much anger inside. If he can't have self-control with a drunken idiot at a bar, what's stopping him from turning his rage on me?"

"Is that why you're ignoring me?"

She spun around, her mouth half open.

I stepped forward. "You think I would hurt you?"

She ignored my question and pointed to the door. "Leave."

"Please, let me apologize." I was close to begging.

"I don't want your apology. There's no apologizing for the way you behaved. That kind of violence is unacceptable." She folded her arms across her chest. "Maybe you should be giving your apology to Shawn instead."

I couldn't stop my face as it twisted in disgust. "That asshole put his hands on you. I did what any other guy would do in that situation."

"He's got a point," Mallory said. "If a guy slapped my ass, I would expect my man to put him in his place."

She's on my side. Maybe there was hope for me after all.

"Tanner is not my man, and he almost choked the life out of Shawn." Charlotte's eyes stared straight into mine. "You were out of control. It scared me."

Her words cut me like a knife. I scared her. She was afraid of me. "Charlotte, I am sorry that I scared you. You're right. I was out of control. I need to get a handle on it." I walked toward her and pressed my palms onto the counter. "But I need you to understand that I would never hurt you."

She wavered for a second, the softening of her face revealing that maybe this wasn't entirely what she wanted. For that second, I had hope. Then, she looked down at her cast. *What did her broken wrist have to do with anything?* Was she looking at Gabe's phone number? Did she like Gabe?

"Please leave."

My shoulders slumped and I hung my head as I turned and walked out the door. That was it. I'd proven to Charlotte that I was the piece of shit I'd always known I was. She didn't deserve this.

I drove away from the bakery in a fury. The more I thought about what happened that night at the bar, the angrier I grew. Shawn was the one at fault. He was the one who put his hands on her. He deserved to have his ass handed to him. Instead, I was the one who was being punished. *Story of my fucking life.*

By the time I got home, I'd worked myself up so much that I was sure steam was shooting out of my ears. As I stalked up the driveway, the front door opened and Chase trotted down the stairs.

"What's your problem?" he asked with his disapproving look that I so badly wanted to wipe off his face.

Words would not form. My hands balled into fists at my sides as I approached him.

"You need to chill out."

"You need to shut your fucking mouth," I gritted through my teeth.

"You can't go in there like this. Dad's asleep on the recliner, and Khloe's still awake. Whatever's bothering you, you need to—"

I shoved him as hard as I could. He caught himself as he stumbled backwards. Chase was slightly bigger than me, but that didn't mean I couldn't still beat his ass—and he knew it.

"You need to calm the fuck down!" he shouted as he shoved me back.

That was all I needed. I slammed into his midsection, tackling him onto the grass. I mounted him and hurled my fist at his face, but he dodged out of the way. He tossed me off and tried scrambling to his feet, but I was quicker. I pushed him back onto the ground and held him down. *This time, I won't miss.*

"You self-righteous motherfucker!" I was about to land my punch on his jaw when I heard my mother's voice from the top of the stairs.

"Tanner!"

My fist hovered over my brother's face as I glared down at him. All I wanted was one good shot.

"Tanner, don't you dare!"

God-dammit. I slammed my fist into the grass beside Chase's head, and I heard my mother suck in a breath.

I stood and left my brother on the ground.

"I don't know what has gotten into you," Mom said, her voice low. "But you'd better get control of yourself."

I didn't respond and I got back in my car.

Mom and Chase watched me pull out of the driveway, both wearing the same worried expression on their identical faces.

I was losing my father, and now I'd lost the girl I was starting to care for. Everything was so fucked up. Everyone kept telling me to get control of myself, but that was just the thing—I had no control over anything. No matter how hard I tried, nothing went my way.

The only place left to go was Big Nose Kate's. When I took my usual seat at the bar, the bartender handed me a shot of whiskey and a bottle of beer. I downed the shot, asked for another, and downed that one, too.

"Rough night?"

I looked to my right to see who was stupid enough to try talking to me. A man I'd never seen before was sitting two stools over. He wore a backwards baseball cap, and he was covered in tattoos—knuckles, neck, everywhere but his face. He looked like a badass.

"You could say that."

"Looks like it." He nodded toward my swollen hand. "I just hope the other guy's still alive."

I laughed once. "Mom made sure of it."

"Ah. Brotherly love."

I signaled for another shot, and the bartender slid it over. Her eyes volleyed between us like she wasn't sure which one she was interested in. All I wanted from her was alcohol. This dude could have her. She was wearing entirely too much makeup; her eyelashes looked like furry tarantula legs, and her face was three shades darker than her neck. *I hate these fake fucking Staten Island girls.* They weren't like Charlotte. She was different.

The whiskey burned my throat, and I hoped it would burn my heart right out of my chest.

"I always wanted a brother when I was little."

Why was this guy still talking? "You can have mine."

"Yeah, well ... that wishing stopped when my mom died." He

looked down at his full, untouched shot glass. "I was thankful I didn't have a sibling to go through what I went through."

Shit. I wasn't expecting that. I nodded in agreement, thinking about what my family was about to endure.

"Life's not fair to anyone. Gotta keep fighting though."

I downed my third shot. "Not in the mood for a motivational speech, man."

"No one ever really is. The ones who refuse it are always the people who need it the most."

I raised an eyebrow as he stood. "You always come to a bar to pay for alcohol that you didn't drink?"

The man winked at the bartender as he placed a twenty on the bar. "I don't drink anymore." He extended his hand. "My name is TJ. What's your name?"

I shook his hand, getting a better look at the tattoos on his arm. "Tanner."

"Tanner, you should come check out my gym sometime." He pointed at the logo on his T-shirt. "I think it would be good for you."

"No, thanks."

"Suit yourself. But whatever you're looking for at the bottom of that glass, I can assure you that you won't find it. You need to get up and fight for what you want."

I chugged the rest of my beer as TJ walked away. *What I want?* What I wanted was for my father not to be dying, but there was no way I could stop that from happening. I wanted Charlotte to forgive me, but she wouldn't, despite my efforts. I wanted to feel something good for a change, but that never seemed to happen.

So, I'd sit here and drink until I felt nothing at all.

CHARLOTTE

"HI, CHARLOTTE," GABE ANSWERED HIS PHONE CHEERFULLY. "WHAT are you up to?"

"I'm finishing at the bakery in a little while."

"Can I see you when you're done?"

"Sure. What do you want to do?"

"Why don't I take you to dinner? I'd like to take you to an actual restaurant this time."

"We close at six- thirty, and then I have to run home and shower."

"How's seven- thirty?"

"Sounds good to me."

"See you then."

Mallory shook her head as she walked around the counter.

"What are you shaking your head at me for?"

"Why force yourself to go out with Gabe when you have feelings for Tanner?"

"I don't have feelings for Tanner."

"Yes, you do. I saw it when you were dancing with him the other night."

"Tanner is not good for me. You said it yourself—he's a bad boy. I don't need someone like that in my life ... and I am not forcing myself to go out with Gabe. Gabe is nice."

"Just because he's nice doesn't mean you have to date him, Char."

"I'm not dating him. We're just hanging out." I vigorously cleaned the countertops, wishing I could scrub everything out of my mind just as easily.

She walked closer and pointed at me. "If you kiss him tonight, and you don't feel sparks fly, you'll have your answer."

"Sparks don't actually fly in real life. You know that, right? That's not a thing."

"It's your first kiss with him! There absolutely should be fireworks and explosions going off in the background!"

I shook my head. "First kisses are awkward. You have to get past all of that to get to the good stuff."

"I do not agree," she said. "First kisses are the best, and if it's not, then it's the kiss of death."

I was not about to broadcast it to Mallory, but I had only kissed one boy. Kyle Tomlin. We dated senior year of high school. He was a football star and I was a cheerleader. I thought we were a match made in heaven; I thought we were in love. That's why I gave him my virginity. Then, he let Angela Coolidge give him hers in the bathroom on prom night, and that was the end of that. That was one memory I was happy to leave in Florida.

"Have you never experienced a magical kiss like that?" she asked.

"Guess not."

"Well, take it from me." She wrapped her arm around my shoulders. "Life is too short to have mediocre make-out sessions."

I smirked. "You should get that printed onto a shirt."

———

"YOU LOOK BEAUTIFUL." GABE'S EYES SPARKLED IN THE candlelight coming from our table.

"Thanks. You look great, too." He did. He was wearing a crisp white polo with dark jeans. His nose and cheeks were slightly red from his softball game this past weekend, giving his face a sun-kissed glow.

"How's work? Opening week must've been busy."

"It was insanely busy. I've had to put my feet up at the end of every shift."

"Busy is good though."

"It is."

"Do you plan to take over the shop when you're older?"

I shook my head. "I want to open my own business."

"Is that what you're going to school for?"

"Yup. Business major. What about you?"

"I'm a computer nerd. I want to design video games."

"That sounds like fun."

"Do you play any video games?"

"I used to love *Super Mario* when I was a kid."

"That's a classic. My brother and I dressed as Mario and Luigi last Halloween."

"I've seen those costumes."

"Do you have any plans for this Halloween?"

I noted his segue. "I hadn't thought about it yet. Mallory will have something planned for us, I'm sure."

"There's usually a big party at my brother's frat house. Everyone starts planning their costumes around this time to prepare." He laughed. "They take it pretty seriously."

"It'll be here before we know it. Summer's already over."

"In that case, I'd better lock you down as my date to the party."

I shoved a piece of bread into my mouth to buy more time. "Like you said, it will be here before we know it."

The waiter arrived with our food, allowing me to stall some more.

Gabe's eyes remained fixed on me as the waiter set our plates down in front of us.

"Thank you."

"You're welcome. Anything else I can get you right now?"

"No, thanks. We're good," Gabe said. He waited for the waiter to leave. "So? What do you say? Come to the Halloween party with me."

"I'll talk to Mallory and see what she wants to do."

"Well, that wasn't a no. I guess I'll take it."

The corners of my mouth pulled down. "I'm sorry. I just ... Mallory is my only friend here, and I don't want her to feel left out."

"I understand. Maybe we can find her a date."

I nodded, biting into my spaghetti before I said anything Mallory would kill me for. I didn't get the impression that she was fond of Gabe's immature friends. Would Derek be there? I know she'd enjoyed her night with him at Big Nose Kate's. Tanner would probably be there, too.

The memory of us dancing suddenly replayed in my mind. The warmth of his muscular body pressed against mine. The touch of his hands on my waist setting fire to my skin. The heat emanating from his eyes as he scorched me.

The butterflies that had been asleep throughout this whole dinner with Gabe were now wide awake.

"How was it at Big Nose Kate's the other night?" Gabe asked, as if he'd read my mind.

I gulped my water. "It was cool. I heard Chase and his band play."

"Yeah, Chase is great. I heard his brother got into it with Shawn at the end of the night. Did you see that?"

My stomach twisted, sending the butterflies back to their hiding spot. "Yeah, he did."

"I've never had any problems with Tanner, but he goes from zero to sixty, you know? The guy can be a real psycho."

"I wouldn't call him a psycho. Maybe he's got a lot going on that we don't know about."

"That's very good-hearted of you, but I highly doubt there's anything going on. The family is perfect—looks, brains, money—Tanner's just an arrogant jerk."

I instantly wanted to defend Tanner though I didn't know why I felt compelled to do so. It didn't feel good to hear Gabe talking about him—about anyone—like that, without knowing the truth. Gabe didn't know about Tanner's father, and it saddened me to hear how harshly people judged him when his family was going through such a difficult time.

Was I one of those people?

The image of Tanner's crestfallen face leaving the bakery today plagued my mind. Who was going to help him through everything that was about to happen? More importantly, why did I care?

"Did I say something to upset you?"

I offered Gabe a reassuring smile. "No. I'm just getting full."

"Me, too." He patted his stomach. "Do you have any room for dessert?"

I shook my head. I just wanted to go home.

Gabe paid the bill, refusing again to let me chip in. Then, we climbed into his Jeep.

"I don't want our night to end. Do you want to come back to my house?" he asked. "My parents will be home, but we can go in the basement and watch a movie or something."

"I'm actually super tired from work today, and I have class early tomorrow morning."

"Okay. No problem."

A silence fell over us as he drove back to my apartment, and I was fine with that. I stared out the window until we pulled into the parking lot of my complex.

Gabe put the car in park and turned to face me in his seat. "You get your cast off this week, don't you?"

"On Tuesday."

"I bet you're excited to be free of that thing."

"You have no idea."

He leaned in, brushing his thumb across my cheek. "I've been thinking about you since that night at the lake."

"You have?"

"I have." His eyes fell to my lips.

I had a choice to make, and I had to make it fast. I could let him kiss me, and fool him into thinking I felt the same way he did. Maybe I would enjoy it. Maybe it would get Tanner off my mind. But I couldn't do that to Gabe.

I pressed my hand gently against his chest. "Gabe ..."

He stopped advancing and nodded as if he understood. "Am I moving too quickly for you, or are you just not interested?"

I paused before answering, unsure of what exactly I wanted to say. "I think you're cute and sweet, and I like hanging out with you."

"That's good." He wore a hopeful smile.

"But I'd like to be your friend." I looked down at my lap. "I don't have very many of those around here."

Gabe lifted my chin with his finger. "You've got me, Charlotte. I hear you, and I won't try to kiss you again. That is, not unless you decide you want me to."

A small smile touched my lips, knowing in my heart that I never would.

Chapter Six

TANNER

The bell sounded as I walked into the bakery. Every morning this week, I'd come for coffee and a doughnut. I hadn't tried to call or text. I didn't even talk to her when I paid for my breakfast. I'd ask for what I wanted, she'd hand me my change, and then I'd leave. I was a masochist, torturing myself by seeing the girl I liked so much, even though I knew I couldn't have her. The worst part was that my heart skipped a beat at the mere sight of her, yet she couldn't bring herself to look at me.

As I walked to the counter, I noticed Charlotte's arm was cast-free. *Don't ask how she is. Just get your shit and get out.*

Mallory watched me with a knowing smirk. Maybe she would talk Charlotte into forgiving me. I needed all the help I could get.

Charlotte placed my chocolate glazed doughnut into the white paper bag and sat it on the counter beside my cup of coffee. Cash. Change. Done.

I was getting into my Mustang when I saw Charlotte coming outside after me.

"Did I forget something?" I patted my jeans to check for my wallet.

"No, you're good. I just ... I want to know why you keep coming here."

She knew exactly why. I raised my coffee cup. "I like the coffee."

She put her hands on her hips. "Come on. It's just coffee." Damn her and that sexy attitude.

"Well, I like it." I pointed to her wrist. "How does it feel to have your arm back?"

"Tanner ..."

"What? I'm just trying to have a conversation with my friend." I didn't know what else to say. I was desperate to keep her talking to me.

She raised her eyebrows. "Oh, we're friends now?"

"Can't we be?"

She thought for a moment. "Well, as your friend, I feel obligated to tell you that starting every day with a doughnut isn't the healthiest choice."

I stifled a smile. "The doughnut isn't for me. It's for my kid sister."

"You have a sister?"

I rested my cup on the roof of my car so that I could pull my phone out of my back pocket and swipe until I found what I was looking for. I held my phone out so Charlotte could see the picture of my blond-haired, hazel-eyed little sister, who I loved with my whole heart.

Charlotte smiled, and I almost melted into a puddle. "What's her name?"

"Khloe."

"She's beautiful." Charlotte's expression changed. Tears sprang into her eyes, and she quickly turned around to hide them from me. "I have to get back to work."

What the hell? "Whoa, where are you going?" I put myself in between her and the bakery door, forcing her to face me. I took a chance placing my hands on her shoulders and lowered my head to see her eyes under the brim of her hat. "What just happened?"

A tear escaped down her cheek. "Please don't look at me. This is so embarrassing."

I took her face gently into my hands, the same hands she had seen violently squeezing Shawn's throat. "Why are you crying?"

"Khloe is too young to lose her father. I remember what that's like. I just wish your family didn't have to go through that."

My heart nearly shattered. She was crying because she was worried

"If you were my girlfriend, I'd want to spend time with you."

"He's not my boyfriend." It came out more defensively than I'd planned. "We're just friends."

"Why didn't you call your friend Gabe when your car broke down?"

"I don't know if he knows anything about cars. You were the first person that came to mind."

"You're dating someone and you don't know if he knows anything about cars?"

"I'm not dating him! Besides, he told me he doesn't know how to drive a stick."

"What kind of man doesn't know how to drive a stick?"

"What is with the third degree?"

"We're friends. I talk to my friends about these kinds of things."

I rolled my eyes. "Yeah, I can really see you and Derek discussing the inner workings of your relationships."

His shoulders shook as he chuckled.

I stood and leaned against the car to get a better view of what he was doing. "So, what about you?"

"What about me?"

"What's your dating situation like?"

"Don't have a situation."

"Have you ever?"

"Depends on what kind of situation you're talking about."

"When was your last relationship?"

"I don't do relationships."

"Why?"

"I keep everything casual. I don't waste my time getting into relationships."

"Why not?"

"Now look who's giving the third degree."

"You said friends discuss these things. So, I'm discussing it."

"Hand me that screw-driver right there by your foot."

"You've never had a girlfriend before?"

He took the tool from me and continued working. "Nope."

"Why?"

"Because there's no point in getting into a relationship with someone I'm not in love with."

"How do you know if you're in love with a girl if you don't take the time to date her?"

"It's easy. I just know."

"It's impossible to fall in love with someone without getting to know them first."

"I go by the feeling I get when I'm with a girl."

"What are you expecting to feel?"

He stood and tossed the screw-driver onto the floor. He ran his fingers through his hair, and set his gaze on me. "I'll feel like everything is going to be okay."

My breath faltered a moment as a mixture of fluttering and aching swelled deep in my gut. His answer was so simple—and revealing. His vulnerability took me by surprise. All Tanner needed in life was to be reassured that everything was going to be okay. *Didn't we all?*

I stared up at him, unable to look away, as one looks up to a starry sky in wonderment.

"What?" He shoved his hands into his pockets.

"I'm just ... I didn't expect that from you."

"Why not? Because I have *anger issues with no self-control?*"

I winced hearing the words I'd said about him. "One minute, you're sincere and sweet. The next, you're ... you're just confusing."

"I know. Look, I'm sorry for what happened that night at the bar. I never want you to feel scared of me. That was the worst thing anyone has ever said to me." He looked down at his shoes. "And people have said some pretty fucked-up things about me."

"I don't feel scared of you right now. And I hadn't until that night with Shawn." I stepped toward him. "If you have that much anger inside you, maybe you need to talk to someone about it or find a way to channel it."

"You think I need a shrink? That's great." He turned away from me and collected his tools.

"Tanner, stop." I tugged on his arm until he turned to face me again. The pain behind his eyes matched the pain behind mine. Maybe, if I could help him move past the hurt and the anger, it would somehow help me move past mine too. "We all have issues. I could lie on a couch and fill a therapist's entire pad with all the things that are wrong with me."

"I highly doubt that."

"Trust me. I have rage inside me, just like you do. I've done things that I can't take back. Things that are unforgiveable." Admitting it aloud, I was hit with a realization: I was no better than him. Actually, I was worse. Much worse. He was impulsive and angry, but I was calculated and deliberate. His flaws were out in the open for all to see. I was the one with the skeletons locked in my closet. I was the one pretending to be someone I wasn't.

He crossed his arms over his broad chest. "What have you done that's so bad?"

If only I could tell him. I wanted to tell him whatever he needed to hear just to make his aching stop.

"Let me guess. Did you wash your clothes without checking the tags first?"

I tried to hold it in, but a laugh escaped. "You're never going to let me live that down, are you?"

"I'll bring it up every day if it makes you laugh like that." He stepped toward me and reached out to caress my cheek with the back of his hand. "I don't think there is anything wrong with you, Charlotte. I think you're perfect, and if I wasn't terrified that you would never speak to me again, I would kiss your perfect lips right here and now."

His touch against my cheek sent a wildfire throughout my entire body. My heart slammed against my chest like a pent-up animal in a cage. I wanted to set it free. *Just one kiss couldn't hurt, could it?* Looking into the black abyss of his eyes, I felt certain that it could.

I took a step back and averted my eyes. "So, did you fix it?" I motioned to my car.

"It's fixed." His intense stare remained on me.

"What do I owe you?"

"You don't owe me anything."

"Tanner, you worked on my car. Let me repay you."

His brow quirked. "You can repay me by having dinner with me."

"What?"

"On Friday."

"You're going to let me repay you by buying you dinner?"

"No. You're going to let me buy you dinner."

My response left my traitorous lips before I could catch it. "Okay."

His lips broke into a wide grin. "Friday, then."

As scared as I was to go further with him, I continued to put one foot in front of the other right in Tanner's direction. I knew I shouldn't let him in. I shouldn't let myself trust him. I knew he had the power to take me down, and when he did—I would be to blame. I'd be the one who handed him the weapon.

Chapter Seven

CHARLOTTE

"Wh at's the difference?" *Is that a dumb question?*

The man eyeing me from behind the counter held up the larger gun. "The revolver is heavier. It holds fewer bullets." He raised the gun in his left hand. "The pistol is lighter and holds more bullets."

"Why would someone pick one over the other?"

"It all depends on your preference. The revolver is easier to use for beginners. I'm assuming this is your first time owning a gun?"

"Yes."

"What is it that you are looking to do with this gun?"

"I'd just feel better if I had it with me. For protection."

The man nodded. "If you're planning on carrying it in your purse, then I'd say go with the pistol." He silently assessed me, and I shifted under his gaze. "Do you have kids?"

"No. It's just me and my dad."

"You can keep it loaded, but you need to make sure the safety is on at all times. With this pistol, you can load it and then lock the safety." He demonstrated. "If someone attacks you, you won't have to fumble around with it. It'll be ready."

That's all I needed to hear. I took a deep breath and nodded. "I'll take it."

With my permit and background check already completed, I paid for the pistol and bullets and left. In my car, I stared at the gun in my lap. Never did I think I would be carrying a loaded gun around with me. I never thought I would need to.

I rubbed my wrist as the feeling of being tied to the oven crept to the front of my mind. My hands trembled as I swiped at the tears spilling down my cheeks. I gasped for air, my skin slick with sweat. I gripped the gun, foolishly trying to transfer its power into my body somehow. But I couldn't. I had to pull myself out of this on my own.

"WHAT ARE YOU WEARING?" MALLORY ANSWERED HER PHONE ON the first ring.

"I'm trying to decide between shorts or a dress." Actually, I was trying to talk myself out of wearing a dress. My brain had conjured at least ten smart, valid reasons as to why a dress was a bad idea.

"Go for the dress. It's a date. You should always wear a dress on a date."

Facing the mirror, I sandwiched the phone between my ear and my shoulder as I held the dress against my body. It was a periwinkle strappy dress with a single ruffle that hung off each shoulder. It hit mid- thigh and was just flowy enough to not be completely form-fitting.

"It's not a date." I laid the dress on my bed.

"A hot guy is taking you to dinner. Of course it's a date."

"He just felt guilty about selling me a car with a broken gas gauge."

Growing up without my mother, I'd relied on my best friend, Carla, for help in the guy department. She'd go through my closet and toss outfits at me. She was also the makeup expert. Dad didn't have the slightest clue how to apply eyeliner, and I certainly couldn't ask him for dating advice.

I knew being without a mom would get harder as my problems got bigger. I glanced at my mother's picture. *I'd love to hear your thoughts about Mallory's firework first-kiss theory.*

"Trust me. It's a date."

I glanced at the clock on my nightstand. My stomach twisted in a nervous knot. "All right. Let me go. I have to finish getting ready."

"Send me a selfie before you leave!"

"I will."

Against my better judgment, I slipped into my dress. I hooked my small silver hoop earrings through my lobes, buckled my white sandals around my ankles, and spritzed myself with perfume.

At seven o'clock on the dot, my phone dinged with a text from Tanner. I snapped a quick selfie for Mallory and grabbed my purse as I made a beeline for the front door.

"Where are you headed?" Dad was on the couch watching television.

"Just going to dinner."

He smiled. "You look very pretty for just dinner."

"Thanks. I'll see you at work tomorrow."

His face fell, and guilt stabbed me in the stomach. "Have fun. Be careful. Call me if you need me."

TANNER

CHARLOTTE STEPPED OUTSIDE, AND MY HEART STOPPED BEATING FOR a few seconds. Her strappy blue dress was just short enough, showing off her long, toned legs. The ends of her hair curled slightly, and I saw something shimmery on her eyelids. She didn't need to do any of this —she was naturally beautiful—but the fact that she did told me she wanted to look good on our date tonight. For me.

I stood outside my Mustang holding a bright bouquet. I tried to steady my breath as she approached, my heart racing faster with every step she took.

"Wow. I would say you look beautiful, but that just doesn't seem good enough."

"I wasn't sure what to wear. Is this okay for where we're going?" She tugged on the hem of her dress.

I leaned over and placed a lingering kiss on her cheek. "It's perfect. You look perfect." I handed her the flowers. "I didn't know what your favorite flower was, so I got an assortment."

She smiled. "I love them. You didn't have to." She pointed to an orange flower in the middle of the bouquet. "And Gerbera daisies are my favorite."

I swung the passenger door open for her. "Good to know." I'd remember that for next time.

I took Charlotte to my favorite Spanish restaurant on the other side of the island. I had fond memories coming here with my family when my father was well. We were seated at a small corner booth in the back of the dimly lit room. It was private and secluded with an intimate vibe. I tried to focus on the menu, but found it difficult to concentrate with Charlotte's bare leg pressed against mine in the booth.

From the corner of my eye, I caught her stealing a glance at me every so often. *What was she thinking?* I was almost too afraid to ask.

"What's going on behind those pretty blues?"

"Just wondering what I should order." Liar. "What do you get when you come here?"

"I usually come with my family. We get a bunch of different dishes, and we share them. The enchiladas are my favorite."

"Can we do that? Order a few things, and share them?"

"We can do whatever your heart desires, sweet girl." I winked as I closed the menu.

The waitress sauntered over to our table. "Are you ready to order?"

"We are."

Charlotte continued to watch me as I rattled off several appetizers and entrees. I'd pay good money to hear her thoughts.

"I'll put your order in right away. Oh, and I just have to tell you: you two make such a gorgeous couple."

I couldn't help but grin. I wrapped my arm around Charlotte's shoulders. "Thank you very much."

Charlotte nudged me with her elbow once the waitress left.

I took my arm back and chuckled. "What? She's right. We look great together."

"I just hope she gets our order right. I don't think she heard a word you said. She was too busy drooling on her notepad."

"I don't care what she brings out, as long as I'm sitting here next to you."

"Do you always have the right words to say?"

"No. My family would tell you differently."

"Why is that?"

"My brother and I are like night and day. Chase was always good at everything. Good in school, good at sports, he's a good singer ... He's the good son. I always got into trouble, and my dad would compare me to him. He didn't mean to, but he did. We don't really see eye- to- eye on a lot of things. I always wanted to go away to college and have something that was my own. Something that I could be good at."

"So why didn't you?"

"Dad got sick, and the hope of me going to college went out the window. We couldn't afford it with all the hospital bills, and they needed my help at the shop. They had already given Chase a chunk of their savings to go to California." I shrugged. "I never got the chance to make Dad proud of me the way Chase did."

"Nobody says you have to be like your brother, and you shouldn't try to be. I don't know Chase, and I'm sure he's great, but you're great, too." Charlotte covered my hand with hers.

That one small gesture, a touch of affection, was more than anyone had shown me. My heart swelled. I turned my hand over and laced our fingers together. "You're pretty much the only person who thinks so."

"The waitress also thinks you're great."

I laughed. "Well, if you like me, then I must be doing something right."

"I do." It was almost a whisper, as if she was afraid to admit it.

What is she so afraid of? "I like you, too, Charlotte."

She looked down at our hands. "You didn't really want to be just friends, did you?"

I smirked, leaning toward her. "Just about as much as you wanted to be mine."

Her cheeks turned pink, but she didn't deny it. She was smiling, too.

CHARLOTTE

THE CONTENTED SMILE SPRAWLED ACROSS TANNER'S FACE AS HE drove me home made his shadowy eyes twinkle. From his long black lashes to his full lips, he was so handsome it made my heart ache—and the boy was charming. He exuded charisma with every word he spoke. Our waitress seemed to be entranced while taking our order, and I had to suppress a giggle. I understood. I didn't know it was possible to sound that sexy ordering food.

More than just looks, though, he had the heart of a lion. He was an incredibly selfless and caring human being. Only, he had no idea. He sacrificed so much for his family, yet he never felt good enough. I wanted to make him feel good enough. I wanted him to see what I saw.

Opening doors and bringing me flowers were romantic gestures that had taken me by surprise. This Tanner was a far cry from the violent version I'd caught a glimpse of. Yet, I knew it was still inside him. Tonight, I realized that he was not one or the other—he was both Dr. Jekyll and Mr. Hyde.

We arrived at my apartment, and Tanner insisted on walking me to the front door of my building.

I turned to face him. "You're sweet. You didn't have to get out. We could've just said goodbye in the car."

"A gentleman always walks his lady to her door. Besides"—he smiled and touched his hand to my cheek—"if I didn't walk you here then I couldn't give you a proper good-night kiss."

All I could hear was the blood pulsing in my ears. I'd known this moment was coming, and I was foolish to let it get to this point. I wasn't supposed to get too close to anyone. Kissing him would make everything that much harder. I knew I shouldn't. *But I want to.* My entire body ached with want for Tanner. No matter how hard I fought it, something kept pulling me toward him.

Tanner leaned in and I was frozen where I stood, stuck inside my head. He kissed me with the softest lips. It was gentle and sweet, exactly how he'd been with me the entire night. He pulled back, and he took my breath with him.

"This is the part where you say good night and walk inside," Tanner whispered, our faces inches apart.

I should listen to him. But my lips were tingling, and I wanted more. I looked into his eyes and swallowed hard. "Kiss me again."

Tanner pulled me against his body and his lips crashed into mine. I dropped my purse and the flowers onto the concrete, stretching onto my toes as I gripped the back of his neck. His tongue rushed inside my mouth, and I felt it throughout my entire body. His hands were lost in my hair as our tongues swirled together in perfect unison.

His passion, this incredible sense of urgency, radiated off him and it poured over me. He kissed me as if my kiss was all he needed to survive. I'd never been kissed like that before. All the cliché descriptions of a spectacular first kiss became my reality: dizzy, heart racing, weak in the knees, and definitely fireworks—the entire grand finale of the Macy's Fourth of July display.

We lost track of time, lost in each other. I jumped when I heard my neighbor's yappy dog on her nightly walk a few feet from us.

"Damn dog," Tanner muttered, grinning and breathless.

I giggled. "You should hear her in the morning." I took a step backwards and kicked my purse onto its side. I knelt down, but froze. *Oh my God. No!*

"Is that ...?" Tanner bent over to get a closer look. "Is that what I think it is?"

My gun was on the ground amidst the spilled contents of my bag. I quickly shoved it back inside along with everything else and stood up. "It's nothing."

"That's not nothing. That's a gun."

"Everyone has a gun down south." I laughed nervously. I knew he could tell I was lying, but I didn't know what else to say.

His eyes narrowed. "Are you in trouble?"

"No. Really. It's just for protection."

"Who do you need protection from?"

I took a shaky breath before answering. I needed to get my story straight so it sounded believable. I did need it for protection; it wasn't a lie. "I come from a small town. I was scared to move to a city like Staten Island. My best friend, Carla, suggested I get a gun." I tried to appear nonchalant as I shrugged. "It's for protection."

The way Tanner looked at me, I could tell he wasn't buying it. "Do you know how to use that thing?"

"Just point and shoot, right?" *Why wasn't he pressing this further?*

He blew out a puff of air and his lips slowly spread into a grin. "You can't give a guy the best kiss of his life and then pull a gun on him."

"Maybe that will keep you in line."

Tanner leaned in, caressing my face. "With a kiss like that, I am putty in your hands." He covered my lips with his, kissing me one last time. "Good night, my sweet girl."

"Good night, Tanner." A shiver ran through me, my entire body covered in goose bumps. "Thank you for tonight."

I took my wobbly legs upstairs and tiptoed quietly into my apartment. Dad had fallen asleep watching TV as he did most nights. He stirred when I locked the door behind me.

"Sorry, Dad. Didn't mean to wake you."

He smiled, rubbing the sleepiness from his eyes. "It's okay. I want to hear how your night was."

I sat on the couch armrest. "It was great."

"You went on a date, didn't you?"

"I did."

"Who's the lucky guy?"

Tanner's kiss had weakened my defenses. My guard was down, and my heart was exposed. "His name is Tanner. His family owns the auto body shop where I bought my car."

"Ah, so that's where you met him."

I nodded. "I'm really tired. I'm going to call it a night."

Dad reached out and gave my arm a squeeze.

Once in my bed, I replayed each second from the night as I stared at the flowers on my dresser. Was Tanner in bed doing the same? As the tingling throughout my body faded away, the guards at the gates of my heart began pulling the drawbridge closed.

Losing a parent at a young age, you learn not to get too close to people. If your own mother could be taken from you, no one was secure in your life. For months, my parents had told me: "Everything is going to be okay." They lied to protect me from the heartbreaking truth. I was only five years old when my mother died, and I couldn't make sense of it. Why did they lie? Why didn't they tell me what was going to happen so I could prepare for it?

The older I grew, I learned it was easier to keep people at arm's length. If I didn't let people in, they couldn't hurt me. If I didn't trust people, I couldn't fall prey to their lies. The only person I'd let get close to me in eighteen years had been Carla. How I wanted to call her right now. She'd have the perfect thing to say to ease my worries. I wanted to share my new life with her.

But what would she say about what I'd done to get this new life?

Moreover, what would Tanner think? He thought he liked me, but he didn't know the real me. He liked the version of me I was portraying. The truth slapped me in the face: I had trust issues, yet I was the one who couldn't be trusted.

The bell on the door sounded, and Charlotte snatched her phone out of Mallory's hands when she saw me walk in. I knew she was showing her my text from this morning. That made me happy to see. She'd never admit it.

"Hi, Tanner," Mallory said in a singsong voice.

"Hi, Mal," I sang back. I curled my finger signaling for Charlotte to come to me.

She glanced at the kitchen door as she scurried around the counter. I wrapped my arms around her and spun in a circle before setting her down. I pressed my lips against hers, and an electric shock zapped through me the way it had last night. I wanted to lay her on the counter and make love to every inch of her body. Mallory could watch. I didn't care.

"Did you come for your coffee and doughnut?"

"I came for your lips. But, I suppose I'll take a doughnut for Squirt, too."

Mallory leaned her elbows on the counter while Charlotte sauntered away to put my doughnut in a bag. "So, when are you asking Charlotte out again?"

"Mal!" Charlotte shouted.

I chuckled. "I was actually going to ask if she wanted to go out tonight."

"Tonight?" Mallory asked. "That's so soon."

Charlotte dug her elbow into her friend's back as she walked around her to hand me the doughnut. "I'm free tonight."

"Pick you up at seven?"

"Sure."

I leaned over and pointed to my mouth. "Give me one more to hold me over until then."

Her cheeks heated. Still, she didn't pass on the opportunity to kiss me again.

My heart was a jackhammer in my chest until I was back inside my car. I was falling for this girl. Hard. She had me in the palm of her hand, and she didn't even know it. With Charlotte by my side, I felt like I could face anything. She made me want to be better. She made me feel better. Calmer. Safer. I only wished I could do the same for her.

She kept me at a distance. Close enough to touch her, but not close enough to touch her soul. I couldn't stop thinking about the secrets surrounding her. She refused to tell me why she had to leave Florida; she refused to tell me why she was carrying a gun; she refused to tell me who she felt she needed protection from.

Charlotte was guarded. Someone had hurt her, and she was scared of getting hurt again. I had to prove myself to her. I had to prove that she could trust me.

CHARLOTTE

TANNER REFUSED TO TELL ME WHERE WE WERE GOING. ALL HE SAID was to dress casual. I brushed my hair and spritzed perfume as I surveyed myself in the mirror for the last time—jeans and a pale-yellow shirt. I jumped when his text came in at seven. I swung my purse over my shoulder as I made my way downstairs.

To my surprise, Tanner was holding another bouquet—a mixture of yellow, orange, and pink Gerbera daisies.

"Tanner, this is so sweet, but totally unnecessary. You bought me flowers yesterday."

"You said these were your favorite. I wanted you to have your favorite." He leaned in and left a lingering kiss on my lips, sending shivers down my spine, all the way to my toes.

"I can't argue with you when you kiss me like that."

He smirked. "Good. I'll have to remember that. It might come in handy the next time you're pissed at me."

As Tanner drove, I watched the turns he took, trying to figure out where we were going. He finally pulled into a parking lot ten minutes later. Looking at the sign on the building, a knot formed in my stomach. We were at a shooting range.

"What are we doing here?"

"You have a gun, and for whatever reason, you won't tell me why. If you don't want to tell me the truth, I can handle that. I don't know why you feel like you need a gun, but I do know that you need to know how to use it. So, I figured it would be fun if we could learn together."

My stomach flopped. He knew I was lying to him, yet he was choosing to help me, anyway. He had my back, regardless of my secrets. He was trusting me. But I didn't deserve it.

"Thank you," was all I could manage amidst the emotion caught in my throat.

Inside, Tanner paid for an hour of practice, along with ammo and paper targets. We were given eye and ear protection, which we were instructed to put on before entering the range.

"It's loud in there, especially for first-timers," said the range officer, Billy. "But don't worry—as long as you follow my instructions and rules, you'll be safe."

Tanner and I exchanged glances and nodded.

The sound of shots firing filled the air as soon as Billy opened the door. Even with ear protection on, I jumped every time I heard someone fire. Loud was an understatement. I noticed that I was only one of three women. The other two women were much older than me. I was relieved that Billy had agreed to help us get started.

Billy gestured to an empty bay beside the older ladies, and we set our things down on the table. He showed us what to do, step-by-step. It seemed easy enough.

"Ladies first," he shouted.

I swallowed hard and took a deep breath. I didn't know what to expect firing a gun for the first time. *Don't completely miss the target. That would be embarrassing.* I took my gun from Billy after he loaded it and stood in front of the table. My hands shook as I raised the gun in front of me.

"May I?" Billy stood behind me and placed his hands on my hips. He moved me where he wanted me to stand, setting my legs in the proper spots. He raised my arms, and I held the gun straight out in front of me. Then, he stepped away.

One. Two. Three. I pulled the trigger. Immediately, I was pushed backwards from the powerful blast, and the sound of the shot vibrated throughout my chest. I didn't hit any of the marks in the middle of the paper, but I hit the paper nonetheless.

I set my gun down on the table and turned around. Tanner high-fived me, a grin stretched across his face.

"What do you think?" Billy asked.

"I think you need to teach me how to hit my target."

He and Tanner laughed. "All right. Take the stance I showed you." I watched as he placed a small red sticker on the target paper where an actual human heart would be located, and sent it back down the track. "I want you to aim for that red sticker. Take a deep breath, and when you exhale, that's when you shoot."

I aimed for the red dot. Inhale. Exhale. Shoot. This time, I wasn't pushed backwards as far as before. I didn't hit the red dot, but I did hit the fake human in his chest.

"Woo!" Tanner hooted.

"That's the trick," Billy said. "If you aim for something small on your target, you'll be sure to hit somewhere close enough."

"I just need more practice."

"Your girl's determined," he said to Tanner.

Tanner just kept grinning. "Yes, she is."

"I think you guys are good to go. Let me know if you need any more help." Billy walked away, leaving me and Tanner alone.

"Your turn." I set my gun down and leaned against the table, watching Tanner take his stance.

I didn't find guns sexy, but Tanner looked sexy holding one. Then again, he would look sexy no matter what he was holding. He oozed virility. His shirt was tight in all the right places, showing off his muscular physique, and his jeans hugged his perfectly round bottom. The only bare asses I'd seen were in movies, other than my ex-boyfriend Kyle's. Kyle's could never compare. From what I could see, I doubted Brad Pitt's magnificent rear could even hold a candle to Tanner's.

"How's the view back there?"

My cheeks grew hot, and I knew my face was as red as a tomato. "Aren't you supposed to be focused on your target?"

"It's kind of hard to concentrate with you checking out at my ass like that. I'm not a piece of meat, you know."

One of the older women next to us poked her head into our bay. "Sugar, with a rear end like that, you should be used to getting ogled everywhere you go."

I burst into laughter, and she winked at me before returning to her side of the bay.

Tanner laughed, and it was the first time I'd seen him blush. He set the gun down. "Get over here. It's my turn to stare at your ass now."

"Careful," I said, gesturing with my thumb. "She might think you're talking to her."

We took turns shooting for the rest of our paid hour and grabbed pizza nearby afterward. Two hours later, we arrived back at my apartment.

"I'd say we could go back to my place to hang out, but my brother ruined that idea." Tanner turned off his car and faced me in his seat.

"What do you mean?"

"I was going to move in to the apartment above our garage. My parents had it furnished for me and everything. Then, Chase decided he wanted to give it to his girlfriend instead."

"He's dating that girl Merritt, right?"

"Yeah, or at least he thinks he is. I'm not sure she's interested in him ... which makes me like the girl instantly."

"Mal told me what happened to her family. She probably needs that apartment more than you do right now."

"You sound like my mom."

"What's she like?"

"She's perfect. She's like Superwoman."

"Most moms are."

Tanner laced his fingers with mine. "Do you remember yours at all?"

"I have some memories of her. Only good ones. She gave the best hugs."

"You don't seem sad when you talk about her."

"I've had a long time to grieve."

"How did your dad handle it?"

I knew Tanner was asking because he was about to go through it himself. Normally, I didn't like opening up about this, but right now I didn't mind. I would stay in the car talking to him until sunrise if I knew it would help him feel even a little better.

"My dad was heartbroken. He still is."

"And you?"

I shrugged. "I was so young, I don't think I really processed it. I focused on cheering up my dad. We were so close."

"Were?"

"We sort of had a falling-out since leaving Florida."

"You didn't want to come here, did you?"

"I didn't really have a choice."

"You're eighteen. You could've stayed there."

I shook my head. "I should get going. It's late."

Tanner leaned closer until the warmth of his breath reached my lips. "If I stop asking questions, will you stay a little longer?"

"Maybe."

"Let me convince you, then." He trailed kisses along my neck. His tongue swept across my skin, followed by a gentle bite that sent a charge through me.

I couldn't move, completely paralyzed and breathless under his spell. Nobody had ever put their mouth on me like that. Then again, nobody I'd met had ever been quite like Tanner Brooks. He was intimidating and exhilarating at the same time, and I was powerless to the way he made me feel.

"Now will you stay?" he whispered as his tongue traced my ear.

"You said you wouldn't ask any more questions."

His laugh was low and husky as he took my earlobe between his teeth. "Smart-ass."

Unable to take the teasing for one second longer, I grabbed the back of his head and pulled his lips onto mine. I opened my mouth, letting his tongue slide inside. Tanner let out a low growl. His kiss was so intense—so electrifying—I felt it in every nerve ending. I slipped my hands under his shirt to feel the ripples on his stomach. His skin was silk, each cube on his abdomen as if carved out of stone. I craved more of him but couldn't get close enough with the center console between us.

"I really hate my brother right now."

I giggled against his mouth. "She needs the apartment, even more than you do right now."

Tanner sighed and touched his lips to my forehead. "Yeah, yeah."

"Besides, I wouldn't let you take me home tonight, anyway."

His eyebrows lifted as he leaned back in his seat. "No?"

"Nope. The last time I gave myself to someone, he threw me away like yesterday's trash. I won't ever let that happen again. The next time I'm with someone, it's going to be someone worthy of me. Someone who will treat me, and my body, like I am something special."

"I'm glad to hear that." He took my face in his hands, and stared straight into my eyes. "Because you deserve to be worshipped, my sweet girl, and I plan on showing you exactly what that feels like."

As soon as the words left his mouth, I felt it. The smallest seed had been planted deep in the soil outside my heart. If I allowed it to remain there—if I let the sunshine in and watered it—it would sprout leaves and twist its vines around my fortress.

Or maybe it already had.

Chapter Nine

TANNER

"Can we watch *Moana*?" Khloe asked. She was jumping on my bed in zebra footy pajamas.

"Not tonight, Squirt. I have plans."

"With who?"

"A girl named Charlotte."

Khloe stopped jumping and bounced onto her bottom. "Who's Charlotte?" Her big round eyes watched me in the mirror as I pulled a T-shirt over my head.

"A girl I know."

"Where are you going with her?"

"To the movies."

"Can I come?" She fell to the floor onto her knees and begged with her tiny hands in front of her face. "Can I, Tanner? Please?"

"Not tonight. It's almost your bedtime." I ruffled her hair before tossing her over my shoulder.

She squealed as I carried her into her bedroom and flipped her onto her bed.

She giggled as Mom walked into the room. "Mommy, Tanner won't let me come to the movies with him. He's going with a girl."

Mom's eyebrows shot up, but she didn't ask me about it. "He probably won't let you come with him because it's your bedtime."

"See? Told ya, Squirt." I leaned over to kiss her on her forehead. "Good night. Sleep tight."

"I love you, Tan-Tan," she called.

"I love you, and I'd love you even more if you stopped calling me Tan-Tan."

"You know she only calls you that because you can't stand it," Mom called as I left Khloe's bedroom.

I winked at her before closing the door.

I trotted downstairs and slipped my wallet into my back pocket.

"Going out again?" Dad called from the living room.

"Yes, sir." I walked over to find him on the recliner. He'd lost so much weight over the past couple months, and his sallow complexion no longer looked like the same olive color as mine. It was hard to see him like this.

"When are you going to let us meet this mystery woman of yours?" he asked with a smirk.

I smiled as I leaned down to kiss him on the top of his head. "Good night. I love you, Dad."

"I love you, too, son."

I knew my parents were curious about who I was spending all my free time with. The past few weeks had been spent either at the shop, or with Charlotte. Chase was bringing Merritt around a lot, and it made me want to bring Charlotte over, too.

But being around my father broke my heart, and I didn't want to be home to witness it. Charlotte was my escape from the depressing reality of what was happening to him. When I was with her, nothing else mattered—not our past lives, and not anything we were going through in the present.

CHARLOTTE

TANNER TOOK ME ON ANOTHER DATE. WE WERE SITTING IN THE

back seat of his car at a drive-in movie. I didn't even know what movie we were here to see. It didn't matter—our eyes were closed as we made out like kids without a care in the world. His Mustang wasn't the most comfortable place to be, but it was better than nothing.

"This is the first time I am actually regretting buying this Mustang."

"I think this is romantic. It's what everybody did in the fifties."

"Oh, yeah? Is an ass cramp romantic to you?"

"It is if you'll massage it out for me."

"One day, I'm going to take you up on that."

I giggled and rested my head against his shoulder. Admittedly, the more time we spent together, the more I wanted *more*. The physical attraction between us was growing by the day.

"We should be taking this time to get to know each other better," Tanner said.

I raised my eyebrows. "Okay. What's your favorite color?"

"Red. You?"

"Teal. It was my mom's favorite. When's your birthday?"

"May 1."

I laughed. "Of course it is."

"What does that mean?"

"You're a Taurus. I could've guessed that one."

"All right, smartass. When's your birthday?"

"March 1."

"We're both on the first. That's pretty cool. What does that make you?"

"Pisces."

"So, I'm a bull and you're a fish?"

"Yup. Two fish swimming in opposite directions." *Which was exactly how I felt most of the time.*

"Okay, enough of these fluffy questions. I want to truly know you. I want to know about your life."

"Well, you already know about my mom. After that, it was just me and my dad. Both of their parents died young, so I didn't have any grandparents or other family members. We had a few close friends. I miss my best friend, Carla, terribly. She is the reason why I know about zodiac signs. She knows all about astrology. She swears by it."

"Do you still talk to her?"

No, because I disappeared in the night, never to be seen or heard from again. "Sometimes."

"Can I ask you something else?"

"Sure." I stiffened, an uneasy feeling creeping into my stomach.

Tanner swiped and clicked on his phone a couple times and then held out his screen for me to see. "Was that your dad's old bakery?"

Acid pooled in my stomach. The picture on Tanner's screen showed a fiery blaze engulfing the storefront of a bakery—my bakery —as firefighters attempted to put the fire out. The headline above the picture read: "Fire Breaks Out at Family-Owned Bakery."

"That's it, isn't it?"

Tears welled in my eyes, and my throat felt like it was closing. The dam I'd built to stop me from remembering that night had sprung a massive leak as the memories rushed forward. I sat, paralyzed, while the terror and guilt washed over me. Just like that, I was back in the kitchen of Dad's old bakery ...

I turned the knob on the stove. The clicking igniter sounded so loud in the silent room. It accompanied the sound of my beating heart. The flame roared to a start, and I stared into it. The red gas can felt light in my hand. I couldn't forget to take it with me when I left.

I was doing this. There was no turning back now.

"What do you think you're doing?" John's voice startled me out of my thoughts. He stood in the doorway at the back of the kitchen.

He was too early. Had he been watching me?

"Stay back!" I shouted. "You can't stop me."

"The hell I can't! You think you're so smart, but you're not smart enough, blondie!" He stomped toward me, but his fancy leather shoes slipped on the lighter fluid I'd poured all over the kitchen. His legs went up as he flew into the air, and his head bounced when it hit the tile.

I held my breath, waiting for him to get up.

But he didn't.

. . .

"Charlotte!" Tanner was shaking me by the shoulders now. "Talk to me, baby. Please!"

I blinked a few times and touched my fingers to my cheek. I was crying. Where was I?

I turned to see Tanner sitting beside me wearing a tortured expression.

"Charlotte? Can you hear me?"

I was safe. I was with Tanner. I flung my arms around his neck and held him as tightly as I could.

"Baby, what the hell just happened? Talk to me. One second, you were sitting here talking to me, and the next ..." He paused. "You were gone. It's like you were sleepwalking."

I tried to control my sobs, wiping my face with the back of my hand. "I ... I get these sometimes."

"These? What are these?" He held me out in front of him so he could look into my eyes. He looked so scared, and I felt awful. I'd scared him.

"I don't know. Panic attacks, I think."

"What are you having panic attacks about?"

I covered my face with my hands. "I can't tell you, Tanner."

"Why not?" He took my hands and held them inside his. "Maybe I can help you. Let me help you."

"There's nothing you can do. It's over now."

"Clearly, it's not over. You just had a panic attack when I showed you the fire from your old bakery. Is it because of the fire? Were you trapped inside or something?"

"Tanner, enough!" I yelled louder than I'd meant to. "Please," I begged with tears streaming down my face. "I need you to trust me when I say that I cannot tell you. I need you to accept me for who I am today. I need my past to stay in the past. I need to move forward. I need to forget."

"And when will these panic attacks end?" he asked quietly.

"I don't know. I don't know what's going to happen in the future, and I can't change what has happened in the past. All I know is that I want to enjoy spending time with you. I want to hold you, and I want to kiss you. That's it. If we continue, I need you to say that you can accept me this way."

Tanner ran his fingers through my hair and drew me in until his lips brushed mine. "I accept you. I will always accept you." He looked at me with such ferocity, I could feel how much he meant it.

I knew it was unfair to ask him for this without full disclosure, but this was the only way. He wouldn't be able to accept my demons if he met them. I wouldn't expect anyone to. The only way I could protect Tanner from my past was keeping him completely out of it. He was innocent. I was not.

Chapter Ten

CHARLOTTE

"I can't believe Tanner Brooks is your boyfriend," Mallory said as we got out of my car.

"He is not."

"You've spent every single day for the past two weeks together. You make out. He brings you flowers and pays for your meals. That sounds like boyfriend behavior to me."

"I don't even know if I want him to be my boyfriend." *He hasn't asked me to be his girlfriend. I can't just assume things.* "What if he's dating other girls?"

Mallory stopped in the middle of the street and gave me a blank look. "He is not dating other girls, and you know it."

I thought I knew, but one never really knows for sure.

"Just think—all of this is happening because I made you look for a hot guy in the cafeteria that day."

"I'll be sure to send you a fruit basket."

"Have you talked to Gabe at all?"

"We texted a few times, but we haven't hung out since I gave him the let's-be-friends speech."

"I'm sure he got the hint. I wonder if he knows you're with Tanner."

"We are not exclusive." I didn't know what we were doing.

I followed her up the walkway to the Beta house and smiled. "Mal, your ass looks great in that costume."

"Fuck yeah it does!" She flashed me a devilish grin over her shoulder before pushing the door open.

A blast of music hit us as soon as we walked in. The party was already in full swing, and people were crammed in everywhere. Elaborate decorations filled the house as if the Halloween Spirit store shipped over everything it had in stock. I'd never been to a party like this. The parties where I came from consisted of a handful of friends sitting around a bonfire on a beach, or in someone's backyard.

"This is insane," I shouted into Mallory's ear as we weaved through the crowd. I noticed a large banner that read, "Happy Birthday, Shelly," hanging from the wall behind the DJ. "Who's Shelly?"

"Merritt's best friend. The redhead. She acts like this whole party was meant for her."

We reached the kitchen, and Mallory wasted no time filling two red cups with beer.

"Cheers!" She tapped her cup against mine. "Let's go find your man."

I scanned the room as we walked through another door at the back of the kitchen. I noticed Chase immediately, his blond hair sticking out above everyone's heads. He was dressed as a mobster with the fake gun and cigar to match. My chest tightened. I inhaled and exhaled several times, trying to push it away. *Relax. It's just a costume.*

I wouldn't have recognized Merritt if Chase hadn't been standing there too. Her sling was off, and her wild curls were tucked under a short black wig. She wore a stunning silver flapper costume ... and a smile. I felt happy that Chase and his family were looking out for her. She'd been through so much tragedy, from what I had heard. Life without my mother was difficult, but I couldn't imagine life without my dad on top of that. Merritt needed people like the Brooks. It was comforting to know that there were good people like them in this world.

Then I spotted Tanner. Standing by the pool tables across from the dance floor, he wore a gladiator costume. I knew I was openly gawking at his bare upper body, but I couldn't find it in me to care. His caramel skin called to me, and I immediately wanted to reach out and touch it. From his blocky broad shoulders to his shredded stomach, with the sought-after V of his lower abdomen, he looked every part the Roman warrior. Moreover, as much as he did not like to admit it, he had the heart of a warrior, as well.

Mallory leaned closer to me. "Pick up your jaw. You're drooling."

Tanner surveyed my body as Mallory and I approached. He wore a wide grin and his eyes gleamed when they locked on mine. He handed his pool stick to Derek and stalked around the table. He grabbed hold of my face and planted one of his mind-blowing kisses on me. My legs threatened to buckle. Though he hadn't claimed me as his girlfriend, this was a public declaration I hadn't expected. *I hadn't expected to like it, either.*

"You look incredibly sexy, Supergirl."

"You look sexy yourself." I ran my hands along his arms and over his chest.

"Get a room!"

Tanner glared at Derek over his shoulder. "Or you could just look away, fuckwad."

Derek held out Tanner's pool cue. "Come on. It's your turn, bro."

"Yeah, let's go. I want to dance," Mallory said. "You can't hog her all night. She was mine first."

Tanner chuckled. "Go dance. Let me finish this game, and I'll find you on the dance floor."

"Good luck!" I said before Mallory dragged me away from him.

We squeezed into a small space on the dance floor. It was hot, and we were sweaty messes in no time. I stole a few glances at Tanner every now and again—and each time I did, he was already looking at me.

"Hello," Mallory shouted. "Earth to Charlotte!"

"Sorry, I was thinking."

"You're at a raging house party. You should be drinking. Not thinking!"

"I'm your designated driver. I had one beer. I'm done."

"We're taking a damn Uber next time!"

"You say that every time."

"Well, next time, I'll mean it!"

A warm body pressed against my back. When I turned around, I was unpleasantly surprised to see Shawn grinding against me. I pushed him away, but he grabbed my waist and pulled me closer.

"Please leave me alone," I said, pushing him backward again.

"I just want to dance with you, sexy," he slurred in my ear.

I wiped his sweat off my face.

"She doesn't want to dance with you," Mallory shouted.

"Why don't you show me what's underneath that skirt?" He reached for my thigh, but Mallory shoved him hard enough to buy me time to escape.

We walked on the outskirts of the dance floor, making our way toward the pool tables. Tanner pushed his way through the crowd to get to us. The darkness in his eyes worried me.

I met Tanner at the edge of the dance floor before he could get any farther. I placed my hands on either side of his face, forcing his eyes off Shawn and onto me. "Look at me. Look at me. Everything is fine. I handled it."

"Did he hurt you?"

"No. Everything is fine. He'll go bother someone else now."

"What did he say to you?"

"Nothing. He's drunk and slurring his words."

"Charlotte—"

I stretched onto my toes and pressed my mouth against his.

His entire body melted against mine as his arms wrapped around me. All of his attention was focused on me now. He walked me backwards and pushed me against the nearby wall. I ran my fingers down his back, feeling the tiny droplets of sweat along his spine.

"Your hands are the only hands I want on me," I said into his ear. "Nobody else is going to touch me."

"Good, because you're the only one I want to touch." He kissed my neck, causing me to exhale and grip him tighter.

A large hand appeared on Tanner's shoulder. Chase was standing beside him. Well, technically, he was *swaying* beside him. I looked around for Merritt and spotted her on the dance floor with her friends.

"Baby brother." Chase's eyes were glassy. "Always the ladies man."

"Fuck off, dick-hole." Tanner shook free of his brother's grip.

Chase only laughed. His eyes had the same sparkle as Tanner's when he smiled, though they were a stunning hazel color.

"Who's driving your drunk ass home?"

"I came with Merritt," he slurred. "The love of my life."

Tanner rolled his eyes. "Here we go."

"One day, you'll understand." Chase's eyelids closed. "You're going to fall in love, and you're going to understand everything." He reached out and ruffled Tanner's hair before he stumbled away.

I bit my lip in a failed attempt to conceal my laughter.

Tanner shook his head. "Drunk bastard."

"He's totally in love with Merritt. I think it's cute."

"Where is she, anyway? She needs to make sure he gets home safely." Tanner glanced around the room, and his smile diminished. "Fuck."

I spun around to see Shawn now attempting to dance with Merritt. He gripped her arm, and judging by the look on her face, he was hurting her. Chase was too drunk to notice.

I held onto Tanner's arm. "Tanner, you can get her away from Shawn without hurting him."

"But I want to hurt him," he said through gritted teeth.

"Promise me you won't hurt him!" I shouted as he barreled through the crowd.

He looked back at me, and his eyes were already far-away. "I promise I'll try."

I searched for Mallory, but she was already coming for me. She grabbed my elbow with Derek in tow. "You know Tanner's going to kill him. Come on."

We followed Tanner as he pushed through the people on the dance floor, tossing them aside like ragdolls. When he reached Shawn, he gripped two handfuls of Shawn's shirt in his fists.

"She doesn't want to dance, bro," he shouted over the music as he glared down at Shawn.

Shawn raised his hands to surrender, and I let out the breath I'd been holding. All Tanner had to do was let him go, and then walk away.

"It's okay, Tanner," Merritt said, trying to calm him down.

Tanner's grip on Shawn's shirt loosened. Then, Shawn leaned in and said something in his ear. In the blink of an eye, Tanner's huge fist smashed into Shawn's face. Blood spewed out of his nose and splattered everywhere. Shawn fell to the ground. Everyone circled around them, chanting for a fight. People pushed against me, and Mallory's hand was slipping out of mine. I squeezed it tighter. There were too many people in here, and we needed to get out.

I lost sight of Tanner. While I was focused on finding him, someone shoved me from behind. Fights were breaking out around us. Drunken frat boys with beer muscles and a mob mentality. I lurched forward and stumbled into someone else. Before I could apologize, the guy I'd knocked into turned around and blindly swung his fist at me.

The last thing I heard was Mallory's scream.

TANNER

"TAKE IT EASY, BABY. DON'T MOVE TOO FAST." I KNELT DOWN NEXT to Charlotte and tried to ease her up.

"Back the fuck away from her, asshole," Mallory said, the sound of her voice like nails on a chalkboard.

"I'm just trying to help her."

Charlotte sat up and the ice pack slid off of her face and plopped into her lap.

"Help her? Look at what you did to her face! That right there is because of you." Mallory knelt on the floor next to the bed. "Hey, girl. How do you feel?"

"My head hurts," Charlotte mumbled.

I extended my hand to touch her, but Mallory intercepted.

"I swear to God." Mallory closed her eyes. "If you don't back the fuck away from her, I am going to break every finger on that hand of yours. Go. Away."

I opened my mouth to fire unkind words back at her, but I thought better of it. I didn't want to upset Charlotte. She'd already been through enough.

"How bad is it?" she asked.

"You've got a nice shiner. Doesn't look like anything's broken, though." Mallory handed Charlotte her phone so Charlotte could look into the camera and see for herself.

A deep purple ring had already begun forming around Charlotte's right eye. Tears welled behind my lids as I watched her look at her reflection. Someone had punched her in the face and knocked her unconscious. I wasn't there to stop it. I was supposed to protect her, but I'd let her get hurt.

"Don't cry, Char. It's okay. You're going to be okay. I know it was scary back there but you're safe now." Mallory glared at me.

It was physically killing me to not comfort her. The fact that I had caused this was not lost on me, but right now, I just wanted to comfort her. I'd never meant for her to get hurt.

"Mal, can you please give me a minute with Tanner?"

Fucking finally. I needed to be alone with her. I needed to hold her and tell her how sorry I was. I needed to make sure she was okay.

Mal's eyes widened. "Are you—"

"Please, Mal." Charlotte held her hand up to stop her. "I'll meet you in the car."

Mallory wavered a moment but then stood and walked away. Derek left with her.

I sat beside Charlotte on the bed, taking her into my arms. "Are you okay? I am so sorry, my sweet girl. I—"

"I know you never meant for me to get hurt," she finished.

I sat back to look at her. "I am so sorry that this happened."

She nodded. "I know you are. You can't help it. It's who you are. I should have never expected you to change."

Worry spread like wildfire throughout my body. She seemed distant. "Charlotte, I can change. I want to change. Tonight was a mistake."

"Tonight wasn't a mistake, Tanner. Tonight was a choice, and choices have consequences. You made the choice to punch Shawn. That choice caused a ripple effect. Now, I have a black eye and probably a concussion." She lifted her face to look me in my eyes, and it looked like it pained her to do so. "Anger is a choice ... and it's the wrong one." Her voice cracked as she said it, hoisting herself out of bed.

"Please don't walk away from me, Charlotte. I will try harder next time. I know I can."

"I don't want there to be a next time. I don't want to be worried about when you're going to fly off the handle again. I don't want you to hurt people. I don't want to get hurt." She pulled her arm free from my grasp. "Please, Tanner. Don't make this any harder than it already is." A tear rolled down her cheek as she turned and left.

I remained there, cemented to the ground. I had Charlotte's trust, and I'd fucked it up. In a matter of seconds, it was gone. I'd let myself fall. I took the leap, only to be splattered at the bottom of the cliff.

Once again, I'd proved that I could be nothing more than a worthless piece of shit.

Chapter Eleven

CHARLOTTE

"What did your father say about your eye?" Mallory whispered as she tied her apron around her waist.

"He asked if Tanner hit me."

"He might as well have. Fucking psychopath."

"Stop. Please. I don't want to talk about this, or him. I just want to forget this weekend ever happened and move forward."

"Has he called?"

I sighed. "No. He knows how I feel."

"How *do* you feel?"

Disappointed. Empty. Hurt. "Stupid."

"Why do you feel stupid?"

"I can't stand the kind of girls who try to change the men they're with. They try to make them act how they want them to act, but then get mad every time they revert back. I've always felt that if you didn't like something about someone, you shouldn't be with them. You can't change people. I was dumb for trying to change Tanner. I was dumb for trusting him. I was dumb for thinking he could be different."

Mallory put her hand on my shoulder. "You gave him a chance, and it was going well for a while. You care about him. That's not dumb."

I pulled the brim of my hat lower as the first customer walked through the door. "I just wish it didn't hurt so badly."

"It will get easier in time. I think you're doing the right thing, getting out now before you're both too invested in each other."

The pain in my chest told me it was too late for that.

Mallory helped the customer and waited until she was gone before turning back to me. "Did you hear what Shawn said to make Tanner punch him?"

I shook my head. I wasn't sure I wanted to know, but I knew she was going to tell me anyway.

"He said if Tanner wasn't going to fuck Merritt, then he would." She shivered. "He's disgusting."

I knew any male would've wanted to hit a mouthy guy like Shawn. He was disrespectful toward women, to say the least. Even I'd wanted to slap him during our encounters. I didn't want to admit it, but part of me felt glad that Tanner knocked him out. Could I be overreacting about it? Or was this a sign from the universe telling me we weren't meant to be? This was the endless mental battle I'd had with myself all weekend.

"So, what are your plans for first Thanksgiving in New York?"

The holidays. I hadn't thought about them. Dad and I had always been surrounded by friends. This year, it would be just the two of us.

I shrugged. "We haven't discussed it yet."

"You and your dad should come to my house. My mom puts out a huge spread. We're Italian, so we'll have more than enough food."

"I'd like that. I'll talk to my dad."

"Talk to your dad about what?" Dad stepped out of the kitchen with a fresh batch of seven-layer cookies.

"I'm inviting you to my house for Thanksgiving," Mallory said. "It'll be me, my mom, my grandparents, my aunt and uncle, and their three kids."

"Sounds like a full house. Are you sure your mother won't mind setting two extra plates for us?"

She blew air out of her mouth and waved her hand. "Please. You guys are like family. She'd love to have you."

Dad looked at me for approval. "What do you say, kiddo?"

"I'm in."

He smiled. He looked genuinely excited. Had he been worried about what we would be doing for the upcoming holidays? We barely talked anymore. It felt odd not knowing everything that went through his mind. More guilt piled on top of my heartache.

When I got home later that evening, I showered and flopped onto my bed with my Kindle. I was in the mood to escape my thoughts and the real world. I hadn't gotten past the first page when there was a soft knock on my bedroom door.

"Come in."

Dad poked his head through the doorway. "Whatcha doin' tonight?"

I lifted my Kindle. "You're looking at it."

"I thought you'd be off with Tanner."

Just the sound of his name was like a knife through my chest. "No. I ended things with him."

"Can I ask why?" He sat on the edge of my bed.

"I got punched in the eye because of a fight he started."

Dad took the Kindle from my hands and set it down on my nightstand. "I always thought your mom would be around to have these talks with you." He chuckled. "You're eighteen, and you're dating. I don't know where the time went."

"I often wonder what Mom would say if she were here. I didn't get the chance to know her well enough."

"Well, I knew her. You can ask me a question, and I can try to tell you what I think she would've said."

I smiled. "I like that idea."

He stuck out his chest and lifted his chin. "Go ahead. Try me."

The way I'd been treating Dad since we'd left Florida was wearing on me. I didn't know if it was due to my recently damaged defenses, or if I was feeling the upcoming holiday spirit, but I felt weakened under the weight of my emotions. My fading resolve had me missing the way things used to be between us.

"Tanner has a huge heart. He's funny, and caring. He's handsome."

"Those are all very good qualities."

"He has anger issues, though. I get where it all comes from. His dad is really sick. He's dying, actually."

"Oh, no. What from?"

"Cancer."

"Ah ..."

"But his anger makes him do crazy things. It's like he's a different person. I'm worried that he could really hurt somebody someday."

"Do you ever feel like he could hurt you?"

I shook my head. "No. It was never directed at me. Then again, we haven't fought. I've only known him for a short time. I don't really know what he's capable of, and that scares me."

"Well, as your father, I will say that his anger worries me, too. Your mother, on the other hand, would tell you to ask your heart what it's feeling."

"All my heart tells me is what I feel for him. Not very helpful."

"Your mom was a firm believer in following your heart. She would say that your head only makes you worry about things, and it could create an entire problem out of nothing. She always said your head is not to be trusted."

"She sounds so brave."

"She was." Dad's eyes gleamed. "She was brave right until the very end."

"I wish I could be more like her."

"You're more like her than you realize. You just have to trust your heart."

"It's not that easy, Dad. You have to listen to your brain. Your brain is what keeps you safe."

"Then I guess you need to decide if you want to play it safe, or if you can try to be brave. Safe will keep you protected, for the most part. Safe will give you a fine life. Brave, on the other hand, could give you opportunities and experiences that you would never have known if you didn't take the chance. Your mother believed that life was about taking chances."

"I am careful. I am safe. I don't know how to be any other way."

"I imagine Tanner feels the same way."

"What do you mean?"

"He's angry and hurting. He doesn't know what to do with it, and he doesn't know how to be any different. You came along and changed his whole world. He needs more time to adjust." Dad looked down at his hands. "People are going to make mistakes, Charlotte. It's how we learn, and grow, and change.

"I know you hate feeling pain; you were so young when you lost your mother. But you can't shut pain out. You can't shut people out. Sometimes, you have to be brave and give someone another chance to prove that he won't do it again."

I knew he was talking about more than just Tanner. I leaned over and wrapped my arms around him. Tears stung my eyes, and I hugged him tighter.

"I'm sorry for ruining things between us," Dad said, his tears wetting my shoulder. "I don't want you to hate me forever."

"I'm sorry, too," I choked out. "I don't hate you. I just want things to be like they used to."

He held me out in front of him. "Then give me that chance. We're all we have. Just you and me. I don't want to lose you. I know I made a horrible mistake, but I need you to forgive me."

We often look at our parents like superheroes. We think they can do no wrong. They raise us, protect us, and care for us. Then, we get to a certain age and realize our parents are only humans. They make mistakes, just like we do. They don't know what they're doing any more than we do. This realization is like a slap in the face. Another betrayal. *First, there's no Santa. Now, you're telling me that my parents make mistakes?*

What we need to practice isn't how to be perfect. We're all trying to figure out our lives, and we're all going to make mistakes. What we need to practice more of is forgiveness.

Looking into my father's eyes, I knew it was the right thing to do. My father was the only man I had ever loved, and he was the only family I had. Even though he'd betrayed my trust, he was still my father. I couldn't control what happened to my mother, but I could control where my relationship with my father went.

And sometimes, when a girl gets her heart broken, the only thing she needs is her dad.

————

"THIS IS GOING TO BE SO MUCH FUN!"

I swallowed hard as I looked at the gym from inside my car.

Mallory's shoulders slumped. "Why do you look like you're going to puke? You're the one who wanted to do this."

I fixed my face and shot her a look. "I'm fine."

I'd seen a flyer at school for a self-defense class at the nearby gym. As a teenager, I'd always wanted to go to one. *It would be fun to learn how to kick someone's ass*, Carla and I would say. I didn't think I would ever need to defend myself in order to stay alive.

Now, I did.

So I asked Mallory to join me, knowing she would be on board, no questions asked.

When we stepped through the gym doors, we were hit with a musty smell. So many things were going on at once in different areas of the open space, I stopped to take it all in. From young co-eds to gray-haired men, all walks of life threw punch after punch at long, black punching bags hanging from the ceiling. Some flipped giant-sized tires, while others slapped ropes against the floor. Everyone glistened with sweat. Everyone looked like they knew what they were doing.

As intimidating as it was, I felt a bubbling in my gut. *Gun, check. Ass-kicking skills, here we go.*

"Hello, ladies. Welcome to my gym."

I snapped my head toward the deep voice. Out of the corner of my eye, I saw Mallory's mouth fall open. I think I even heard a gasp escape her lips. Before us stood a tall, muscular man covered in tattoos. Arms, legs, ribcage. Even his knuckles and neck were tattooed. The only place that wasn't inked was his face. Chiseled jaw, ice-blue eyes, and dimples that framed his Colgate commercial smile. His cut-off tank top revealed his incredible physique. I'd heard of a six-pack before, but this man's stomach had muscles I didn't even know existed. He was an odd mixture of beauty and badassery.

He held his hand out. "I'm the owner. My name is TJ."

I slipped my hand inside his, bracing for a hard squeeze. "I'm Charlotte. This is Mallory."

TJ shook my hand gently and turned to do the same to Mallory. She shook his hand like a robot, still speechless. "Nice to meet you both. What are you ladies here for?"

"I saw a flyer about a self-defense class."

TJ nodded. "You're right on time. Follow me."

Mallory grasped my arm as we followed behind him. "Please tell me he's the instructor."

I stifled a giggle. "I can't believe someone was able to render you speechless."

"I feel as if I've seen a unicorn. A big, sexy, muscular, tattooed unicorn. Who looks like that? Seriously. His six-pack has a six-pack! I bet his dick has a six-pack, too!"

The laugh I'd been suppressing burst from my throat.

TJ turned around with a curious smile. "What's so funny?"

Mallory's nails dug into my forearm. "Nothing, sir. Sorry."

"Sir? I like the sound of that." He winked and gestured to the three women standing in the mirrored corner of the gym. "Are you ready to begin?"

They nodded eagerly, looking just as awed by him as Mallory and I probably looked. The two younger women looked like sisters in their early twenties. The older woman looked to be their mother. Unlike the other gym members, they didn't have exceptional muscles nor did they look tough or menacing. They looked like regular women, just like me and Mallory.

"You can leave your coats and purses on the bench in the corner," he instructed. "Spread out, and we'll get started."

For the next hour, TJ led us through a series of maneuvers. He took turns working with each of us, explicitly explaining what he was going to do before he did it. The moves started out simple. How to jab someone in the throat. How to break free from someone's grip on your arm. How to use your attacker's weight to your advantage. Everything led to the final maneuver, when we were taught how to flip an attacker over our shoulders and slam him onto the ground. That move was my favorite.

At what I thought was the end of the session, TJ instructed us to sit in a circle with him. We wiped our sweat with the free towels he'd provided and gulped from our water bottles while we caught our breaths.

"I always start my class with the physical moves. That's what everyone expects out of a self-defense class. We all have fun slamming people onto the ground, don't we?"

We nodded in agreement.

"But I am going to teach you something that will help you more than any of the exercises we just did. Defense is only half of the lesson. You need to learn how to play offense, too." His eyes narrowed, and he pointed his index finger around our circle. "Each one of you has inner strength. You might not know it. You might not believe me right now. But it's there. You need to remember this always. Your attacker is going to be strong. He, or she, is going to have confidence. Predators see victims as weak. They believe they can take advantage of you. Don't let anyone think they can take advantage of you. Don't give them a reason to think you are weak."

Instantly, the image of my father and I tied to the oven in our Florida bakery flashed through my mind. As if I was looking in on myself from the outside, I saw a scared, vulnerable girl.

"What are you thinking about right now?" TJ was looking directly at me.

"Huh? I, uh ... nothing. I was just listening."

TJ gave me a knowing smile. "Were you ever in a situation where you felt weak?"

I tried to swallow the lump in my throat as I nodded. "Yes. Once."

"Will that situation ever happen again, after today?"

"I hope not."

"Hope isn't enough, Charlotte. You need to believe that it won't happen because you won't let it happen. You need to believe in your-self. Do you understand?"

Again, I nodded. *But how?*

TJ pointed to the mother of the two girls sitting beside Mallory. "Jessica, would you like to share your story with our new classmates?"

"Of course." Jessica turned to face us. "Ten years ago, I worked in Manhattan. I had to take the subway to and from my job five days a week. I was a secretary for a law firm. I always dressed professionally. Heels, skirts, blouses. Anyway, some nights I stayed late and had to take the subway during the less-crowded hours." She laughed once. "Sounds nice, right? Most people would love an empty subway car to themselves."

My stomach twisted as I anticipated where this story was headed.

"One night on my ride home, I was listening to music on my phone with my earbuds in. People got off at their usual stops, leaving me and a man who I thought was asleep a few seats down. When we started moving again, the man stood and lunged at me, grabbing my arm and pulling me onto the floor in the aisle. I thought he wanted my purse, so I tried to give it to him. It was when he tossed my purse aside that I realized what was about to happen."

Jessica's daughters took each of her hands as she told us the rest of her horrific story. Tears streamed down my face. Mallory's, too.

"I kept it from my family. I felt embarrassed. Dirty. Used. Pathetic. I quit my job and told my husband that I'd been let go from the firm. I never wanted to step foot on that subway again." Then, something in Jessica's somber expression changed, as her chest swelled and her chin tilted upward. "Last year, I met TJ. I've been training with him for ten months."

"And now?" TJ asked.

"Now, I'm in law school. I'm going to be a lawyer."

"And she takes the subway," Jessica's daughter added.

"I never want my daughters to experience anything close to what happened to me. I allowed myself to be a victim for a long time." She shook her head. "Not anymore. I'm a survivor."

"Victim versus survivor. Do you understand the difference between the two?" TJ asked, looking around our circle. "A victim is the result of a situation. The *result*. The end. Your story doesn't have to end after something heinous happens to you.

"A survivor is someone who remains. Someone who copes with the aftermath and rises above it." TJ looked at me, a soft yet determined expression on his face. "Are you going to be the victim for the rest of your life, Charlotte?"

Acid boiled in my stomach. The burning crept up my body, spreading out into my arms, and simmered in my throat. "No."

TJ slowly broke out into a Cheshire grin. "And why is that?"

"Because I am a survivor."

Chapter Twelve

TANNER

"*Moana! Moana! Moana!*"

"Can't we watch something else? You've seen this movie a hundred times." I stood and cleared plates from the dining room table.

"Why don't you put *Frozen* on?" Mom asked on her way into the kitchen.

"Let it go! Let it go!" Khloe sang as she twirled.

I covered my ears. "Forget what I said. I'll watch *Moana*."

Khloe giggled. "Yay! *Moana*!"

"You are a tiny tyrant, you know that?"

"But she's my tiny tyrant," Dad said, standing from his chair at the head of the table. He held his hand out for Khloe to take. "Lead me to the living room, Kokomo."

"Daddy, what does tyrant mean?"

I watched with a smile as they made their way into the living room. I stacked as many plates as I could, and was about to bring them into the kitchen when I saw something out of the corner of my eye.

Dad collapsed onto the floor.

"Daddy, get up. Daddy! Are you okay?" Khloe shouted.

I slammed the plates down on the table. I ran into the living room and scooped my father into my arms.

"What's going on?" Mom asked. Her hands flew to her mouth when she saw her unconscious husband in my arms. "What happened?"

Tears streamed down Khloe's face as she wrapped her arms around my mother's leg. "Daddy fell! I didn't do anything. I promise! He just fell!"

I shifted Dad's weight in my arms and snatched my car keys off the table near the front door. "Take your car and meet me at the hospital. I don't want Khloe with me while I drive. I'll call Chase on the way."

Mom just stood there, nodding and blinking.

I carried my lifeless father out the door. I wasn't waiting for an ambulance. I'd get there faster. I clipped my father into the passenger seat, and his head fell forward. I reclined the seat and positioned his head more comfortably. I couldn't bring myself to check for a pulse. He had to be alive. *This can't be it.*

I called Chase's phone when I was on my way, but it kept going to voicemail. I made one last attempt before I arrived at the hospital.

"Hello?" he answered, huffing.

"Meet me at the hospital."

"What's going on?"

"I'm on the way to the hospital with Dad."

"What do you mean? You're heading there now?"

"Yes! Get your head out of your ass and listen to what the fuck I'm saying!"

"Okay. I'll be there soon."

I dropped my phone into my lap and glanced over at my father in the passenger seat. "Please hold on, Dad. Hold on. We're almost there."

Several minutes later, I screeched to a halt in front of the emergency room entrance. I lifted my father out of the car and carried him into the waiting room as fast as I could. Two people wearing scrubs came running out from behind the double doors.

"What happened?" the woman asked, while the man signaled for a gurney.

"He just collapsed. He has cancer." I didn't know what else to say. I didn't know what the fuck was happening.

A third person pushed the gurney toward us, and I carefully placed my father onto it. They rolled him away from me, shouting things to each other. I didn't understand any of it.

"Sir, you have to wait here," the man ordered.

"The fuck I am! That's my father."

The man remained calm while the others wheeled my father farther away. "If you want us to help him, you need to stay here."

I was tempted to knock him out and chase after the gurney. *Don't do anything stupid. He's going to help Dad.* I remained where I stood, watching the doors close slowly behind them.

"Sir," the receptionist called. "You can have a seat and start filling out paperwork, if you want. It'll help take your mind off things for a bit while you wait."

I stared at her blankly, and turned my head back to the double doors. Mom would be here soon. She would be able to fill out the paperwork. I needed to stand right here and wait for Dad.

CHARLOTTE

I RUBBED MY EYES AS I TURNED OVER IN BED. THE ALARM CLOCK ON my nightstand read 3:00 a.m. I reached over for my phone, irritated that it was going off in the middle of the night. Fumbling to find the right button, I declined the call and set it back down. Why do wrong numbers always seem to call when you're sleeping?

Buzz. Buzz.

This time, I sat up and looked at the number calling on my screen. I almost dropped the phone when I saw who it was.

"Tanner?"

"Did I wake you?" The sound of his deep voice sent a familiar zing through my heart.

"It's three in the morning."

"I know. I'm sorry."

"Is everything okay?"

"Can you come outside for a minute?"

My spine stiffened. "Outside?"

"Yeah. I'm downstairs in my car."

"Why are you downstairs? Tanner, what's wrong? You're scaring me."

"I just ... I really need you right now. I don't know who else to talk to."

At the sound of the desperation in his voice, I tore the covers off and swung my legs out of bed. "I'll be down in two minutes."

I threw my hair into a ponytail and gargled with mouth wash. In my fuzzy slippers and flannel pajamas, I ran down the stairs and into Tanner's car.

"Where's your coat?" he asked, fighting to get out of his jacket.

"I keep forgetting how cold it gets here."

When he reached over to wrap his jacket around me, that's when I saw his eyes. Wet and bloodshot.

"Tanner, what's going on?"

"It's my dad. He ... he's in the hospital."

I sucked in a gasp. "What happened?"

"We'd finished eating dinner. He went into the living room with Khloe to watch *Moana*, and he just collapsed." Tanner shook his head in disbelief. "Right there on the floor. In front of Khloe. He collapsed. I carried him to the car, and I drove like a madman to the hospital."

My gut twisted thinking about Khloe having to witness that. "Where was Chase?"

"With Merritt. They're at the hospital now."

"What did the doctor say? How is your dad now?"

"The doctor ran a bunch of tests. Everyone just keeps saying how weak his body is." A tear rolled down his cheek as he averted his gaze out the windshield. "He's not strong enough to fight the cancer anymore."

I swiped his tear away with my thumb, and held my palm against his face. "I'm so sorry, Tanner."

He leaned over and buried his head in my neck. I wrapped my arms around him, stroking his soft hair as he cried on my shoulder. Words would always fail in a situation like this. I knew from experience. I knew what Tanner needed most: to be reassured that everything was going to be okay. I was thankful to be the one to give that to him. I wiped my own silent tears as I held him.

"I'm sorry I woke you. I couldn't take being in that hospital any longer."

"I'm glad you called me. You shouldn't be alone right now."

"You should go back inside. You're going to be exhausted when you have to wake up."

"Why don't you come in?"

His eyebrows pressed together. "Right now?"

"You can have my bed. I'll sleep on the couch until my dad leaves for work. I don't have to be at the bakery until the afternoon."

"You have class in the morning, don't you?"

"I can skip it."

He shook his head. "Don't skip class for me. I can go home."

"The thought of you in that house all by yourself would kill me."

"Your dad wouldn't mind me in your bed?"

"As long as I'm on the couch, it's all good. He knows about your dad."

"You talked to him about me?"

I nodded and looked down at my lap. "He wanted to know why I've been so sad lately."

Tanner touched his lips to my cheek. "I'm sorry for hurting you, Charlotte."

"Don't worry about me. You've got enough on your plate to deal with." I looked into his watery eyes. "Please say you'll come inside."

Tanner ran his fingers through his hair and exhaled a long breath of air. "Okay."

Once we were inside, I led him into my bedroom. I turned on my nightstand lamp and gestured to the bed. "All yours. Do you want some water or anything?"

"No. Thank you."

I closed the door behind me and stretched out on the living room couch. Wrapping myself with a fleece blanket, I didn't feel tired anymore. I thought about how lucky I was to have lost my mother at such a young age. It sounds crazy to think about it like that, but I was so young when it happened—I didn't have much to miss.

Chase and Tanner had almost two decades of memories with their father. Everything from this point on would be filled with reminders that their father was missing, that he should still be here. People wouldn't get to say that he went peacefully, or that he lived a long and happy life. They would say he was taken too soon. It wasn't fair. My heart broke for Tanner. How much more would he have to endure before his father's fight was over?

I watched the hours tick by until my father emerged from his room. The sun had not even begun to rise, and he was ready to leave for work.

"Charlotte? What are you doing out here?" he asked, sitting at the edge of the couch cushion next to my feet.

"Tanner's father is in the hospital. He's having a hard time, and I didn't want him to be alone. So, I told him to sleep here. Hence, me on the couch."

"Is his dad going to be okay?"

"I don't know how much longer he has. He's in the phase where his body is shutting down. It's just so sad."

Dad wrapped his arms around me and kissed my forehead. "You're a good kid. I know this is hard for you."

"I wish there was something more I could do."

"I know. But you can't save everyone from heartache. All you can do is be there to help them through it."

"I know."

"Well, let him know that he is always welcome here. I'm off to make the doughnuts. I'll see you in the afternoon."

"I love you, Dad."

"I love you more."

I watched as he gathered his wallet and keys before heading out. Once I heard the door lock, I sprang from the couch and into the hallway. I cracked my bedroom door to check on Tanner.

His head immediately lifted off the pillow.

"Did you get any sleep?"

His red eyes told me the answer before he could. "No."

Hurt for him constricted my chest, compelling me to comfort him. I climbed into bed beside him and slipped my legs under the covers. He still had his clothes on.

"You can't possibly be comfortable lying in a bed with jeans on."

"I didn't know if your dad was going to chase me out of here with a shotgun when he woke up. I figured, if you're packing heat, he must be, too."

"He doesn't know I'm packing heat, and I'd like to keep it that way. Now, take off your pants." I grimaced when I heard the words come out of my mouth. "I mean, you know ... get comfortable."

He chuckled as he stepped out of bed. I was glad to see him smile, even if it was at my awkward expense.

Don't look. Don't look. But I couldn't tear my eyes away. I watched as he pulled his shirt over his head and then unzipped his fly. He pushed his jeans down over his ass and let them drop to the floor before sliding back under the covers in nothing but his tight black boxer briefs.

I wrapped my body around Tanner, intertwining my legs with his, and melted against his smooth, warm skin. My head nestled perfectly in the crook of his neck, and I inhaled his scent as deeply as I could. I didn't know what I was doing, but my heart exploded with emotion. *Follow your heart.*

Tanner lifted my chin just slightly to look at me. "I miss you so much." He said it as if he still missed me, even though he was holding me. "Does this mean you're not mad at me anymore?"

Being this close to him after not seeing him for weeks felt so right, it was impossible to deny it. To deny him. "I miss you too much to be mad."

Unable to hold myself back any longer, I pressed my lips against his. It was the first time we were kissing without anything standing in our way—no console in the car, no neighbors with barking dogs. I kissed him with reckless abandon.

I crawled on top of him, feeling certain from his hardness that he wanted me there. I pressed myself against him as his hands made their way to my hips. His grip on me tightened as I rocked back and forth, our breaths becoming shorter with each passing second.

Tanner pulled my face just far enough away from his to speak. "I don't want to stop, but I'm afraid that once you leave for work later, we'll go back to not speaking. I don't want that." He squeezed me tighter. "Please tell me this isn't a one-time thing. I don't want your pity."

"This is not pity."

"What is it, then?"

The question lingered between us. *What was I doing? What was this?*

"Charlotte, whatever it is that's holding you back from me, please, just let it go. I don't care what you've done in your past. No matter what it is, it will never change the way I feel about you. You are the one for me. I want you to be mine."

That was the moment everything became clear. I knew I would never tell Tanner about the things I'd done in my past. I couldn't. I wouldn't be able to stand him looking at me in any other way than he was looking at me right now. Tanner accepted me with my secrets—he always had. Now, it was my turn to accept him.

I was going to follow what my heart wanted and throw caution to the wind. I didn't have the strength in me to care about the consequences any longer. Tanner needed me, and my heart was telling me that I needed him, too. If being safe meant being without him, then I didn't want to be safe. I'd have to be brave.

"I am yours."

He kissed me softly. "Say it again."

"I. Am. Yours." He hardened against my panties again as he opened his mouth and deepened our kiss. Our mouths melded together, hot, wet, and frantic, until we couldn't breathe. He pulled me back greedily each time we broke away panting.

I tore my lips away from his and kissed his neck, making a trail down his incredibly sculpted body. I took my time, running my lips and fingers over each of his perfectly cubed abs, until I reached the elastic waistband of his boxers. I slid them off, enjoying the hungry look in Tanner's eyes as he let me take control.

I took him into my mouth slowly and swirled my tongue around the head as Tanner exhaled a low groan. I drew him back into my mouth, gliding over his sensitive skin again and again. The louder he groaned, the more turned on it made me and the deeper I wanted to take him. Never before had I wanted to do this for anyone as much as I did right now. He needed this release, and I was determined to bring it to him.

I could feel him pulsating against my tongue, and I knew he wouldn't last long. I pulled him all the way to the back of my throat, and he gripped the back of my head with both of his hands.

"Holy fuck, baby." He tried to get me to stop, but I brushed his hands away and kept going. When he realized what I wanted him to do, his head fell back onto the pillow and he let go. Calling out my name followed by a series of curses, Tanner came in my mouth. Then, every muscle in his body went from tense to completely relaxed.

I crawled on top of him, laying my head on his chest and listening to his heavy breathing.

"I didn't expect that."

"Good."

"Once I get the feeling back in my legs, it's my turn."

I smiled. "Or we could just lie here together. You need to get some rest."

"If you think I'm going to be able to sleep after what you just did ..." He shook his head.

Tanner's phone vibrated on my nightstand and we both jumped.

"Hey," he answered. "What's happening?"

I watched his facial expression closely, straining to hear what Chase was saying on the other side.

"Yeah. I'll be there soon." He ended the call. "My dad's stable. Chase said they're keeping him for the rest of the day to monitor him, and then he should be able to go home."

"That's great news."

Tanner wrapped me tightly in his arms. "I don't want to leave you."

I kissed his temple. "You need to be with your family right now. I can see you later, after work."

"You promise?"

"I promise." I pulled him in for a kiss. "You have nothing to worry about. I'm not going anywhere."

Chapter Thirteen

TANNER

"You're welcome!" I dropped to my knees and spread my arms out wide for the big finish.

Khloe loved it when I sang along with The Rock. She doubled over, eyes closed, as she laughed hysterically. I loved the sound of her laugh, but it was not only her that I did this for. Dad was laughing, too.

"No matter how many times she asks you to do this, you sing it with as much enthusiasm as if it were your first time," Dad said, still chuckling.

"Well, you've gotta commit when you sing a song like that." I sprawled out on the couch next to him, slightly out of breath.

"You're breathing kind of hard, brother," Chase called from his recliner.

"We just ate a twelve-course meal. I have a cramp." I rubbed my full stomach.

I got to spend another Thanksgiving with my father, and I would soon be picking up Charlotte for a special night I had planned. Not even Chase's comments would put a damper on my mood. Not tonight.

"I didn't know you could sing like that," Merritt teased. "I guess it runs in the family."

"Just because I don't doesn't mean I can't."

Mom laughed. "I should show you the videos I have of the two boys singing in the bathtub when they were little."

"No!" Chase and I both exclaimed.

Merritt laughed. "Oh, I would pay to see that."

"Shh!" Khloe held her tiny finger to her lips. "Watch the movie!"

We watched the rest of the movie in silence. Time seemed to crawl. I couldn't wait to see Charlotte. To hold her. To kiss her. To gaze into her eyes. Whatever happened or didn't happen tonight, I just needed to fall asleep with her in my arms.

I'd never felt anything like this before. I loved my parents. I loved my siblings. I'd do anything for them. But this was different. Charlotte set everything in my life into place. For the first time, I felt certain of my future. I felt certain of my place in the world. I would spend all of eternity giving her everything she deserved. I'd sacrifice my life to prove to her that I could be the kind of man she needed.

I sprang to my feet when the movie finally ended. Everyone was busy tucking Khloe in for bed, and I was able to slip out the front door without any questions. Tonight, I was going to forget about everything. Everything except for her.

CHARLOTTE

"WHERE ARE WE GOING?"

"Like I told you the last seven times you asked: you'll see when we get there." Tanner grinned from the driver's seat and reached his hand out for mine.

I sighed as my knee bounced. "I can't imagine anything is open on Thanksgiving."

"Stop trying to figure it out and tell me how your day was."

"It was great, actually. Dad and I spent the day at Mallory's. It felt nice to be surrounded by a family."

"I wish you could've been with mine." He kissed my hand.

"Me too."

I was slightly jealous that Merritt got to spend so much time with Tanner's family. Although, I knew she didn't have a family of her own. She was lucky to have them. Tanner and I hadn't discussed meeting each other's families. I knew he had a lot going on with his dad being sick. *Would I ever get to meet him?*

As Tanner pulled into the parking lot, I craned my neck to see the sign above the building. We were at a bed-and-breakfast. A slow smirk formed on my lips.

He turned off the engine and faced me in his seat. "I just want to fall asleep holding you."

"We have a room all to ourselves. I hope we do a lot more than sleep."

Tanner chuckled. "We will do whatever you want to do, my sweet girl."

I took his face into my hands and kissed him tenderly. "I love this idea."

Inside, the woman at the desk handed Tanner our room key with nothing more than a smile.

"That was quick," I whispered as we walked up a winding staircase.

Tanner didn't respond. He led me down the hallway like he knew where he was going.

Maybe he did. *Oh, God.* My heart sank. *Had he been here before?* I suddenly remembered Mallory warning me about Tanner's promiscuous past.

He looked back at me, and his eyebrows furrowed. "Are you okay?"

"I know I'm going to regret this question, but I have to ask it." I shoved my hands into my coat pockets and looked down at my boots. "Have you been here before?"

He looked confused. "What do you mean?"

"You seem to know your way around this place, and you didn't even have to check in at the front desk. She gave you the key like it was your own." I lifted my eyes to meet his. "Is this where you take girls when you want to have sex with them?"

Tanner laughed once, and then even harder when he realized I was serious. "I have been here before. At about eight o'clock this morning."

My eyebrows shot up.

"I was here to book the room for us for tonight. I've wanted to do this for a while now. I think you'll understand when you see the room." He tugged on my hand, and I followed.

Tanner stopped in front of a door at the end of the long hallway. He turned the key in the knob and held the door open for me to walk through.

The room was dimly lit. I walked inside to find dozens of battery-operated candles scattered around the room flickering in the dark. My hands flew to my mouth when I saw rose petals formed into the shape of a heart atop the bed. A bottle of champagne stuck out of an ice bucket on one of the nightstands, with two glass flutes beside it. A small iPod dock played soft music on the other nightstand.

Tanner's hands wrapped around my waist from behind me. "You said you had a bad prom night experience. I thought we could make a better memory together."

The tears that had been threatening now slid down my cheeks. "Tanner, I can't believe you did all of this." I turned around in his arms and looked up at him. "This is amazing."

"You are amazing, my sweet girl." He unzipped my jacket. Letting it fall to the floor, he knelt down and slid my boots off each foot. Standing again, he cupped my face in his hands and kissed me. "I'm going to make you feel so good tonight."

My skin hummed with anticipation. I yanked the hem of his shirt until it was over his head, and made quick work of his pants, peeling his boxers off before standing again. I ran my fingers along his smooth, broad chest. My tongue followed everywhere I touched. I stopped when I reached his protruding hip bone and bit it gently.

Tanner pulled me up with an impatient growl. He tore my dress off and slammed his lips into mine. His hands that had started in my hair traveled down my back. He unhooked my bra and I let it slide down my arms before tossing it onto the floor. He immediately took my breasts into his hands and then dropped to his knees so he could reach them with his mouth. I exhaled loudly when I felt his warm tongue.

"You have the most perfect body," he murmured. He continued licking his way down my body. The closer he got to my panties, the wetter I got inside them. My entire body was on fire. I watched as he pulled my panties to the side and lightly ran his tongue over my throbbing skin.

"God, you taste so good," he said as he rubbed his tongue against me. "You are my sweet, sweet girl."

I moaned, gripping handfuls of his hair as my knees buckled.

Tanner picked me up and laid me on top of the rose petals on the bed. He slid off my underwear and positioned his head between my legs again. He teased me with his tongue ever so lightly as he watched me.

"Tanner, please." I raised my hips to get closer to his mouth.

He flashed me a wicked smile and spread my legs further apart, slipping his hands under my ass to get a firm grip. His tongue swirled in between my folds, causing me to moan even louder. I never knew anything could feel this good. He worked magic with his tongue, and all I could do was press myself into his mouth and beg for more. I moved my hips in rhythm against his tongue.

Many people fear fire. Understandably so. It's a powerful force, too painful to touch. It spreads within seconds, reckless and out of control. It destroys homes. Forests. Lives. Fire takes everything, leaving nothing but ash in its wake.

Still, we welcome its warmth. We need it to survive. We harness it. We fuel it. It's exhilarating, the heat that spreads over you when you're near it. The power you feel when you possess it. When it belongs to you.

Being with Tanner was like playing with fire. I'd known it from the beginning. I am flammable. Combustible. I'm the moth to the flame. And I let it scorch me.

The slow burn between my legs turning into an explosion. "That feels so good, Tanner. Keep doing that."

His tongue moved faster, and my knees fell completely open. He hit the perfect spot, causing an explosion throughout my body. I screamed his name several times, and my entire body shook as I came apart. Pure bliss blanketed me. When it was over, I couldn't move.

Tanner crawled on top of me, kissing my neck as I tried to catch my breath.

"I'm sorry," I panted.

"For what?" He jerked his head back to look at me.

"Did I pull your hair too hard? Was I too loud? I had no control over my own body. That has never happened before."

Tanner's eyes narrowed. "What do you mean that has never happened before?"

"Nobody's done that before."

"Charlotte, have you ever had an orgasm?"

I covered my face with my hands. "No."

Tanner sat up and moved my hands away. "But you've had sex before."

"We were in high school. I don't think he knew what he was doing. Not like you, anyway."

A wide grin spread across his face as he leaned in to kiss me. "You will always orgasm with me, my sweet girl. I don't unless you do."

I leaned onto my elbow. "Can you get my purse for me?"

Tanner hopped off the bed and I enjoyed the view of his naked body as he brought my bag over.

I pulled out a strip of condoms and dangled them in the air. "I hope I brought enough."

Tanner

Charlotte kissed me with yearning. The kiss was deep and passionate. All of our emotion spilled onto each other.

I got on top of her and pressed myself between her legs. I was hard as a fucking rock, and she was so wet. I needed to get inside her, fast. I was about to finish before we even got started.

"I need you inside me," she murmured.

I ripped open a condom and rolled it on. Charlotte watched as I traced my tip around her entrance, teasing and waiting for her reaction. She wrapped her legs around my hips and dug the heels of her feet into my ass cheeks.

We let out simultaneous gasps as I plunged inside her. I held her in my arms, kissing her over and over again as the light from the candles danced around us.

"Are you okay, baby?" I gently caressed her face. "I won't move until you tell me to. I don't want to hurt you."

"You can move," she assured me. "Just stay right here. I want you close to me."

Looking down into her eyes, I was overwhelmed by the amount of love I felt emanating from them. I had fantasized about this moment for so long, and now it was finally happening. Charlotte was giving herself to me—I was one with her. No one had made me feel this way before, and I was certain that nobody ever would again.

I slowly pulled out before pushing inside her a second time. As much as it was killing me to go slow, I was going to take my time. I wanted to make love to her.

She let out a moan and bit my bottom lip, digging her nails into the muscles on my back. She lifted her hips to meet each of my thrusts. Then her angelic eyes looked up at me as another moan escaped her lips. "Fuck me, Tanner."

I stopped holding myself back and took her hands in mine, pressing them above her head into the mattress. I drove myself deep inside of her, over and over again.

"*Fuck*, you are so tight. You feel incredible."

Droplets of sweat had formed in between her tits, and her skin glistened in the dim light. I lowered my head so my tongue could graze over one of her perfectly hardened nipples. Charlotte's back arched and she gripped fistfuls of my ass, pushing me deeper inside.

"You like that, baby? Tell me what else you like. Tell me what you need."

To my surprise, she guided my hand down her body, placing it exactly where she wanted it to be. "Touch me," she breathed.

I rubbed her sensitive skin in small circles, watching the ecstasy wash over her face. Her thighs squeezed my hips as she writhed underneath me. Her moans got louder and closer together, before turning into screams. She called out my name, and I felt her insides clench around my dick as her entire body shuddered. The feeling of her orgasm instantly brought me to mine.

It was the most intimate moment I had ever experienced. She held my face so close to hers while I shook from my release. My body tensed as I grunted a slew of words that made no sense when I strung them together. When I finished, we remained still, letting our breaths slow down. Then, I rolled onto the bed beside her.

Charlotte showered my face with kisses, and curled around my body. "That was the best sex of my life."

I grinned. "You don't exactly have much to compare it to, but I'm still taking that as a compliment."

"Sorry I don't have all that experience like you do." She rolled her eyes and jabbed my side.

I took her hands in mine and looked at her with complete serious-ness. "Tonight was the best night of my life."

She giggled. "Because we had sex?"

"Because it was with you."

Her eyelids closed as she pressed her forehead to mine. When she opened them, something new sparked in her eyes.

"Tanner, can you make love to me again?"

"Yes, my sweet girl. I can."

Chapter Fourteen

CHARLOTTE

My mom died in the springtime. It was April. I hadn't known our last Christmas together would be our last. All I remembered of the few holidays with her was that she loved them. She loved to decorate the house and bake dozens of pies and cookies. So each year, that's how Dad and I honored her memory.

Tonight we were decorating our Christmas tree, and Tanner was coming over to help. The two most important men in my life were going to meet for the first time, and I couldn't be happier. My relationship with my father was back to normal; Tanner's anger was seemingly gone; my old memories were finally staying in the past; and my panic attacks had almost disappeared completely.

I jumped up when I heard the knock at the door. Tanner was standing in the hallway with a bouquet of Gerbera daisies for me, and a bottle of red wine for my father. He was dressier than usual, wearing a black sweater with dark jeans. I had memorized every inch of him under that shirt. I couldn't get enough of him, and whenever he was near me, all I could think about was getting him naked. Visions of him making love to me flashed through my mind, making it hard to concentrate on words.

"Hi, handsome."

"Christmas is not about what people need. My aunt Cathy sends me a toothbrush in the mail every year. Everybody needs to brush their teeth, but nobody wants a toothbrush for Christmas."

"She really sends you a toothbrush?"

"In bubble wrap. I shit you not."

"Well, I don't know what he wants!"

"I'm taking you to the mall right now."

"What's at the mall that Tanner wants?"

"Two words: Victoria's Secret."

I shook my head. "But that's not for him."

"It's for his viewing pleasure."

"I know, but I want to get him a gift, too."

"Guys are so easy. Get a bow and slap it on your vag. Boom. Instant gift. That's all they really want, anyway."

I laughed. Though Tanner would love that idea, I had to figure something else out. Something special. I just didn't know what.

TANNER

I HAD SUCCESSFULLY STOLEN THE BATTERY OUT OF CHARLOTTE'S CAR while she was in class. I knew Mallory would be there to drive her home. Chase drove me to pick up the car from the parking lot and didn't ask too many questions about who I was doing this for. He had his head so far up Merritt's ass, he couldn't see anything except her. I didn't give him a hard time. The same could be said about me with Charlotte.

Over the next few days, I worked as fast as I could to buff out the dents and scratches on Charlotte's car. She was relentless with questions, asking if I'd figured out what was wrong with it. I had to make excuse after excuse to cover my ass when I sent it to my buddy's paint shop. I couldn't wait to see the look on her face when she realized what I'd been doing all along. I knew she was going to love it.

On Christmas Eve, it was finally ready. I waited until I was the only one left at work, and then I called Charlotte.

"Hey, baby," she answered. "Did you finish at work?"

"I'm all finished. Can I pick you up? I want to show you something."

"Sure. You sound weird. Is everything okay?"

"Everything's fine. I just want to show you something."

"Okay. I'll be here waiting for you."

When I arrived at the bakery, Charlotte was bundled in a hat, scarf, coat, and gloves. I had to laugh. It was only December. She hadn't even seen winter in New York, yet.

"What's so funny?"

"You. You look like the abominable snowwoman."

She smacked my shoulder though she was laughing. "It's cold, okay? I'm not used to this kind of weather."

"I can't wait to see what you wear in February."

"You love me. You're not supposed to make fun of me."

"I love you, and that's why I make fun of you."

"Fine. Now, what is this thing you have to show me? I have to get home to get the food started for tonight."

"I need you to come with me to the shop. We'll be quick. I promise."

She raised a skeptical eyebrow but sat back in her seat without another word. I could see the wheels turning in her mind.

Five minutes later, we were walking through the door to the garage. "You have to close your eyes."

Again, she gave me a look, but she didn't argue. Her leopard fuzzy gloves covered her eyes.

"No peeking."

"I'm not peeking, but you're going to have to help me here."

I guided her through the garage door and positioned her in front of her new-and-improved GTO. "Okay." I took a deep breath. "Open."

Her hands left her eyes and quickly flew to her mouth. "Is that my car?"

"It is."

She was frozen where she stood. "Tanner, I can't believe you did this! It looks like a brand-new car."

She wore a festive red velvet dress with white fur trim around the hemlines. I couldn't help but smile as wide as she was smiling.

"You're Charlotte?"

"I am. You must be Chase, right?"

She giggled the most perfect little giggle. "No, silly! I'm Khloe!"

"Oh, Khloe. That's right. I got confused. You guys look so much alike."

She put her small hand in mine and pulled me into the house.

A tall, slender woman entered the foyer from another room. Like Khloe, she was another spitting image of Chase. Did that mean Tanner looked like his father?

She smiled and opened her arms as she approached me. "Charlotte, it is so nice to meet you. I'm Beverly."

Her hug instantly made me feel comfortable and welcome. "It's nice to meet you, as well." I held out a box of assorted cookies. "My dad baked these."

"Oooh, cookies!" Khloe took the box and scampered into another room.

"Thank you. You didn't have to bring anything. Let me take your coat."

Tanner finally emerged at the top of the stairs while I was slipping out of my coat. He was beaming, and I knew he was excited for me to be there.

Tanner wrapped me in his arms so tightly, I could barely breathe. "Merry Christmas," I choked out.

"Merry Christmas, beautiful." He gestured with his thumb to a doorway to my right. "Dad's really tired. He fell asleep in the recliner. You'll meet him when he wakes up."

"I'm glad you didn't wake him just for me. He needs to rest."

Tanner laced his fingers with mine and led me into the dining room. Beverly had prepared coffee, tea, and several pies.

"Mom's an amazing baker." Tanner pulled out my chair for me.

"Not like your father, I'm sure," she added.

"This all looks wonderful. Thank you for having me over."

Khloe was busy piling a tower of cookies onto her plate. I stifled a giggle when Beverly's eyes widened as she saw what her daughter was doing.

"How was Merritt?"

"She put on a smile, but I'm sure she was sad." Beverly looked down at her lap. "It was her first Christmas without her father."

"This is going to be our last Christmas with our dad," Khloe said matter-of-factly.

"Oh?" Her bluntness took me by surprise. Was I the same when I lost my mom? I'd have to remember to ask Dad.

"Yeah. Dad has cancer. Do you know what cancer is?"

"Yes. My mom had cancer."

"Did she die?" Khloe's eyes were wide with curiosity.

"Khlo," Tanner interrupted. "You can't ask people that."

I put my hand on his shoulder. "It's okay. You can ask me anything you want to know. I'll tell you whatever I remember. I was only five, so it's not much."

"I'm almost five!" She shoved a powdered cookie into her mouth. "And you have blonde hair like me. It's like we're the same. Merritt's hair is super curly. Do you know Merritt? She's Chase's girlfriend. I gave her a necklace for Christmas that says sister on it, because we're sisters now. She's going to marry Chase one day, and—" She stopped mid-sentence. "Oh, no!"

"What's wrong?" all three of us asked in unison.

"I didn't get a present for you, Charlotte! I didn't know you were coming over." Her big round eyes welled with tears, and her bottom lip trembled.

"No!" I rushed over to her chair. "It's okay. I didn't bring you anything either. We'll have plenty of time to give each other gifts one day, I promise."

She hugged me, squeezing me with her tiny hands. "You can come to my birthday party, and then I can come to yours!" She returned to her cookie, happy that she had come up with a solution.

I bit my bottom lip to keep from laughing as I returned to my seat.

"I'm sorry Tim's not here to meet you," Beverly said. "He's just been so tired lately."

"It's fine. I understand."

I stood, smelling the coffee brewing in the kitchen. "I need coffee. You want me to get you a cup of tea while I'm in there?"

Dad reached out and took my hand. "You have made me so proud, Tanner. Do you know that?"

I swallowed hard. "Have I?"

"You have worked your ass off in that shop every single day. I wished you could've gone to college. I know how badly you wanted to go away. But you put your family before yourself, and we wouldn't have survived without you."

"I didn't do anything. I just—"

He squeezed my hand as hard as his weakened body would allow. "You deserve all the love and happiness in the world. I appreciate everything you've done for this family. You are a good man, Tanner. You've made me so proud."

Tears flooded my vision. "I love you, Dad. It means the world to me to hear you say you're proud of me."

"Ah, don't start blubbering on me." He wiped his eyes as he chuckled.

"I'll be right back with your tea." I walked into the dining room feeling stunned.

"How is he?" Mom asked.

"He just told me he's proud of me. I think he's delirious."

She smiled. "He just wants you to know how much he loves you."

"I told him I'd bring Charlotte over again today," I called from the kitchen. I filled my mug with coffee and Dad's mug with hot water. "I really want her to meet him."

"That would be great. Invite her over for dinner."

I walked back into the living room and set Dad's mug in his cup holder. His head was slumped forward, and his mouth was open. He'd fallen completely asleep in the few minutes I'd been gone.

I took my phone out just as Khloe came bouncing into the room. She babbled on and on about her Christmas gifts from Santa while I typed out a text to Charlotte. I was only half listening. Then, I heard three words like a siren blaring in my ears:

"Daddy's breathing weird."

I looked up from my phone before clicking Send. "What do you mean?"

"Come listen."

I set my coffee down on the side table, and leaned over to listen for what Khloe had heard. Dad's breaths sounded like he was gasping for air.

"Hey, Dad? Are you okay?" I asked. Normally, he would pick his head up when he heard someone talking to him. He didn't respond.

"Khlo, go get Mommy. Tell her I need her to come in here." I pressed two fingers against his neck. His pulse was so faint, I could barely feel anything at all.

"What's wrong?" Mom asked, looking concerned.

"His breathing doesn't sound good, and his pulse is ... not good either."

Mom sat beside him on the couch. "Tim, honey. Wake up. I need to know if you're okay."

The three of us sat in silence, waiting for him to respond. When he didn't open his eyes, I knew something was very wrong. I immediately stood. "Get Dad's coat. I'll warm up my car."

"What's going on?" Chase asked as he came downstairs.

"I'm taking Dad to the hospital. Something's wrong." I flew out the door and started my car.

When I got back inside, Chase was helping Mom get Dad's jacket on. No one was talking. Khloe sat on the couch, watching.

I lifted Dad into my arms and carried him out to my car. "I'm going to get you to the hospital, Dad. Everything's going to be okay," I whispered. Dad looked like he did the night he collapsed. I tried to remain calm. The doctors had helped him before; maybe he would be okay again.

It was like déjà-vu when I arrived at the ER. The nurses took Dad from me and rolled him through those same double doors. Within minutes, Mom walked into the waiting room, followed by Chase holding Khloe. We waited and waited, still silent. Even Khloe was quiet. I think we were all holding our breaths, hoping for a miracle. But Christmas was over, and the time for miracles had run out.

A doctor emerged from the double doors only five minutes later—

much sooner than I'd expected. That was when I knew. His face was a dead giveaway. So was the breath he inhaled when he sat beside my mother. Mom covered her mouth before the doctor said a word. She knew, too.

I heard the doctor say, "We lost him." His mouth kept moving, but the sound of blood pounding in my ears was all I could hear. I pulled my hood over my head and slumped into the chair. Mom cried, rocking Khloe who was crying now, too. Chase covered his face with his hands. I couldn't look at them. It was too painful to watch. My own pain was slicing through my chest.

How could Dad be gone? He talked to me as if everything was fine this morning. He'd told me he was proud of me. Now, I would never hear him say those words again. He'd said he wanted to meet Charlotte.

Now, he never would.

I lifted my eyes to watch my mother stand and follow the doctor. She was going to say goodbye to her husband. Tears spilled over my eyelids. What would she feel when she saw him lying there? She was now alone. A widow. Her life partner was gone.

That's when it hit me. Reality was a freight train—a ton of bricks. Everyone dies. Life ends. All of our lives will end. We're going to have to bury our father. Eventually, we will have to bury our mother. There was a chance I would even have to bury Chase or Khloe.

Charlotte. One day, Charlotte is going to die. I suddenly couldn't imagine a world—my life—without her in it. I made her my every-thing, and one day, she's going to take it all with her when she goes. I will be left here with nothing. Alone.

As if sensing my downward spiral, Khloe crawled out of Chase's arms and into my lap. She placed her tiny hands on either side of my face and kissed my forehead. I couldn't offer her any words. There was nothing I could say to help her make sense of this. I just wrapped her in my embrace and held her as we cried.

After several minutes, Mom came back into the waiting room, her puffy eyes red. She kneeled and brushed Khloe's tears away. "Do you want to say goodbye to Daddy?"

Khloe nodded and took Mom's hand as she stood. Chase stood, too. I remained in my seat.

"Are you going to come in?" Chase asked. The usual self-righteous tone was absent from his voice.

I shook my head.

Mom placed her hand on Chase's shoulder as they walked away. "He doesn't have to come with us. He can have his time alone with Dad after."

I couldn't be in there while they cried over his body. That wasn't Dad. Not anymore. He was gone. Nothing would ever be the same again.

I could feel my demons closing in. They'd broken free from their cages. All this time, I'd only suppressed them, unable to defeat them. I'd tried so hard to fight. Charlotte made me want to try. But now ... I was just tired of everything in my life being *so fucking hard*. I could feel myself slipping into the darkness as the demons dragged me away. It felt oddly comforting—familiar.

The automatic doors to the waiting room opened as Merritt ran inside. One look at me, and she knew. She knelt on the floor in front of my chair.

"I'm so sorry, Tanner. I'm so sorry." She wrapped her arms around my shoulders.

I buried my face in her sweatshirt. She'd lost her mother when she was thirteen, and then she lost her father. She knew what this felt like. She understood what I was about to endure. So much death surrounded us. Death was everywhere. It was coming for everyone. Not one of us stood a chance against it. What was the point in falling in love and building families when we would only be torn apart by death in the end?

My phone vibrated in the pocket of my hoodie. I pulled away from Merritt and looked at the screen. It was Mom.

"Yeah," I answered, clearing my throat.

"Can you call Merritt for me? I want to get Khloe out of this place. Maybe she can take her for a while."

"She's already here."

"Okay. We're coming out."

I shoved the phone back into my pocket and wiped my tears quickly. "Mom is coming down with Khloe."

Mom was carrying Khloe in her arms when she came through the doors. There was no sign of Chase. I didn't wonder why he wasn't coming out to see his girlfriend. He'd figured out what I just had.

"Thank you for coming," Mom said as she approached.

Khloe turned her head to see us, her big eyes red. More searing pain cut through my chest. Khloe was too young to lose her father. The same age as Charlotte was when she lost her mother. Charlotte's mother died from cancer. Charlotte could get cancer one day. I could, too. It was in our genes.

"Merry," she whispered as she was transferred from Mom to Merritt. "My daddy went to heaven, like yours did."

"I am so sorry, angel girl."

"Do you think he will see your dad? Do you think he knows what he looks like?"

Merritt smiled as the tears spilled down her cheeks. "I think he will see my dad up there. I think they'll be good friends."

"I do, too."

"Do you mind taking her for a little while?" Mom asked. "She shouldn't have to stay here for this part. I don't know who else to ask." I watched as a tear escaped Mom's eye. It only made me angrier. She shouldn't have to feel pain like this.

"Of course I'll stay with her. I'll do anything you need. Just say the word."

"Thank you. You can take the car seat out of my car. I'm sorry to bother you."

"Don't be sorry. I'm glad I can be here to help."

Merritt left, and Mom sat down next to me. "I need you to come in with me and your brother. I want us to be all together."

I shook my head.

"Tanner, please. I need you with me. I can't do this alone."

I made the mistake of looking into her eyes. My mother's beautiful eyes, now dull and broken, were imploring me to go with her. This was the worst day of her life—and she needed me. It didn't matter what I wanted or needed. I had to be there for her. I had to help her through this.

So, I stood, and followed her to say goodbye to my father.

CHARLOTTE

"HEY, TANNER. IT'S ME AGAIN. JUST CALLING TO SEE IF EVERYTHING is okay. Call me as soon as you can, please."

It was unusual for Tanner to ignore my texts and calls. He always had his phone on him. The more time went by, the more worried I felt. Something was wrong.

I decided to drive to his house. When I arrived, there were no cars in the driveway. *Where were they?* Even Merritt's car was gone. There was no way Tim would've had enough strength to go out, and they wouldn't ever leave him home alone. Then, my heart sank.

I drove as fast as I could to the hospital. Looking around the waiting room in the ER, I didn't see anyone I knew.

"Excuse me. Are you able to tell me if anyone with the last name Brooks has been admitted?"

Her face fell at the mention of his name. "Are you family?"

"I'm his son's girlfriend. I can't get a hold of anyone, and they're not home. I'm worried."

She looked like she was thinking about what she should say. "You should talk to your boyfriend, miss."

"He won't answer me. Please. Can you tell me anything? Is Tim okay?"

The receptionist looked at her coworker sitting next to her, and the woman nodded her head, granting her permission. "Miss, I'm sorry to tell you this ... but Mr. Brooks passed away this morning. The family just left a few minutes ago."

Oh, God. "Thank you." It came out as a whisper.

I knew it was coming, yet I wasn't prepared for it. How was that possible?

I made my way back to my car in complete shock. I checked my phone as I drove out of the parking lot. Tanner still hadn't tried to contact me. My heart ached. I wanted to be there for him, to hold him. I wanted to tell him everything would be okay.

I dialed him again. No answer.

TANNER

MY PHONE BUZZED ALL DAY, BUT I COULDN'T BRING MYSELF TO answer it. I didn't want to tell Charlotte. I didn't want to say the words. Once I said it, it would all start happening. Funerals. Black suits. A hearse. I wasn't ready for any of it. I thought I would be, but I wasn't. Not since we'd returned from the hospital with one less family member.

Chase locked himself in his room. I wanted to do the same, but my father's last words resonated in my mind: *You put your family before yourself, and we wouldn't have survived without you.* Mom needed me. Khloe needed me, too. She needed to see that our family would be okay. So, I buried my own feelings. I was used to it.

Merritt had gone grocery shopping for us and brought pizza for dinner. I couldn't think about eating anything until I smelled the aroma wafting out of the box. My stomach growled, and I remembered that I hadn't eaten all day.

The four of us were eating quietly together when Chase stepped into the dining room.

"Thanks for bringing all this," he muttered as he sat next to Merritt.

"Are you having a slice?" she asked, motioning with an empty plate.

He shook his head. "Not hungry."

"Chase, you haven't eaten anything since dinner last night. You need to eat something," Mom said. I could barely look at her. It killed me to see her so dejected.

"I'll eat when I feel hungry," Chase snapped. Without saying another word, he walked out of the room.

"He's just tired." Mom always made excuses for him.

"This isn't something he can just sleep off. Dad's gone, and the sooner he comes to terms with that, the better off he'll be." I left the room with my plate before I said something inappropriate in front of Khloe.

I walked into the living room and sat on the couch. I stared at Dad's empty recliner, reminding me that he was no longer here. I felt the hot tears return. I couldn't be here.

I ran upstairs to my room. I had dozens of calls and texts from Charlotte. I stared at her number on my phone, blinking back the tears as scary thoughts filled my mind. She was the love of my life; she was everything I'd been searching for. *What would I do if I ever lost her? How would I go on without her?*

It was a fear I'd never known before. I couldn't bear the thought of going through what Mom was going through. It would kill me—literally tear me open and rip me apart.

I needed something to take this pain away. Something to make the aching stop. I left my phone on my nightstand and dug my car keys out of my pocket.

Chapter Seventeen

CHARLOTTE

*H*e texted me once. Once, and then nothing after that. The text said very simply that his father had died, and that he needed to spend this time with his family. I was shocked at his reaction, at his coldness toward me. I'd been there for him when his father was sick. He'd needed me, or so I thought. *Did I not say the right things? Why did he feel like he couldn't lean on me now? What changed?*

Millions of questions crowded my mind. I didn't know what to do to make things better for him. I felt helpless. I couldn't understand why he was pushing me away, but I had to respect what he wanted.

I told myself that he would snap out of it soon. I sent flowers and a tray of food to his house. I texted him every day, reminding him that I wasn't going anywhere. I tried to be a part of this awful time in any way I could. Even if that meant hiding at the back of his father's funeral.

I sat in the last row. With my scarf pulled up to my chin, I shivered in my coat. Even with the sun shining in the middle of the clear blue sky, it was no match for the bitter winter air. The funeral had already started as I craned my neck to see Tanner sitting in the front row.

I watched his expressionless face and wondered what he was thinking behind his stone-cold eyes. My heart sank when I saw Merritt sitting with them, holding Chase's hand. I wished I could do the same for Tanner ... but, he didn't want me there.

The service was beautiful. Everyone was crying. Everyone except Tanner. When it was over, I watched as the Brooks family piled into Beverly's car, Khloe clutching her father's urn in her tiny hands.

Then, I headed home.

TANNER

"LET ME HAVE IT IF YOU'RE NOT GOING TO DRINK IT."

TJ covered his glass. "You've had enough to drink."

I waved my hand to summon the bartender. "I'm just getting started."

I heard TJ's sigh of disappointment over the music. "I really don't feel like taking your drunk ass home again. Why don't you quit while you're ahead?"

"I never asked for your help." I was slurring. Even I could hear it, and I was drunk.

"You know I can't let you drive like this. When is enough going to be enough for you? Drinking isn't going to bring your dad back, you know."

I glared at him.

"It's the truth. You need to hear it."

I tried to flag down the bartender again, but she continued to ignore me. "I'm sick of the truth. The truth hurts too much. I'm no good for her. I can't protect her." I covered my face with my hands. "I can't lose her."

"You're going to lose her if you keep acting like this. You're a fucking mess. You need to get your shit together."

The bartender handed a beer to the man standing next to TJ's stool.

"Hey, what the fuck? I've been waiting for another drink for ten minutes!" I shouted angrily.

"She's cutting you off, bro. Take the hint," the stranger shouted back at me.

I stood, swaying as I tried to balance myself on my own two feet. "Why don't you mind your own fucking business?"

TJ put his hand up, signaling for the man to back off. "He's not worth it. He's wasted."

The man shook his head at me before he turned and disappeared into the crowd.

"I'm not breaking up another one of your pointless fights," TJ said. "I'm also not paying your tab. You should be paying me to sit here and listen to this pathetic bullshit."

"Fuck you," I grumbled as I slumped back onto my seat. "What's the point of it all? We try and we try, but nothing is in our control. Dad died. He died and I couldn't stop it. I have no control over anything. If the same thing happens to Charlotte, I'm useless. I can't help her. I can't save her. The way Mom lost Dad? All those years together, and now what? She's all alone." I rambled on and on, spewing my pain and sorrows to TJ.

"Death is a scary thing, man. I get it," TJ said. "But you can't stop yourself from having a life just because you're afraid of what it will bring. You can't let fear rule you. Fear isn't real. It's all in your head. The sooner you realize that, the sooner you can heal."

TJ was right about one thing—the fear was in my head. It had taken command, and was now running the show. Every thought I had, every move I made from here on out would be controlled by fear. Fear had taken all of my love, joy, and hope and tossed them into the dumpster. I had nothing left. Fear had completely numbed my heart. I was now empty inside.

CHARLOTTE

"GET UP AND GET DRESSED. WE'RE GOING OUT!"

I let out a frustrated sigh. "Mal, I really don't feel like going out tonight."

"It's been two weeks. I want my friend back. There's nothing you can do right now. You need to get your mind off him for a little while."

A loud, crowded bar would hardly help get my mind off of Tanner. Admittedly, I couldn't take another night of sitting in my room and wondering if he was going to call. If he would ever call. My heart was breaking—for him, and because of him, all at the same time.

"So get dressed, or I'm coming in there to get you dressed!"

I stared at the phone after she ended the call. I had no doubt that she would live up to her word, so I quickly swung my legs out of bed.

Big Nose Kate's was filled with the usual crowd for a Friday night. No bands were on tonight, so the DJ's dance music played straight through. Mallory bought the first round of drinks and then dragged me onto the dance floor.

"You could not look more miserable right now," she shouted in my ear.

"I'm sorry. I just want him to call me."

"I know you do. This will all blow over. You'll see."

I hoped it would, but what would that mean for us? Would Tanner push me away every time something bad happened to him? I didn't think our relationship would be like this, but we had met during such a tumultuous time in our lives. *What if we couldn't withstand the chaos?* The more I thought about it, the sicker it made me.

Mallory was right. I needed to forget about everything. Just for one night. I tried to fix my face and mustered a smile for my friend. She was the only thing I had to help get me through this, and I was grateful to have her.

We danced to songs from a mixture of decades. Soon, we were back at the bar for our second round. Mallory ordered happily as she bopped to the beat. Then, I watched as her expression suddenly changed.

"I don't fucking believe it," she spat.

I spun around to see what she was looking at, surprised by the two dark eyes looking back at me a few stools over.

Tanner. He wasn't home with his family. He wasn't crying in his room. He was *here*.

Tears instantly filled my eyes. I couldn't help it. Did he lie about needing space? What was he doing here? I whirled around and pushed my way to the exit. I didn't stop until I reached Mallory's car.

Mallory was not far behind me when I saw Tanner shove past her. The closer he got, the more apparent it became that he was drunk. *Had he been here drinking by himself?* I didn't remember seeing anyone with him. His eyes were glassy and bloodshot. He stumbled as he ran in a crooked line to get to me.

"Charlotte," he breathed, taking my face aggressively into his hands. He covered my mouth with his, but he tasted like whiskey, and his kiss was too forceful. This wasn't the Tanner I knew.

"Tanner, stop." I pushed him off me.

"I've missed you so much," he slurred.

"Have you?" Mallory snapped. "Because you sure as fuck have a funny way of showing it."

Tanner squeezed his eyes shut as he swayed back and forth. "Please just let me explain."

"I will let you explain when you're sober. Not like this." I yanked on the door handle of Mallory's car.

Tanner grabbed my arm, stopping me from getting into the car. "Charlotte, wait. Please don't leave."

I tried to shake myself free from his grasp, but he was holding on too tightly. "Tanner, you're hurting me. Let go!"

Mallory tried prying his fingers off my arm, but that only made him hold on tighter. "Get off her, you asshole!"

"You don't understand! I can't lose you, Charlotte!" he yelled, pulling me closer to him.

"You're going to lose me if you don't let me go, Tanner!" I felt a familiar panic twisting around my lungs as he clutched my arm.

When he didn't let go, I did what I had to do. I kicked him in his kneecap and twisted his wrist until he released me.

"Oh, shit!" Mallory exclaimed.

Suddenly, TJ appeared out of nowhere. He spun Tanner by his shoulders and shoved him away from me. "Get in the fucking car." Then, as if nothing had happened, he turned his striking eyes to me and smiled. "Nice work, Charlotte."

"Where did you even come from?"

"I was having a drink with your boyfriend."

"You know Tanner?"

"Right now, we have a love/hate relationship. Mostly the hate part, but … I think I'm growing on him." He winked.

"Oh. Well, thank you for your help."

He raised his hands in the air. "I didn't do anything. That was all you, baby girl."

"That was fucking amazing," Mallory said. "I wish I'd gotten that on camera."

I rubbed my arm. "I'm really worried about him, TJ."

"He's going through a hard time right now. I'm trying to help him work through it."

"Great. He's pushing me away, but taking the help of a stranger. No offense," I quickly added.

"None taken. I'm going to sober him up and give him a ride home. Something tells me he'll be calling me in the morning. Your man has got a lot of anger inside."

"Tell me about it."

"I'm going to help him channel it."

"Maybe you can channel him to call me while you're at it."

TJ grinned. "Don't you worry, sweetheart. He is completely and utterly crazy about you. He's just having a hard time dealing with the loss of his father. Death scares the shit out of people like that."

"I really hope you can help him."

"He's a stubborn little shit, but I think he'll be ready after tonight." He waved. "Get home safely, ladies."

"That man is fucking delicious," Mallory murmured.

TANNER

I COULD FEEL THE POUNDING IN MY HEAD BEFORE I EVEN OPENED my eyes. Sunlight streamed through my window. *Why is my knee throbbing so much?* The alarm clock read past noon. Then, the memories from last night came flooding back. *Fuck. Me.*

I went to reach for my phone, but jumped when I saw Khloe's big round eyes staring at me from the foot of my bed.

"Jesus Christ."

"Not Jesus. Just me." She shrugged.

"Why is it so bright in here?"

"Your blinds are open." She climbed on top of my pillow and stretched onto her toes to reach the string on the blinds. "There. That better?"

"A little bit. Thanks, Squirt."

"Mom says you got home late last night. She said you were drunk. What does drunk mean?"

"Drunk means you're a dumb fu—" I caught myself. "A dummy."

"That's okay. If you were acting like a dummy last night, then you need to change your behavior today. Every day is a new chance to start over. That's what my teacher says to Aiden when he doesn't listen."

I couldn't fight the smile that tugged at the corners of my mouth. "You're very wise, little Yoda."

Her face scrunched. "What's a Yoda?"

I tickled her belly until she squealed. "You're a Yoda! Now, scram. I have to get dressed." There was somewhere I needed to be.

Twenty minutes later, I found myself standing inside TJ's gym. Punching bags outlined the massive room. To the left was an area with several giant tires; to the right, a woman with larger muscles than I had was coaching a man to slap thick ropes against the ground.

TJ emerged from the octagon-shaped ring in the center of the room. He shook hands with an older balding man who looked like he had just taken a shower with his clothes on. The poor dude was winded. Meanwhile, TJ hadn't broken a sweat. He made everyone else around him look tiny.

"I gotta be honest, bro," TJ called out. "I wasn't sure you were going to show."

"Yeah, well, I'm here."

"I like it when people prove me wrong. Doesn't happen very often." He gestured to the ring behind him. "Step into my office. Lose the socks and shoes."

I did as instructed. I hoisted myself over the ropes and stood inside the ring. It was a lot bigger than it looked on TV.

"You're scrappy." TJ bounced back and forth. "You've got tenacity. That's a dangerous thing."

He swung and missed.

I put my fists up, ready to defend myself against whatever TJ was going to throw at me. *No warm-up? Shouldn't I be taping up first? Maybe a mouth guard?*

"You're quick, too." He swung again. I blocked it and landed a punch to his rib cage.

TJ smiled, unfazed. "I bet your pretty little girlfriend can hit harder than that."

This time, I swung at his face. He dodged it effortlessly and rammed into my midsection, sending us crashing onto the floor. He instantly popped back up onto his feet and held his hand out to help me stand.

"And there it is."

"There what is?" I asked as I stood.

"Your anger. You let it control you, and it makes you weak."

Weak? "I'm not weak."

"You are, and that's okay. You won't be once I get done with you. Recognizing your weaknesses will help you work on them. Then, they become your strengths."

I raised my fists again. "I'm not fucking weak." I wanted to knock the smug smile off his face. He didn't know a damn thing about me.

"You got drunk every night this week because your dad died. That sounds pretty fucking weak to me."

I lunged and slammed him onto his back. I threw punch after punch, each one harder than the last.

TJ blocked every single one.

"Are you done yet?" he asked, sounding bored. He pushed me off, spun around, and twisted my arm backwards in the blink of an eye.

It felt like my elbow was going to break in half. I tapped out within seconds, and TJ released me.

"Just because you beat up the punks in high school doesn't mean you're tough. All you have are muscles and rage. If you don't learn how to channel them, you've got nothing."

I wanted to tell this guy to go fuck himself, and then leave the gym.

"I get you're upset about your father," he continued. "You've been looking for something quick and easy to mask the pain. Instead of confronting your feelings, you ran from them. You looked for an escape. If you decide to train here, with me, you're going to have to stop running and deal with your shit. You have to feel everything if you want to get over it."

I hated hearing him out my flaws into the light like that. It made me sound even more pathetic than I felt. "Is that what this is about? We hold hands and sing 'Kumbaya'?"

"This is about you, Tanner. This is about facing your problems head-on. If you want to keep wallowing in your pathetic bullshit, be my guest. If you want to conceal your fear with snarky remarks, go right ahead. But last night, you put your hands on your girlfriend. You didn't mean to, but that doesn't matter. You did. So, if you're ready to step up and be a man—the kind of man who will make his father proud as he looks down on him—then get the fuck up and let's fucking go."

The last thing my father said to me was that he was proud of me. TJ's words hit home. I got to my feet, and squared my shoulders. "I'm ready."

———

BEING WITHOUT CHARLOTTE HAD BEEN HELL. EACH DAY THAT passed hurt more than the one before. I needed to talk to her. I had to explain. But what would I say? I was terrified to be with her because I was terrified to be without her. I couldn't live without her, yet I didn't know how to live knowing that I could lose her. I was stuck on a torturous merry-go-round of fear, unable to step off and see straight.

Still, the way I'd behaved was unacceptable. She deserved more. So, I bravely clicked on Charlotte's name on my phone and listened to the ringing, praying she would answer.

"Hello?"

"You answered."

"Yeah, well ... I wanted to make sure you weren't dying in a ditch somewhere," she said flatly.

"More like wallowing in guilt."

"Good."

"Good that I'm not dead, or that I'm wallowing in guilt?"

"Both."

"I love it when you're mad."

"Is that why you make me mad so often?"

"Charlotte, I need to see you. I don't want to do this over the phone."

She paused. "Do what?"

"Apologize. Explain."

"I know you're sorry, Tanner. I don't want to keep hearing apologies from you. They don't mean anything unless you stop doing the things you're sorry for."

"I know. I just—"

"No," she interrupted. "If you're truly sorry, then you'll prove it."

"How? Tell me. I'll do anything."

"I want you to call that TJ guy and tell him you're going to start training at his gym."

"That will make you forgive me?"

"It's a start."

"I already went there today and had my first session."

"Good. I have to get back to work."

"Wait."

I heard her soft exhale. She was always so patient with me.

"I want to see you later. I need to explain what's been going on with me ever since ... since Dad."

"Train with TJ for a week and I'll think about seeing you."

"Are you kidding me?" Mallory yelled in the background.

"Shh!" Charlotte hushed her friend. "Tanner, I gotta go."

Then, she ended the call.

Chapter Eighteen

TANNER

"He's a selfish prick!"

"Tanner, calm down." Mom rubbed her forehead as I paced the dining room like a caged animal.

"How could Chase leave us at a time like this? How are we going to survive? I can't fix every car that comes in. I can't do it all by myself!"

"We will figure it out."

Chase and Merritt were moving to California. Chase had gotten a call from an old friend who knew someone at a record label, and now they were off to follow his dreams of being a rock star. Once again, Chase was putting himself first instead of his family. How would Mom and I manage the shop without two of our workers? How could he even think about leaving Mom? A month ago, Khloe lost her father, and now she was going to lose more family members. I stand by my statement. *Chase is a selfish fucking prick.*

"I knew something was up with him last night at dinner, but I didn't expect this! And Merritt doesn't even want to go!"

Mom's eyes narrowed. "How do you know that?"

"She said she wanted to stay here until we had time to interview and hire new employees ... but I could see it in her eyes. She doesn't want to go."

"It must be scary for her to move across the country. Away from everything familiar." She cleared her throat. "Like Charlotte. Where has she been, by the way?"

My chest heaved with each breath. "I'm going to take a ride to the gym."

Mom nodded. "That sounds like a good idea." She stood with me and gave my arm a squeeze. "Everything is going to be okay. Whatever life throws at us, we will get through it together."

I wondered if she believed that. It sounded like she was trying to convince the both of us.

———

"You're fired up tonight."

I threw punch after punch against the pad TJ was holding. "My brother has that effect on me."

"You shouldn't let him."

"How can I not?" *Punch. Punch.* "Everything he does affects my family. His selfish actions affect my life. Yet, he doesn't seem to care."

"You focus too much on what other people do. That's why you're always so angry."

Punch. Punch. Punch. "Then tell me, O Wise One. What should I do?"

TJ dropped the pad and started sparring with me. He bounced from side to side, light on his feet, planning his first attack. "You should focus on yourself. On what you're going to do to move forward."

I ducked as he threw his first punch. "What the fuck am I going to do when I'm down two workers? We're going to drown."

TJ grinned devilishly as I evaded his next few throws. "If you think you're going to drown, then you will." He slammed into my midsection, and I fell on my back. Effortlessly, he popped back up and resumed bouncing. "Focus on the moves you need to make to succeed."

I grunted as I got to my feet. "I'll need to find new employees. People who know what the fuck they're doing. That could take months."

TJ shrugged. "It could."

"Easy for you to say when it's not your business on the line." I swung and landed a punch to TJ's ribs.

"You think it was easy getting to where I am now?" He returned a punch to my gut. "You have no fucking clue what I went through."

I kept my mouth shut for the remainder of the session. TJ was right. I had no idea what his life had been like. He was tough as nails, and I could tell he hadn't been born that way. *You don't cover your entire body in tattoos if you've had an easy life.* TJ enjoys the pain because he's come out on the other side.

I thought about what TJ said for the rest of the night. In my living room, I took Dad's urn off the ledge and sat with him on the couch. I couldn't control what Chase did. I could only control my own actions. *I'll have to put an advertisement in the paper for a mechanic. I'll have to set aside time for interviews.* I sighed heavily as I patted the sky-blue urn in my lap.

"I want to make you proud, Dad. I just don't know how we're going to do this."

CHARLOTTE

"YOU'RE RUNNING TOO FAST," MALLORY CALLED FROM SEVERAL FEET behind me.

"If I ran any slower, I'd be walking."

"I don't like sarcastic Charlotte. I really thought I would, but I have to say ... not a fan." Mallory rested her hands on her knees, hunched over on the sidewalk.

I giggled, jogging in place. "Come on. We're almost there! You've got this."

"Remind me why we're doing this again?"

"You said, 'Let's start being healthy.' I said, 'What should we do?' Then, you said, 'Let's start exercising,' and I said—"

"Okay, okay. I get it. It was all my dumb idea." She stood upright with a determined expression on her face. "Let's go."

I used to run every day in high school. I'd wake up extra early and run for miles. It felt exhilarating to get back to doing what I loved—especially here in the freezing February temperatures. Running always helped clear my mind. Lately, it needed a lot of clearing.

Thirty minutes later, Mallory was sprawled out on my living room carpet.

I handed her a water bottle. "I'm proud of you."

"Just tell me this gets easier," she huffed.

"It does. Everything's always hard in the beginning." I sat on the floor next to her.

"Are you sure you don't want to come out tonight?" she asked, a slight whine in her voice.

"I just haven't been in the mood."

Mallory grunted as she sat up. "Look. You need to hear this, and I wouldn't be your best friend if I didn't say it. So, open your ears. You are letting a boy control your happiness. You're great when you're together, but you're all sad and moody when you're not. Whatever happened between the two of you, just let it go. If it's meant to be, it will work out in the end, regardless. Enjoy the time you have now, in other ways."

"How did you get to be so smart?"

"I don't know what the fuck I'm doing any more than you, or anyone else. No one has it all figured out. Knowing that will set you free."

I smiled. "I like that."

"So, whaddya say? Let's go out tonight."

"I'll go, under one condition."

Her eyes widened. "Anything."

"I don't want to go to Big Nose Kate's."

"Done! I've got an idea that will blow this tiny island out of the water."

I hugged her tightly before she turned to go. "Thanks for being my friend."

"Thanks for being mine."

"I'll walk you downstairs. I think I'm going to keep running for another couple of miles."

"There is something very wrong with you."

———

"I SHOULD'VE TAKEN YOU TO MANHATTAN A LONG TIME AGO. I don't know what I was thinking!"

I craned my neck to see the giant billboards and LED lights surrounding us. "Wow," was all I could say. Seeing the city on TV was nothing like walking amongst the crowded streets. Again, the smell left a little to be desired, but I didn't care. I was in New York City.

Mallory chuckled. "Looking at your face, all I hear playing in my head right now is Journey."

"I certainly am a small-town girl. This place is incredible."

Mallory linked arms with me. "I'm so glad I brought you here. The bar is right down the block."

Session 73 was a small bar on the Upper East Side. Patrons in suits and ties lined the bar. The place even had a coat check. It was a surprisingly stuffy atmosphere, especially when compared to Mallory's youthful, bubbly personality.

"You've been here before?"

"Yep. My friend Jason's band plays here on occasion. They're playing tonight." Mallory motioned to the stage against the window. Four guys were setting up their equipment. "That's Jason. He plays bass."

"You're into beards, huh?"

Mallory grinned. "Beard is the new black."

We found a space at the bar and waited for our drinks.

"Well, if it isn't Charlotte Thompson."

My spine stiffened and my pulse accelerated. *Who had recognized me here, of all places?* I slowly turned around, gripping my purse, preparing to make a run for it. I let out a relieved exhale when I laid eyes on the familiar face.

"Kyle! Hi. What are you doing here?"

"I live here. What are *you* doing here?"

"I live here, too. Well, not *here* here. I live ... I live ..." *Do I tell him where?*

"Nearby," Mallory said. "I'm Mal. You are?"

"Kyle Tomlin. I'm Charlotte's high school sweetheart." He offered me a sly smile.

"Ex," I corrected. "Ex-high school sweetheart."

Mallory's eyes widened.

Oh, no. Is she going to say what I think she's going to say?

"You're the douchebag who cheated on her! On prom night!"

Yep. She is.

"You told her about me?" Kyle's smile deepened.

Mallory turned to me, gesturing to Kyle with her thumb, as if he wasn't standing right there. "This guy, Char? Seriously? You definitely upgraded with Tanner."

"Tanner?" Kyle shoved his hands in the pockets of his dark slacks.

"Her boyfriend." Mallory crossed her arms while she surveyed him from head to toe.

I love her. I cleared my throat. "So, you live in New York?"

"I do. Going to school here. Trying to secure myself a spot on Wall Street."

"You always said you'd get out of Apalachicola."

Kyle winked. "What brought you up north? New York doesn't really seem like your scene."

I tugged on the hem of my dress. *Why am I nervous around him? It's just Kyle.* Sure, he'd broken my heart, but that seemed so long ago. Plus, he'd left for college before the bakery burned down. Hopefully, he hadn't heard anything about it. "Dad wanted to grow his business. He figured we'd do better in a bigger city."

"How is Frank?"

"He's good."

"Good, you're all caught up now." Mallory tugged on my elbow. "Come on. Let's go say hi to the boys."

I bit the inside of my cheek to keep from laughing.

"It was nice running into you, Charlotte. I'd like to buy you a drink later. If that's okay with your bodyguard."

Mallory rolled her eyes.

"Sure." I waved as Mallory dragged me away.

"God, what a loser," Mallory said once we were out of earshot.

I giggled. "He's not a loser."

"Don't defend him! What did you ever see in that guy? He's like a skinnier, dorkier version of Tom Cruise."

"I think he kind of looks like Shawn Mendes, actually."

"Do not insult that beautiful boy like that. Kyle is scum as far as I'm concerned."

I laughed. Then, I couldn't stop. Mallory looked at me like I'd lost my last marble. I doubled over, clutching my stomach.

"What the hell are you laughing at?"

I wiped my eyes as the hysterics died down. "I just realized something. You're like Rizzo, from Grease ... and I'm Sandy."

Mallory chuckled, shaking her head. "Yeah, right. You'd never let me give you a makeover."

I burst into a laughing fit again, picturing the extreme makeup and outfit Mallory would try on me. She must've pictured the same thing because she started laughing, too.

Then, I realized something else: I was lucky to have found a friend like Mallory. I missed Carla immensely ... but Mallory had saved me from the dark pit of fear when I arrived on Staten Island. I owed her so much.

"Let's do shots."

Mallory's eyebrows nearly launched off her forehead and her jaw dropped open. "You want to do *shots?*"

I shrugged, trying to appear nonchalant. "I mean, unless you don't want to."

"No, no! I want to. Come on, Sandy!" Mallory dragged me clear across the room, making a beeline to the bar.

Chapter Nineteen

CHARLOTTE

*N*ote to self: *five shots is too many.*

After nursing my hangover all day with Gatorade and ibuprofen, I forced myself to go for a run. The sun was setting, and my breath puffed out in front of me like a cloud of smoke. I needed to feel the high. Once I got there, nothing else would matter.

In the middle of my thoughts, I heard a car rolling slowly behind me. I hadn't noticed anyone following me, but I also hadn't been paying attention. I didn't have mace, my gun, or my phone with me. My heart pounded faster. I wanted to look over my shoulder but felt too nervous. *Was someone following me?*

I picked up the pace, wanting to break into a sprint, but not wanting to alert the driver. With every block I turned down, the sound of the tires rolling over the pavement followed behind. Finally, I stopped and pretended to tighten my shoelaces. When I bent down, the sound of the moving car stopped with me. Panic set in. *TJ taught me what to do. I can handle this.*

As I tied the knot on my laces, I casually looked around. A shiny black Cadillac SUV was stopped in the middle of the road. The windows were tinted so dark, I couldn't see inside. The reflection from the streetlights on the windshield made it impossible to make out the driver. If I was being followed, that could only mean one thing: Tommy was coming back for revenge.

I couldn't go home. I would lead him right to my father, if he didn't already know where we lived. My heart beat in my throat as I ran thinking about what I should do next.

Then, a car horn split the air, causing me to jump. I spun around and saw Tanner's Mustang behind the SUV. Tanner was beeping and waving his hand out the window.

"Come on, asshole! You're blocking the road! Drive!" he shouted.

The SUV took off, whizzing past me. I strained my eyes as hard as I could to get a glimpse of the person inside, but it was no use.

Tanner pulled alongside me wearing a grin. "Hey, hot stuff. Want a ride?"

I quickly threw his passenger door open and hopped inside. "Drive. Hurry!"

TANNER

CHARLOTTE LOOKED AS IF SHE'D SEEN A GHOST.

"What's wrong, baby? Are you okay?"

"I think that car was following me. I just need you to drive away from here." She frantically locked her door.

"Are you serious?" I stepped on the gas and turned left at the first intersection I approached. She was a beautiful girl, running alone at dusk. Joggers were abducted all the time in New York. There was a scary possibility she could be right.

Charlotte covered her face with her hands. "I don't know what would've happened if you hadn't shown up when you did."

"It's okay, my sweet girl. I'm here. Everything is okay." *Thank God I took the long way home from work.* Tears streamed down her face, and her hands shook in her lap. I wanted to console her, but I needed to get her somewhere she felt safe.

"It doesn't matter. All that matters is that you're here, with me. You're okay, baby. I'm going to take you home with me. You'll be safe."

"No!" she exclaimed. "You can't go to your house. He'll follow you there."

"Who is he?" She said it like she knew who he was.

"The ... the driver of the SUV. He might still be following us."

I watched her from the corner of my eye. She could tell me she was in love with me and bare her body to me, but she still couldn't tell me the truth about who she was running from.

Charlotte calmed down once we'd driven around for a while. No one was following us. I'd made sure of it. I pulled the car onto a side street and parked. I lifted her chin as I spoke. "You're safe, baby."

She sighed against my touch. "How are you?"

"I'm all right. Miss you like crazy though."

"Do you?"

"It kills me that you have to ask that."

Her bottom lip trembled, and it was easily the saddest sight I had ever seen.

"Why did you shut me out? Why couldn't you let me be there for you? That's all I wanted. We didn't have to talk about anything. I just wanted to hold you. I want you to be able to lean on me."

I rubbed the stubble that had grown in on my jawline, preparing to bare my soul to her. As it turns out, telling someone you love them isn't all that hard. I'd never had difficulty telling anyone how I was feeling at any given time. However, confessing my deepest, darkest fears and insecurities ... that shit was hard. Once you reveal the skeletons in your closet, there's no more darkness left to hide them in. Light shines like a spotlight on your worst imperfections. You're left with nothing but hope. Hope that people can forgive you for all your wrongs. Hope that people will love you in spite of them.

"When my father died, something struck me. Something that I'd never thought about until that moment. You're going to die one day. I can't stop it. That's life. It sounds crazy when I say it out loud, like I shouldn't be thinking so morbidly ... but it consumed me. I'm not strong enough to withstand losing you. I don't want to live in a world where you are not in it—with me.

"I watched my mother lose the man she loves. I watched her become a shell of her former self, going through the motions, trying to stay afloat for the sake of her kids. It kills me, Charlotte. Absolutely kills me. I don't want to go through something like that." I stopped to swallow the lump in my throat. "I'm terrified of losing you because I love you."

Charlotte's body stiffened. I couldn't read the expression on her face. Then, I saw tears in her eyes.

Shit. I just fucked this all up.

"Are you sure?"

"Yes, Charlotte. I've been in love with you since the moment you told me that you washed my shirt according to the instructions on the tag."

Her tears fell, but she was smiling. "You didn't know you loved me then. You didn't even know me."

"I knew, and I've known every day since then."

Charlotte closed her eyes as she touched her forehead to mine. After a moment of tortured silence, she pulled back and looked into my eyes. "I love you, too, Tanner."

"I just don't know how to handle the paralyzing fear of losing you."

"You know, I was very young when I lost my mom. I learned early on that people die, and there's nothing you can do about it. It hurts like hell, and you never fully get over it. But that doesn't mean you can turn off your heart and refrain from loving anyone ever again." Her eyes lifted to meet mine. "Life is short. Each moment is fleeting. We're all destined to die, one way or another. You need to decide if you can handle that certainty. Follow your head, and live in fear, or follow your heart, and live in love. What kind of person are you? Do you choose to play it safe, or can you choose to be brave?"

I nuzzled my face in between her neck and shoulder, breathing in the familiar scent of her hair. "I choose you. No matter what."

"I'm so sorry about your father. I'm sorry you felt like you had to go through that alone. I wanted to be there for you. I always want to be here for you." She touched her lips to the corner of my tear-stained eye, and then sprinkled soft kisses all over my face.

After a moment, Charlotte pulled away and straightened herself in the passenger seat. "I guess you can take me home now. I'm sorry I freaked out. It was probably nothing. The driver must've been looking

for an address or something, and I just assumed he was following me."
She laughed her nervous laugh, trying to throw me off. "Now you can
see why I bought a gun. I'm so paranoid."

More lies. It nagged at my gut as I navigated back to Charlotte's
apartment. Something I couldn't ignore. "You know how you said you
want me to be able to lean on you?"

"Yes. I meant it."

"Well, I want you to feel like you can lean on me, too."

"I do feel that way, baby."

I cleared my throat. "I want you to be able to tell me about your
past. I want you to open up to me."

"You know I can't."

"No. I don't know anything. I know that you *won't* tell me, but
what I don't understand is why? What's the big deal if you tell me? It's
not like I'm going to tell anyone."

She closed her eyes and squeezed the bridge of her nose. "I can't do
this, Tanner."

The sound of irritation in her voice caused my anger to trickle out.
I tried to breathe through it. "You're keeping something from me.
How can you tell me you love me if you can't tell me the truth?"

"Oh, that's great. So, you're saying I don't really love you if I don't
tell you?"

"I've let you into my heart. I've shown you all of my cards. You
know the good, the bad, and the ugly. I have nothing to hide from you.
I don't get why you feel like you have to hide anything from me. I love
you, no matter what."

"It was just a fire. Dad and I wanted to start over somewhere new.
Now we're here. That's it."

The more she lied to my face, the angrier I grew. "I read the arti-
cles about your bakery in Florida. They were dated right before you
showed up here in New York. Something happened in that bakery, and
you know exactly what it was. Are you and your father in the Mob?
Are you criminals on the run? Are you serial killers?"

"Tanner, please slow down. You're going too fast."

"Don't change the subject. I want you to tell me the truth."

"You told me you could accept me without knowing the truth! You told me you could do this!"

"I can't do this if you don't let me all the way in, Charlotte. I can't be the only one who—"

"Tanner! Watch out!" Charlotte braced herself against the door.

I'd blown through a stop sign without even realizing it. I swerved onto the sidewalk so an oncoming car wouldn't smash into Charlotte's side of the car. The driver blared his horn at me as he skidded out of the way.

"Holy fuck. I am so sorry." I flung my seat belt off and pulled Charlotte into my arms. "Are you okay?"

She pushed away from me. "Just take me home. I want to go home."

I heaved a sigh, raking a hand through my hair in frustration. "Fine."

CHARLOTTE

TANNER DIDN'T CALL OR TEXT ME THAT NIGHT. NO VOICEMAILS TO say he was sorry. Though I was disappointed, I knew what he knew: he didn't have anything to be sorry about. He was completely justified in everything he'd said. It was foolish to think I could be in a serious relationship with someone while I was on the run from my former life. It was unfair to give him my heart with stipulations. Love is all or nothing, not secrets and lies.

Could I go back to a life without him after he'd woven himself so intricately into my life? Every part of my new life had Tanner in it. Maybe this is why people on the run stayed on the run. Maybe Dad and I should've kept moving instead of trying to create a new home here. *Shoulda, coulda, woulda.*

I spent the remainder of the night typing out a text, trying to figure out a way to explain things to Tanner without telling him the truth.

I would tell you, but ...

I can't tell you what happened, but ...

I want to tell you, but ...

Nothing sounded good enough. None of it was what he wanted to hear. Maybe I could tell him. Maybe no harm would come to him if he knew the truth. Maybe I was just scared to tell him. Scared of Tanner seeing me in a less-than-perfect light.

Since the day I met him, Tanner has always looked at me in a special way no one else has. What if he heard the truth and never looked at me the same again? I couldn't bear that.

If I don't tell Tanner the truth, he won't forgive me for it. If I tell him the truth, there's a chance he won't forgive me for it. Either way I sliced it, the end result was the same.

Chapter Twenty

TANNER

"What do you mean Merritt is coming home?"

"Merry's coming to visit?" Khloe shrieked.

Mom sighed heavily. "She's not coming for a visit. She's coming back for good."

"Yay! Merry and Chase are coming back!"

"No, baby. It's just Merritt."

"Why isn't Chasey coming, too?"

I searched my mother's eyes for an answer to Khloe's question. *What the hell is going on?* They hadn't been gone for more than a couple months.

"Kokomo, why don't you go play in your room for a bit? I'm going to talk to your brother, and then I'll be up to play with you."

Khloe bounded out of the room and upstairs. She was such a good kid. After everything she'd been through, she always listened and always had a smile on her face. I'd have to do something special for her.

Mom spoke once Khloe was out of earshot. "I just got off the phone with Shelly. Merritt is already on a flight back here. She's been drinking a lot."

"Drinking? Why?"

"I don't know. That girl's been through hell and back. Truthfully, I don't think she wanted to go to California."

"No shit. I said that."

"You did. You were right. She was trying to do the right thing for Chase, and I guess it was too much for her to handle. Especially with everything that happened with her mother before she left." Mom covered her hand with mine. "She's going to need you, Tanner."

"Me?" *What the fuck could I do?*

"You were in a bad way after Dad died. Now look at you." She moved her hand to my face. "You've come so far. I think you could help Merritt get through her issues."

"Why can't her selfish boyfriend come home and help her? He should put someone before himself for a change."

"Chase is torn between following his dream and his love for Merritt. She needs to learn how to help herself. Chase doesn't understand how to help her do that. I think you'd be able to get through to her."

I nodded slowly. "I can bring her to TJ's gym."

"That's what I was thinking."

"Not gonna lie, Mom. I'm glad she's coming back. We need the help at work."

"I agree, but we need to get her healthy first."

———

As bad as I felt about Merritt being home, it was a huge relief having her back at work—even if she came in every day looking like a train wreck and smelling like a liquor store. I had a plan, but I knew she wouldn't accept my help willingly. She was even more thickheaded than I was.

I walked up the concrete stairs to her apartment. Her car was parked out front, but there was no light coming through her window by the front door. I knocked and waited. Nothing.

"Merritt, it's Tanner. Open the door if you're in there."

I waited another minute, straining to hear any kind of noise or movement from inside the apartment. Finally, I turned around and trotted back down the stairs. She could be out with her best friend, Shelly. Then, a sinking feeling came over me. There was a party at the Beta fraternity tonight. Shelly's boyfriend, Brody, was a member. *Guess I'm going to a party tonight.* There would be alcohol there. Lots of it. I needed to stay focused on finding Merritt. I needed to do this. I pulled my car keys out of my back pocket and got into my Mustang.

Ten minutes later, I was scanning the packed room inside the frat house. I spotted Derek playing at our usual pool table. It felt like forever since I'd seen him. He nodded as I approached.

"What's up, man? Haven't seen you in a minute."

I nodded. "I know. Been busy."

"Where's Charlotte?"

"Not here."

"Uh-oh. Trouble in paradise?"

I shot him a look and he held his hands up. I wasn't about to explain that Charlotte and I were not on speaking terms. I'd texted her once in the past month and told her I missed her, and that I'd be here when she was ready to tell me the truth. She never responded.

I thought I could stand my ground and demand that she tell me her secret. I thought when faced with the choice, Charlotte would tell me instead of walking away. I thought I'd proven myself enough to her. Every day without her hurt a little more than the last. It was like a slow death. *Death by a million little paper cuts.*

"I'm here on business. Have you seen Merritt?"

Derek nodded toward the kitchen. "She just got here a few minutes ago. I didn't see your brother. Is he back from Cali already?"

I shook my head. "He's still there. I'll be back in a few."

I peered into the kitchen and found Merritt with her friend, Tina. She was holding a glass in her hand. Tina was the last person Merritt needed to be hanging out with.

"I came by your apartment before."

"Why, what's wrong? Is Chase okay?"

"He's fine. I just spoke to him an hour ago."

Merritt's cheeks flushed. "Well, at least he's talking to somebody."

"What do you mean?"

"He hasn't responded to any of my texts."

I sighed. What was it with people ignoring the ones they loved? "He's just having a hard time," was all I could offer.

"So, it's okay to ignore somebody when you're having a hard time?"

"Hey, don't kill the messenger."

Before I could stop her, Merritt threw the shot back and held her glass out to Tina for a refill. I wanted to get her out of here, but I knew she wouldn't stop until she learned on her own. I needed to take this slow. I nudged Tina with my elbow. "Watch her tonight."

"I don't need anybody to watch me!" Merritt yelled as I walked away. I shot her a knowing look before disappearing into the next room.

For the remainder of the night, I played pool with Derek and watched Merritt gulp down shot after shot. She would disappear into the kitchen to get a refill for Tina, but sneak one for herself. By the end of the night, her friends had caught on, but it was too late. Way too late.

As I walked over to where they were standing, I heard Tina and Shelly trying to convince her to leave. Merritt was putting up a fight.

She crossed her arms over her chest, swaying like she was standing on a boat. "I'm not leaving."

The hell she wasn't. In one swoop, I hoisted Merritt over my shoulder. Then, I turned toward the door. She was practically family, and I was going to take care of her.

TJ had been there to dust me off and set me straight. Hopefully, he could work his magic on her, too.

———

THE NEXT WEEK WAS A BORING BLUR. WORK. THINK ABOUT Charlotte. Train. Think about Charlotte. Sleep. Repeat. Life without Charlotte was killing me. The only thing to occupy me was keeping Merritt on the straight and narrow. I'd been driving her to and from the gym so she could train with TJ. I didn't know if it was working, but at least she was focusing on something other than alcohol.

I woke up Sunday morning dreading the lazy day ahead of me. I needed something to do. Something different to break up the monotony. I reached for my phone and typed out a text to TJ:

ME: WHO DOES YOUR TATTOOS?

TJ: My buddy John. I'll send you the link to his shop.

FOR THE NEXT HOUR, I LAY IN BED LOOKING AT PICTURES OF tattoos until the smell of pancakes summoned me.

Merritt was cooking breakfast with Khloe's help. I watched in horror as Khloe attempted to flip a pancake, flinging batter everywhere.

At the dining room table, Mom was surrounded by her usual stack of paperwork. Dark circles framed her dull eyes, and her hair was tossed into a messy ponytail. She only got dressed to go to work. On the weekends, she remained wrapped in her robe. Here I was complaining about my boring life—meanwhile, Mom was taking care of the house, the bills, the business, and Khloe, all by herself. I needed to get my head out of my ass and figure out a way to help her. She deserved more of my time and attention.

After we ate, I pulled Merritt into the kitchen. "We need to figure out how to help Mom with the shop. It would kill her if we had to sell it."

Merritt grinned. "Don't worry, little brother. I've got an idea. And it's going to help you get Charlotte back, too."

Ten minutes later, Merritt and I were in the car on the way to the gym. My heart pounded in my throat as she dialed Charlotte's number. *Would Charlotte go for this?* If she did, it would force her to see me every day. Maybe that would melt her reservations.

. . .

CHARLOTTE

"ARE YOU GOING TO ANSWER IT? YOU'RE WATCHING IT LIKE IT'S A bomb."

"I don't recognize the number."

"Maybe Tanner got smart and is calling you from a different phone." Mallory winked as she stuffed another Dorito into her mouth.

"I'll just see if the person leaves a voicemail."

Mallory snatched my phone off the table and slid her orange thumb across the screen.

My jaw dropped as she handed my phone to me with a smirk.

"Hello?"

"Hi, Charlotte. It's Merritt."

My stomach dropped. *Why was she calling me? Was Tanner okay? Something had to be wrong if she was calling me.*

"Uh, hi, Merritt. What's up? Is everything okay?"

"Yeah, everything is fine."

Fine? Why was she calling if everything was fine?

"I'm calling because I have a business proposition for you."

My confused facial expression made Mallory scoot next to me so she could hear what was being said.

Merritt went on to explain how rough things had been for the Brooks since Tim's death. Their business was struggling. I bit my tongue, though I wanted to tell her how she hadn't helped matters much when she and Chase left for California. She was reaching out for help. My help. She wanted me to help Beverly in the office since I had experience running my dad's bakery. Part of me knew Tanner most likely had something to do with this, but I couldn't say no if Beverly really needed my help.

I told her I'd do it.

Mallory was smiling when I ended the call. "I'll give it to him. Tanner's a smart little shit."

"He wouldn't use his mother's strife to his advantage. That just doesn't seem like something he'd do."

"Maybe not, but either way—he's going to win you over like he always does. You might as well call him now and make up with him."

I shot her a look but said nothing. I hadn't told her that Tanner was the one who walked away from me this time. Technically, I'd pushed him away, but still ... he'd put his foot down and wasn't budging. Now, I'd have to face him every day. *Could my heart handle this?*

Chapter Twenty-One

CHARLOTTE

*M*erritt and Tanner got out of the car and walked toward the shop. Beverly sat beside me at the counter, so I tried my best to remain outwardly calm. On the inside, I was anything but. My heart had dropped into my stomach that was sloshing around like a turbulent sea. I'd barely gotten any sleep last night, knowing I'd see Tanner for the first time in over a month. *Would he ignore me? Would he be happy to see me?* I sucked in a breath as he stepped through the door.

Merritt spoke first. "Morning, ladies."

"Good morning!" *Oh, God. That was too cheerful. It's seven o'clock in the morning. Tone it down, Thompson.*

"Your hair looks great curled like that." Merritt hit Tanner in the arm. "Doesn't her hair look nice?"

Tanner barely looked at me as he grabbed a water bottle out of the mini-fridge. "Her hair always looks nice."

Beverly's and Merritt's eyes were on us, and I could feel my cheeks turning pink. I didn't know where to look. I didn't know what to do with my hands.

"Have a great day, guys!" Merritt walked out of the front office and into the garage, Tanner close behind. As he turned away from me, I noticed a bandage on his arm sticking out of his sleeve. *What happened?*

"Well, that wasn't too bad, was it?" Beverly asked, a knowing smile on her face.

I let out the breath I'd been holding. "I suppose it could've been worse."

TANNER

MY EARS STRAINED TO HEAR WHAT SHE WAS SAYING. IT WAS ALMOST closing time, and Charlotte was talking to Merritt on the other side of the garage. We hadn't spoken all day. Not since the awkward encounter when I'd arrived this morning. *That was fucking painful.*

"Bye, little bro." Merritt walked out the door, leaving me and Charlotte alone in the garage.

Charlotte had to walk past me to leave. My heart pounded faster with every step she took. Should I pretend like I don't see her? Should I say something?

"What happened to your arm?"

I stood and rolled my sleeve higher to show her what I'd done. TJ's tattoo artist was talented. I told him I wanted a tattoo of my father's tombstone. He added clustered roses on either side to complete it. I loved it.

Charlotte's eyes widened. "Oh my God! You got a tattoo?" She stepped closer, and my entire body hummed with excitement. I wanted to reach out and run my fingers through her hair. To gently caress her cheek. My gaze involuntarily dropped to her lips. How I missed kissing those perfectly puckered lips. Sweat beaded along the back of my neck.

"It's beautiful," she murmured.

"You're beautiful."

She took a step back as the pink of her cheeks deepened. "You don't mind me being here?"

"My mom needs the help. I appreciate you doing this for her."

"She's not the only one I'm doing it for."

I set my hand free, reaching out to twirl a golden strand of her hair. "Thank you."

The heated look in Charlotte's eyes cast flames throughout my entire body. All she needed to do was tell me. Then, my lips would be on hers. My hands would be undressing her, feeling every inch of her soft, bare skin. I'd be able to taste her hot, aching sweetness, and plunge myself into her depths. But not if she couldn't tell me. Not if she couldn't give all of herself to me.

My love for her outweighed the secrets she kept. That was never the question. I was all in. I was wholeheartedly hers for eternity. But I had to know that she felt the same. I'd done everything I could to prove my love. Now, it was Charlotte's turn to give me what I needed. Charlotte had to prove herself.

CHARLOTTE

I WALKED INTO THE BAR, ALONE. *HOW FAR I'VE COME.* MALLORY WAS babysitting her cousins tonight, and Merritt had asked me out for a girls' night. I could sit home and daydream about Tanner for another night, or I could make new friends and dance. It wasn't a hard choice.

Merritt waved me over as soon as she spotted me. "Hey, Charlotte! I'm so glad you came!"

"Thanks for inviting me." I waved to her friends.

"Charlotte, this is Shelly." I recognized her as the bouncy redhead who I'd always seen with Merritt.

Shelly stuck her hand out. "I'm the incomparable best friend."

A tall girl with short, black hair rolled her eyes and extended her tattooed arm toward me. "Incomparable, my ass. I'm Tina. I'm the bitchy friend."

I shook her hand as my eyes roved over her colorful ink. "Your tattoos are beautiful."

"Thanks. You have any?" An eyebrow arched as she searched my bare skin.

I shook my head. "I'm not a fan of needles."

"Shame. You have the perfect pale skin for ink."

Shelly's face scrunched. "Did you just call the girl pale?"

"I said she had the perfect skin for tattoos. It was a compliment."

A pretty blond stepped forward and put her arm around my shoulders. "My sister is the queen of backhanded compliments. Don't pay her any mind. I'm Kenzie."

"It's nice to meet another blond around here." I returned her genuine smile.

"We don't know where she came from," Tina said. "I'm pretty sure she's the milkman's daughter."

Kenzie's middle finger shot up and Tina grinned.

We danced in a circle for a good hour, laughing the entire time. Winter was on its way out, and it seemed like everyone was celebrating the city finally thawing.

Everyone, including Tanner.

TANNER

OPERATION: CHARLOTTE WAS UNDER WAY. MERRITT PLANNED A girls' night, and Charlotte had taken the bait. TJ and Derek were on board with pretending like we had no idea the girls would be here. All that was left to do was convince Charlotte to dance with me.

I thought giving her space would make her miss me and see that we needed to be together. After a week of working in close quarters at the shop, I realized that being around me was chipping away at her resolve. People had it all wrong: Absence didn't make the heart grow fonder; undeniable sexual tension did.

"Merritt's bringing her over now," TJ said.

Merritt practically dragged Charlotte through the crowded dance floor by her wrist. *Way to be subtle, Merritt.*

"Hey, little brother." Merritt slapped me on the shoulder.

"Hi." I looked into Charlotte's eyes, trying to read past the smile on her face. *Was she happy to see me or just being polite?*

TJ acknowledged the girls and then turned to Shelly. "How's your night going, Red?"

Shelly's cheeks turned as red as her hair. "It's good. We're having a girls' night."

"Well, we were." Tina nodded in my direction. *She is such an asshole.*

"Nice ink." TJ gestured to Tina's colorful arm. "When are you getting yours, Merritt?"

"You're getting a tattoo?" Tina shouted. "You tell me nothing!"

Merritt rolled her eyes. "I haven't decided yet. Calm your tits."

TJ and the girls continued to talk about tattoos. I didn't care to listen. Charlotte was here, and I needed to be close to her. I needed to remind her what she was missing.

"Wanna dance?"

"Uh ..." Charlotte looked at Merritt. "It's a girls' night. I don't want to break the rules."

Merritt gave her a nudge. "We can make an exception."

Charlotte's face lit up as her attention returned to me. "Okay. Lead the way."

We spent the remainder of the night wrapped in each other's arms on the dance floor. We didn't talk. We didn't need to. All that needed to be said was conveyed through our eyes as we gazed at one another.

Every now and again, I'd run my fingers through Charlotte's hair, or touch my fingers to her cheek. As much as it killed me to be this close and not kiss her, I had to pull out all the stops. I had to get her back.

CHARLOTTE

I WALKED THROUGH THE GARAGE DOOR TO HAND MERRITT AND Tanner their lunches. It had become my favorite part of each day. We'd order lunch, and I'd bring it to them when it got delivered. I'd bring Merritt her food first, just so I could sneak a peek at Tanner for longer. Actually, it was much more than a peek. It was open gawking, but I couldn't help myself. The way the muscles in his arm moved and stretched as he cranked the wrench. The way he bit his bottom lip in concentration. The greasy black streaks along his sweaty skin. *God, he's beautiful.*

I walked toward him, gripping the container in my hands. The memory of dancing with Tanner the night before replayed in my mind. We didn't kiss. We didn't talk. Our bodies did the talking.

Every molecule inside me burned with desire. All I had to do was tell Tanner the truth about my past. It seemed so simple. My resolve was wearing thin.

"Is that for me?" he asked.

My body? Yes. Take it. Please. "Yup. Lunch is served."

"You okay?"

Oh, you know. Just daydreaming about you naked. "Yeah, I'm fine."

His eyebrow arched as he stepped closer. "Are you sure?"

I nodded. "Enjoy your lunch!" I backed up, right into his toolbox—cringing as the handle dug into my back. I spun on my heels and walked out of the garage.

Smooth, Char. Real smooth.

I buried myself in work until it was time to leave. Before I knew it, Beverly was flipping the sign to Closed.

She waved. "See you Monday."

"Bye. Have a good night." I slung my purse over my shoulder and took my keys off the hook on the pegboard. Merritt had already left. She and Tanner usually left together, but he was still in the garage. I peeked through the door to find him underneath the car he was working on.

I walked over to where he was and leaned against his toolbox. "It's closing time, you know."

Tanner jumped at the sound of my voice, banging his head on the metal underneath the car. "Fuck!"

"Oh, God!" I knelt down as he sat up.

He rubbed his head. "You're like a ninja. I didn't even hear you come in."

"I'm sorry. I didn't mean to scare you. Are you okay?"

He smiled. "It's going to take a lot more than that to stop me."

I ran my thumb lightly over the knot forming on his forehead. "You should ice it."

Tanner's eyes closed as he leaned into my touch. "This feels better than ice."

Those pesky butterflies flitted around my heart as it thumped in my chest. I allowed my fingers to thread through his hair, gently massaging his scalp.

Tanner's dark eyes opened, hungry as they locked with mine. He lifted his hand to my face, tracing my bottom lip with his thumb.

Instinctually, my lips parted and a breath escaped. My hand slid to the back of his neck and I pulled him closer. I was no longer in control of my body. The need to kiss Tanner, to touch him, overrode any sense I had.

"Charlotte, I miss you."

"I miss you, too." I gripped the collar of his shirt and tried to pull his lips to mine. I had no intention of stopping.

Apparently, Tanner did. "I want to be with you."

"So then be with me," I pleaded, pressing myself against him.

He closed his eyes as he let out a low groan. "You know what I mean."

My shoulders slumped and I rested my head on his shoulder. I did know what he meant. I just couldn't give him what he wanted.

"I don't know why it's so hard for you to just tell me the truth." Tanner lifted my head, taking it into his hands to look me in the eyes. "Whatever happened, whatever you did, none of it matters. All that matters is who you are right now, and that we are together."

"If it doesn't matter, then why do I need to tell you?"

"It matters that you feel like you can't tell me. I want you to give me every part of you. Even the parts you don't like. I want to show you that my love for you is unconditional. I don't know what you're so scared of."

"What happened in my past has nothing to do with the way I feel about you. I made a new life here, and this is it. *You* are it. I have given you all of me. My heart. My body. You consume my mind. I love you, Tanner. I love you so much. All I want is to forget about every bad thing that has ever happened to me, and just look ahead to the good things that are coming. I want to look ahead with you."

The torture in his eyes killed me. I was doing this to him. My secrets. My lies.

"It hurts that you won't tell me." Tanner stood, quietly cleaning up his tools.

I searched for the right thing to say to make this better. I searched as Tanner turned his back and walked away. I searched as he stepped through the garage door and left. I searched as I drove back to my apartment. I searched for the rest of the night, as I showered, as I lay in my bed, as I tried to fall asleep. I searched into the late hours of the night … until the only answer I was left with was the one thing I swore I would never do.

ME: I'M READY TO TELL YOU EVERYTHING.

Chapter Twenty-Two

TANNER

onight was going to be special. I was taking Charlotte out to dinner, and she was going to tell me the truth about her past. I was surprised when she'd texted me late last night. I hadn't expected her to give in. The wall she kept between us was finally going to come down.

I stopped at the florist to pick up the giant bouquet of Gerbera daisies I'd ordered, and then texted Charlotte that I was on my way to her apartment. I pulled up to her place several minutes later, listening to the sound of my rapid heartbeat. I couldn't wait to see her.

Charlotte emerged from her building looking like the angel she was. The curled ends of her hair bounced as she walked toward me in her floral dress.

I left my car running and got out with her flowers in hand. I was so fixated on Charlotte's stunning beauty, I didn't notice the man walking briskly toward her. The rest of the world always faded away whenever she was around. Her eyes left mine and became glued to the suited man as he approached her. It wasn't until I saw Charlotte's face morph from happiness to horror that I realized what was happening.

I dropped the flowers onto the pavement, and ran across the

parking lot as fast as my legs would carry me. As I ran, I watched Charlotte scramble to get her purse off her shoulder. *The gun.*

The man got to Charlotte before she could get what she was looking for. He covered her head with a black sack, and I heard her scream as he tossed her over his shoulder.

"Hey!" I bellowed across the lawn. "Put her down!"

The man turned around, revealing horrific scars covering the entire right side of his face. His eyes locked with mine, and he grinned.

That gruesome face was the last thing I saw before it all went dark.

CHARLOTTE

ALL I COULD DO WAS CRY. THE MAN I THOUGHT I'D LEFT TO DIE inside the burning bakery in Florida was very much alive—and he had come back for revenge. Part of me always knew my past would catch up to me. After what I'd done? People didn't get to start a new life somewhere else and actually be happy. How foolish I was.

The worst part was that Tanner had gotten caught in the crossfire. The last thing I saw was Tommy running behind Tanner, a metal bat in his hands. Then, John slammed a sack over my head and carried me away. I heard a hollow cracking sound that pierced through me like a bullet. I prayed that it was the sound of Tommy's skull being struck with the bat, and not Tanner's.

My hands were now zip-tied behind my back as I lay across the back seat of the moving vehicle. My guess was that it was the same black SUV that had been following me. *I should've known. I should've left when I had the chance.*

Amidst the panic of being kidnapped, and the terror of not knowing if Tanner was okay, an odd sense of relief consumed me: *I am not a murderer.* Although, it might not matter anymore. I wasn't sure if I'd be alive for much longer.

I felt the vehicle stop. John and Tommy were silent as they opened their doors and pulled me out. I was yanked out by my ankles and hoisted over someone's shoulders again.

"What should I do with him?" I heard Tommy ask.

My heart thumped hard against my chest. *Tanner was with us.*

"Bring him in. We can't chance him waking up and escaping."

"I don't think he'll be waking up," Tommy said with an amused tone.

"Please," I pleaded. "Leave him out of this. He has nothing to do with any of this."

"Shut up, blondie," John snapped. "You did this to him. This is on you now."

I said nothing because I knew he was right. If I wasn't a murderer before, I would be now. Tanner's blood would be on my hands. His family would be torn apart all over again. My heart shattered in my chest as the tears spilled over.

A door creaked open. It was not much warmer inside wherever we were. We'd only been driving a short while, so we had to still be on Staten Island. I shook with fear, wondering what was going to happen next.

John sat me in a cold metal chair and zip-tied my ankles tightly to the legs. He then ripped the sack off my head. I frantically searched the darkened room for Tanner while my eyes strained to see where we'd been taken. The familiar sweet smell confirmed where we were.

Dad's bakery.

When I spotted the red gasoline jug by the door, John's plan unfolded in my mind without needing further explanation.

John sat another chair directly in front of me, and Tommy sank Tanner's lifeless body down onto it, tying his wrists and ankles like mine. His head hung forward, and I let out a loud sob when I saw the stream of blood down the side of his face and neck.

Tommy slapped Tanner's cheek several times in an attempt to wake him. Tanner's eyelids fluttered, and he slowly lifted his head. I was filled with mixed emotions, thankful he was alive, but panic-stricken for what he was about to endure. Guilt filled every inch of my body. I'd gotten him into this, and I wasn't going to be able to get him out.

TANNER

. . .

"Aww, look. Blondie is crying. Let me wipe those tears for you." The man with the scarred face swiftly backhanded Charlotte, sending lava shooting through my veins. I tried to stand, but my arms and legs wouldn't budge. I looked down in confusion and saw that I was bound to the chair. *What the fuck was going on?*

"Easy, tiger," the second man said. He was undoubtedly the fucker who'd knocked me out from behind. The immense throbbing in my head paled in comparison to the seething rage inside me.

"You're going to wish I was a tiger when I get my hands on you," I growled.

Both of the men burst into laughter, only spiking my anger. I yanked my limbs as hard as I could, trying to break free from the zip ties.

"Please," Charlotte whimpered. Her cheek was bright red where the man had struck her. "Please let him go. He's innocent in all of this. You have me. You can let him go."

That was the moment I realized that Charlotte knew exactly who these men were. Looking around the room, the pieces of the puzzle began to fit into their respective places. These men were from Charlotte's past; they were the men she and her father had run from; they were the reason she carried a gun; and, judging by the gas can, they definitely had something to do with the fire in her old bakery.

The man with the yellow teeth and mangled face lowered himself until he was nose to nose with Charlotte. His voice was low. "Look at what you did to my face, you little bitch. Do you really think I'm going to show mercy and let your boyfriend go?"

Charlotte didn't respond. Her eyes returned to mine, and my gut wrenched. "I'm so sorry, Tanner."

"Don't be. We're going to get out of here. Don't you worry, my sweet girl." I didn't know how, just yet, but I needed to make her feel better somehow. She was shaking, tear-stained, and terrified. I had to get her out of here, away from these men.

"You're even dumber than you look," the taller man said, "if you think you're getting out of here alive."

I ignored him and continued to pull against the restraints.

"Does he know what you did?" the other man asked Charlotte.

She shook her head, dropping her gaze to the floor.

He laughed once. "Well, then. Let's fill the boy in, shall we?" He leaned against the stainless steel countertop in the middle of the kitchen and crossed his arms over his chest, wearing a smug expression.

Charlotte didn't argue with him. *She thinks we're going to die. She's giving up.* I was curious about what she'd been keeping from me all this time, but these were not the circumstances I wanted her to tell me under. "You do not have to tell me anything. I don't care what you did. I love you, and you don't owe me any explanation."

Charlotte took an uneven breath before lifting her eyes to mine. "No. You deserve to know the truth."

Quiet descended upon the room while we waited for Charlotte to continue.

"My father owed them money," she began. "He got involved with gambling, and lost a lot of money. They bailed him out, so he owed them. One night when we were closing the old bakery in Florida, John and Tommy showed up looking for the money." She took another breath as she retrieved the memories from that night. "Tommy broke my wrist, and told Dad that he would be back in a couple days to collect the money he owed them."

Another puzzle piece snapped into place. Tommy had broken her wrist. *I will beat his ass first.*

"I knew Dad wouldn't be able to get that kind of money. So, I decided to burn down the bakery. I figured we could disappear before John knew we were gone, and we could collect the insurance money from the fire. We could start over somewhere new." Charlotte's shoulders shook as she cried, her eyes now far away. "Dad couldn't bring himself to burn down my mother's bakery. It was all we had left of her. So, I had to do it. I doused the kitchen in gasoline. That's when John showed up." Charlotte wept even harder.

"Go ahead," John urged. "Finish the fucking story."

"He stepped into the kitchen, but he slipped on the wet floor. His head hit, and he was knocked unconscious. I ... I left him there, on the floor. I stepped around his body and set the bakery on fire ... with him inside it." Her eyes implored me to understand. "It was the only way. It was the only way we could get away from them!"

"Your sweet little girlfriend isn't so sweet. She left me there to die!" John exclaimed.

Now, it all made sense. The puzzle was finally complete. Charlotte thought she'd killed John. The guilt must've been eating away at her. No wonder she was having panic attacks and carrying a loaded gun. She didn't want to tell me because she thought I wouldn't be able to forgive such a crime.

I shook my head. "You almost killed him. I'm so disappointed."

Charlotte's face crumpled.

"I'm disappointed that you didn't succeed in killing this piece of shit when you had the chance." I swung my head to look at John. "She might have failed, but I can promise you that I won't."

"I don't see you getting out of your chair to come and get me," John said, snickering. He nodded at Tommy.

Tommy bent down for the gasoline tank sitting at his feet.

I fought to break loose, my wrists and ankles raw from the plastic digging into my skin. We didn't have much time.

"Please, Tommy!" Charlotte wailed as Tommy dumped gasoline in a circle around our chairs. "Please let Tanner go! Please!"

Tommy smirked and doused Charlotte with the foul-smelling fuel. I fought so hard to break the zip ties that I thought my shoulders were going to pop right out of their sockets. Tommy turned around to dump gasoline on me next. I did the only other thing I could think of, and rammed my head into his midsection while I pushed myself upward with the chair still attached to me. He was caught off guard, and fell backwards.

John charged toward me, but Charlotte mimicked what I had done and knocked into him as he passed her. He shoved her backwards with one hand, sending her tumbling. I continued to yank on the zip ties, ignoring the fatigued feeling in my muscles. Defeat was creeping into the place where my hope once was. *How could I get Charlotte out of here if I couldn't get myself out of this fucking chair?*

Tommy and John were both on their feet, but Charlotte wasn't moving.

"Get the car started," John instructed. "I'm going to light this place up."

Tommy walked out, and John lifted his hand in front of his face to reveal a lighter, the flame dancing. The light illuminated his distorted face, and a triumphant grin spread wide. He tossed the lighter onto the floor, and the fire roared instantly.

"Uh, John," Tommy called from the door. "We have a problem."

John and I turned our heads in unison to find Tommy walking back into the bakery, his hands raised up to his ears. Behind him stood Charlotte's father, pressing a gun to the back of Tommy's skull. A tsunami of hope rushed over me.

"Hey, Frankie boy. Nice of you to join us," John said, sounding unfazed. "Now, you and your daughter can burn together."

"Let the kids go, and I won't blow both of your brains out."

"Frank, there's a pocket-knife in my pocket. Cut me free so I can get Charlotte out of here."

Frank walked around the men slowly. He cut one of my wrists free while aiming the gun at John the entire time.

I cut my other hand free, followed by my ankles. I ran over to Charlotte and cut her loose, too.

"You won't shoot us," John dared. "You don't have it in you."

I scooped Charlotte up and carried her toward the door.

"Where do you think you're going?" Tommy snarled behind me.

"Tanner, watch out!" Frank shouted.

Pain sliced through my back and I dropped to my knees, still cradling Charlotte in my arms.

CHARLOTTE

I WOKE UP, COUGHING UNCONTROLLABLY. MY EYES BURNED AS I looked around the smoke-filled room. Tommy was lying on the floor several feet away from me. My heart sank when I spotted Tanner lying dangerously close to the fire. A small pool of blood formed beside his body, and I felt sick. *Oh, God. No!*

"Not so tough without your gun, are you, Frank?"

Frank? His name ripped through my body. On the other side of the flames, I saw my father. He was on his back on the ground while John stood over him with a gun pointed at his head. *My gun.*

I wanted to curl in a ball and cry for help. The fire was so hot, it felt like my skin was melting. I could barely see, barely breathe. Tanner was knocked out, possibly dead, and my father was about to be shot right before my eyes. I said I would be prepared if they ever found me. I said I'd be ready for them. But I wasn't.

That's when I remembered: I am not a victim. I'm a survivor. This was not the end of my story. This was my chance. I needed to do something. Anything.

I got up and ran toward John as fast as I could.

I twisted his arm the way TJ had taught me. The gun dropped from his hand and my father kicked it across the room. I kicked John's knee, but he recovered quickly and took hold of my throat. I gasped for air. His grip around my neck was so tight, I could feel my eyeballs bulging out of my head.

Dad stood and attempted to break John's hold around my neck, but John simply shoved him to the ground. Dad hit his head on the counter on his way down. I felt light-headed from the lack of oxygen. I wasn't going to be able to hold on for much longer.

Don't give up. You are not weak.

I lifted my arms and jabbed my thumbs into John's eyes with whatever strength I had left.

"Ow! You bitch!" John's hold on me loosened, so I squeezed his neck, digging my fingers into his flesh as if I was going to rip out his jugular. He finally released me, and I fell to the ground gasping for air. John bent over and clutched his throat.

Get up! You don't have time to waste!

I kicked John in his kneecap again, and he collapsed in front of me. I took one of the chairs Tanner and I had been tied to and swung it at John's head with all my might. Blood splattered from his mouth and he hit the floor, completely knocked out.

I ran over to my father, taking his wrists in my hands, and pulled. Choking on the thick black smoke that filled the room, I ignored the tightening in my lungs. *Just keep going.* I dragged my father to the door, and didn't stop until we were in the parking lot. The frigid air felt good against my sweaty body. I coughed, gasping for the fresh air. I could hear the sound of sirens in the distance. I hoped they were coming here.

I tied my jacket to cover my nose and mouth and ran back inside to get Tanner. Just as I'd done with Dad, I took hold of Tanner's arms and pulled. He was much heavier than my father, and it was a struggle to drag him to the exit. Blood smeared in a trail on the tile floor behind us. I couldn't help but cry at the sight of it. *I'm going to get you out of here, baby. Please be okay!*

When I emerged with Tanner, I dug his phone out of his pocket and called 911. The wailing sirens sounded closer, but I couldn't be sure they were coming for us. I rattled off the address and dropped the phone onto the pavement. I looked back at the kitchen door, smoke billowing out of it. *I have to go back in.*

My lungs were burning, but I knew I had to do this. It was the right thing to do. I couldn't have their deaths on my hands. I couldn't live with the guilt like I had for the past year.

John was lying on the floor closest to the door. I grabbed him first, dragging him out as I had done twice already. Every muscle in my body was fatigued, but I couldn't stop.

Outside, several firetrucks were pulling into the parking lot. Two firefighters ran over to me when they saw me dragging John.

"Miss, is there anyone else inside?"

My throat burned when I tried to speak, and all I could do was cough. I nodded my head and held up one finger. Help was here. I had gotten Dad and Tanner out of the fire. My knees buckled under me.

We were safe.

Chapter Twenty-Three

TANNER

"**M**r. Brooks, you cannot get out of bed right now."

"The fuck I can't." I sat up, and surging pain split through my skull. The room tilted, and it felt like I was going to fall out of bed. I squeezed my eyes shut and gripped the rails next to me.

The nurse sighed. "Like I said: You cannot get out of bed. You have a concussion, and you inhaled a lot of smoke. You need to rest right now. You can see your girlfriend later."

All I heard was constant beeping. *That fucking beeping.* I was about to get up and unplug every wire that could be responsible for the incessant sound. "I need to see if she's okay."

"I promise you, she is in good hands. We are taking the very best care of her. Like you, she needs her rest."

"What about her father?"

"He's also in good hands. You're all very lucky to be alive."

Alive. We were all alive. I was alive because of Charlotte. The pain in my head was too much to keep it up. I lay back and closed my eyes. *I just need to close them for a minute. One minute, and then I'll go find Charlotte.*

. . .

CHARLOTTE

I OPENED MY EYES TO THE SOUND OF BEEPING. I TRIED TO MOVE, but something heavy weighed me down. My chest burned, followed by involuntary coughing. Something was attached to my face. *Where am I?*

"Hi, my sweet girl."

I turned my head to find Tanner curled up beside me on the bed. A hospital bed. I was in the hospital. Fragments of the night came back to me. *John. Bakery. Fire. Dad.*

My eyes widened. "Where's Dad?" I choked out before more coughing ensued. I tugged at the annoyance on my face.

"Leave that on, baby. You need oxygen to help you breathe right now." Tanner stroked my face with his hand. "Your dad is fine. I just checked on him a little while ago."

Tears stung my already burning eyes. "He's okay?" My throat felt like I had swallowed a thousand razor blades.

Tanner sat up, careful to not upset the tubes connected to me. He wore a bandage around his head, and his face was still stained with blood and soot. He reached over to get my water and the back of his hospital gown loosened, revealing a large bandage covering his shoulder blade.

I touched a shaky hand to my mouth in an attempt to muffle a sob. Tanner almost died tonight. And it was because of me.

"Don't cry, baby. It's okay. I'm here. Your dad is here. Everything is okay." He lifted the oxygen mask and tilted the cup toward my lips. I gulped the water.

A nurse popped her head through the doorway and heaved a sigh. "He's in here, Mary. Never mind." She sat her hands on her hips, giving Tanner a stern look. Her expression softened when she turned to me. "That's one stubborn boyfriend you've got there, Ms. Thompson."

I crossed my arms over my chest and looked at Tanner for an explanation.

He held his hands in the air. "Nurse Mary told me I could see my girlfriend later. It's later."

The nurse fought a smile. "Mr. Brooks, you need to stay in bed until you've been cleared. You can't go unhooking yourself from our machines."

My eyes widened, followed by more coughing.

Tanner handed me the water again. "Look at her. She needs me. I'm fine. I had a CT scan, an MRI, and I've been stitched up." He stretched his arms out wide. "Good as new."

The nurse rolled her eyes. "I'm giving you five minutes. If you're not back in that bed, I'm calling security and having you handcuffed to it."

"Kinky." Tanner grinned.

I used the little strength I had to smack his arm.

"Thank you, Ms. Thompson." The nurse shook her head and turned back out the door.

Tanner chuckled as he made himself comfortable beside me. He rested his head on my chest, and I raked my fingers through his matted hair.

"Did Dad say anything when you saw him?"

"He asked how you were. He has a concussion, but they have him on pain meds."

I struggled to swallow. "I can't believe they came back."

"How did they find you?"

"I don't know."

He looked at me, exuding nothing but love and sincerity. "You saved my life, Charlotte."

I shook my head. "You almost died because of me. Your family would've been devastated all over again."

"But I didn't die. I'm right here. Everything is fine. Stop focusing on what happened, and just look at me. Look at me, Charlotte."

I lifted my eyes to meet his.

"The nightmare is over. You get to put everything behind you, and move on with your life. No more fear. Everything you went through, every choice you made, has lead you to this very moment. If you hadn't left Florida, we never would've met."

"Yeah," I said, laughing once. "If you'd never met me, you wouldn't be in this hospital bed."

"If I'd never met you, I don't want to think about where I would be right now. I was angry and fucked up. Then, my dad died." He shook his head. "You are the only good thing in my life. You saved me from the fire tonight, but you also saved me from my miserable life."

I always thought Tanner wouldn't be able to love me if he knew the truth about my past. How could you love someone who left a man to die in a burning building? Now, my secrets were all out in the open. Tanner saw me for who I really was, yet he didn't love me any less. I didn't deserve it. I didn't deserve him.

I lay my head back on the pillow, but every time I closed my eyes to try to sleep, visions of Tanner bleeding on the bakery floor flashed in my mind. With dried blood on his face, a stab wound in his back, and black sooty smudges all over his skin, it was an image that would forever be burned into my memory.

Tanner had almost died, and I was the reason why.

———

"WHAT ARE YOU THINKING ABOUT?" DAD ASKED, SNAPPING ME OUT of the broken record of self-loathing playing in my head.

I offered him a half- smile from the chair beside his hospital bed. "Just how thankful I am that you and Tanner are all right. How do you feel?"

"I'm fine." He grunted as he sat up in the bed. "I wish you'd stop asking me that." He looked me square in the eyes. "Now, tell me what's going on in that head of yours."

I shrugged, breaking eye contact. "I can't help thinking that Tanner almost died because of me."

"How is any of this your fault?"

"I decided to burn down our old bakery. I left John in there to die, and it was my idea to run. I started a new life, and put everyone who met me in danger. What if Tanner had died? How would I have been able to live with myself?"

Dad's eyebrows pressed together. "Charlotte, I am the reason that all of this happened. It all stems back to me and my poor decisions. You did what you could to survive. You can't punish yourself for any of this. Tanner didn't die. You saved him. You saved all of us."

I knew Dad was the first domino to set this whole situation into motion. However, my choices thereafter are what caused the events of last night. I was responsible for Tanner's injuries. I couldn't stop thinking about it.

"Did you talk to the police yet?"

I nodded. "I gave my statement earlier this morning."

"You're a hero, Charlotte. Everyone's been talking about it."

I raised an eyebrow. "Everyone?"

"The nurses. The police officers I gave my report to. They can't believe you saved four men from a burning building. I was especially proud to tell them about the part when you stopped John from shooting me. Where did you learn those moves?"

"I took a self-defense class. Somehow, I think I always knew they'd come back to find me."

"Is that why you bought a gun?"

I nodded. "How did you know where to find us?"

"When I got home from work, I saw Tanner's car in the parking lot. The door was open and it was still running, but he was nowhere to be found. That's when I noticed the flowers on the pavement, and your purse in the grass. Something inside me knew. There was only one place you could be. Those men wanted revenge. Of course they would go to the new bakery. It was the only place that made sense."

"Back at square one again."

"One of the officers said as long as the damage isn't structural, we'd be able to have it back up and running in no time."

"I wonder how long John and Tommy will be in jail for."

Dad shrugged. "Good riddance. It's all over now. It's all behind us."

Behind us.

It's over.

They're gone.

It hadn't truly sunk in. Not until now. All my guilt over Tanner almost dying had been the only thing consuming my thoughts. The adrenaline was wearing off. The aftershock was settling down. It hit me: nothing was holding me captive in my past.

I could look back without regret.

I could *go* back.

Back to Florida.

Carla.

Chapter Twenty-Four

TANNER

"Hello?"

"Hey, Tanner. Can you come outside for a minute?"

Outside? Why was Charlotte outside my house at ten o'clock at night? She should be resting like the doctor advised. "Do you want to come in instead?"

"No. I can't stay long."

"Okay. Be right out."

I jogged to her car and sat in the passenger seat. "Everything okay? Are you okay?"

She nodded. "Everything's fine. I just wanted to tell you that I'm leaving for Florida early tomorrow morning."

"What?" It came out just as loudly as it exploded inside my head.

"I'm going to visit Carla. Now that John and Tommy are out of the picture, I can finally go home."

Home? "You're going for a visit?"

"Yes. Just for a week."

I breathed an audible sigh of relief. "Okay. Do you want me to come with you?"

Charlotte covered my hand with hers. "No, but thank you for the offer. I haven't been home in so long. I need to do this on my own."

Every time she said the word *home,* it sliced me like a sheet of paper —subtle, yet painful. "Well, have a safe trip." I didn't know what else to say.

What if she didn't want to come back? What if she *didn't* come back? What if she missed her old life too much to return here to her new one?

Fear gripped my heart as Charlotte leaned over the console and kissed my cheek.

"I'll see you when I get back."

All I could do was nod.

CHARLOTTE

I COLLECTED MY LUGGAGE AND ROLLED IT OUTSIDE INTO THE WARM air. I breathed it deep into my lungs; it didn't smell like garbage. I made a visor with my hand as I searched for Carla's beat-up Toyota. The palm trees lining the street made me smile as I waited. *Finally.*

Carla pulled up several minutes later. She flung her car door open and ran around the front end to where I was standing at the curb. Gripping my shoulders tightly, she stared at me as tears rolled down her cheeks.

"I never thought I would see you again," she whispered.

I pulled her in for a long hug, unable to speak over the emotion in my throat.

After a minute had passed, Carla pulled away from me, quick to wipe the evidence of her sentiment. I imagined how Mallory would've reacted in this situation, and I couldn't help but smile. The two were so different, yet both had become my best friends.

It was quiet on the ride to Carla's. All I had told her when I called yesterday was that I was coming to see her, and that I would explain everything. One second, we were best friends dancing at prom; the next second, I'd vanished. The stoic expression on her face told me she was waiting for me to start talking.

"You look great," I offered. Her caramel hair fell in loose waves, much longer than I'd ever seen it. Her pencil skirt and buttoned-up blouse made her look even more mature than she already acted.

"Don't mind the work attire. I took a half- day today."

"Where are you working?" It felt odd not knowing the answer to such a simple question.

"The registrar's office." She glanced at the yellowish-brown bruise fading on my cheek. "You look like you've been through hell."

I looked down at my lap, picking at the fringe on my jeans. "It has definitely felt like hell."

"Yeah, well, it was no picnic for me either."

"I'm sorry, Carla. I've wanted to call you every single day since I left."

"Why didn't you?"

"It's complicated. A lot happened."

"We have a long ride home. Start talking."

For the next hour, I carefully went over every detail since the moment I met John and Tommy for the first time at the bakery that fateful night. Every now and again, I would see Carla's hand lift to swipe a tear off her cheek. Then, she'd readjust her large sunglasses and smooth down her already smooth hair. She didn't ask any questions. She didn't make any comments. She just listened. I expected nothing more from her.

"Is anyone going to be home?"

"Yup." Carla turned down her street. "The fam is very excited to see you."

Seeing the familiar houses on the block I used to ride my bike up and down, I suddenly wondered who was living in my old house. Part of me wanted to see it, and part of me didn't. Maybe I was better off not taking that stroll down memory lane. There was no sense in going back. Yet, ironically enough, here I was at the one place I never thought I'd be again.

Carla's parents were sitting on the porch when we pulled into the driveway. Everything looked the same: the mess of bicycles, sports equipment, and action figures strewn about the front lawn; the matching rocking chairs that creaked whenever people sat in them, and the rusty old car parked in the open garage.

Carla's twin brothers, Sam and Lucas, bounded down the porch stairs. I knelt and opened my arms wide.

"Charlotte!" They tackled me simultaneously and I was knocked onto my back on the pavement.

"Oh, God! What have you two been eating?" I'd only been gone a year, yet they looked like they'd aged three.

They flashed matching wicked grins as they tickled me.

"Help!"

"This is your punishment for leaving," Carla stated, lifting her chin as she strutted by.

"All right, boys! That's enough. Let Charlotte get up." Robert stood from his rocking chair. His hair was more than sprinkled with gray, and he sported dark rings under his eyes. The twins were not planned and certainly gave Carla's family a run for their money. Still, I couldn't imagine their lives without them. *Everything happens for a reason,* her mother, Beth, would say.

I let the boys pretend to pull me up, and I dusted off my backside. "You should enroll them in football."

Beth wagged her finger at me from her chair. "Oh, no. My babies will not be playing that brute sport."

"It's not a brute sport," Robert argued. "It's a man's sport. You just don't understand."

Beth rolled her eyes and smiled at me as I approached the porch. "Charlotte Elaine Thompson, I can't believe you're walking up those steps looking like a woman."

"I can't believe she's walking up those steps at all," Carla said.

I wrapped my arms around Beth as tears sprang into my eyes. I'd forgotten how much I missed her hugs. How much they felt like my own mother's. How much this felt like home.

"We were so worried about you," she whispered into my hair as she squeezed me tightly.

"I'm sorry."

"All right, dear. Don't suffocate the poor girl." Robert placed a gentle hand on her shoulder.

She loosened her grip and touched the palm of her hand to my cheek. "You're even more beautiful than the last time I saw you. My girls are all grown up. I feel so old."

"That's because we *are* old."

"Speak for yourself, Robert!"

I slipped my hands around Robert's midsection and remained there until he patted me on the back.

"I could make this a lot worse, you know," I teased.

"For God's sake, Rob. She's been gone a year. Just hug her!"

Finally, I felt Robert's arms return the hug. "We missed you, kid."

And just like that, I was back. I was home.

———

AFTER DINNER, CARLA AND I SAT IN THE ROCKING CHAIRS ON THE porch, rocking in silence. Though she was normally a woman of few words, she'd been extra quiet today. I thought we'd pick up right where we left off. I didn't anticipate her being angry with me.

"You think you'll be mad at me forever?"

She waited a while before answering, keeping her gaze on the setting sun. "I'm not mad. I was worried about you for so long. Confused. How could my best friend just disappear like that, you know? Then, Kyle came back for a visit and ran his mouth about how he ran into you in New York. I almost didn't believe him. Everyone knew you'd vanished, but their lives went on. You became old news. But for me? My life wasn't the same without my best friend. Everything changed after that. Now, you're back." She shrugged. "It doesn't seem real."

"I wish it weren't. Believe me. Many times I cried myself to sleep, wishing I could wake up from the nightmare."

It was quiet again. Finally, Carla faced me. "So, tell me about this Tanner dude."

"What do you want to know?"

"I want to know if he's worth staying in New York for."

"Ah, now I see."

"What do you see?"

"You're mad at me because you know I'm not back for good."

One corner of her mouth twitched. "Like I said. I'm not mad."

"Carla, I missed you every single day. I thought about you all the time."

"Ditto. I'm just glad you're okay. Or better than okay, it seems."

"Is it that obvious?"

"Completely. You're different. I guess love will do that to a person."

"Maybe it was being hunted down and kidnapped by two psychotic criminals. Puts things into perspective."

Carla laughed for what seemed like the first time all day. "Or that."

I hated admitting it, but I actually missed Staten Island. I'd been forced to start a new life there, and it never quite felt like home. However, being away now made me realize that home had nothing to do with a physical place. Home was about the people you surrounded yourself with. I didn't want my old life back. I wanted the people in my new one. One tall, dark, and handsome person, in particular.

"I wish you could come to New York with me."

"Maybe I'll come for a visit one day. Maybe I'll move up there."

"What?"

She shrugged. "There's nothing here for me anymore."

"Uh ... what about Joe? And your family?"

Carla's eyes dropped to her lap. "Joe and I broke up."

I gasped. "Carla! When? Why? What happened?"

"Last month."

"That answers the when. What happened?"

She ran her fingers through her hair and sighed. "We graduated, and I guess things got too real for him. He wasn't ready to step up and be a man."

"That doesn't sound like him. What did he say? He just broke up with you?"

"Look, I really don't want to talk about it. It's behind me. You've been gone a long time. Things have changed."

I swallowed hard. "I'm sorry, Carla. I'm sorry I wasn't here for you when you needed me."

"It's fine."

"No, it's not."

Silence descended upon the porch once more. Carla was shutting me out. There was more to the story than she was telling me.

Before I left Florida, Carla was with Joe, her boyfriend of three years. High school sweethearts. They'd had a plan to move in together after graduation and then get married.

Carla was different now. Sad. She had this faraway look in her eyes. I couldn't imagine Joe walking away from what they had. Something didn't add up.

TANNER

"PUNCH! COME ON! YOU'RE SLOWING DOWN! PICK UP THE PACE!"

I dropped my arms at my sides. "I just can't right now."

TJ lowered his pads, and sighed. "Your head isn't here tonight. What gives? Is your back all right?"

"My back is fine."

"Did they take the stitches out?"

"Yup."

"Still nothing from Charlotte?"

I shook my head. "Nothing."

Charlotte hadn't called all week. The only texts were in response to the ones I sent first. She was supposed to come home tonight, but a nervous feeling pooled deep in my stomach. I checked my phone all day, waiting to receive a text stating that Charlotte would be staying in Florida. For good. I tried not to jump to conclusions. I tried not to think about what I'd do if that happened. Still, the feeling was there.

TJ tossed the pads to the floor of the boxing ring. "Why don't we go grab a slice of pizza?"

"I'd rather go grab a drink instead."

"So go." He crossed his arms across his chest, challenging me to ruin all the progress I'd made.

"Fuck you."

"Give her some time. Remember when that was what *you* needed?"

"Thanks, asshole. Now I feel even worse."

"So glad I could help." TJ grinned as I turned to leave.

As I made my way home from the gym, my phone rang. I pulled over, too nervous to even see straight.

"Charlotte?"

"Hey. I landed."

I released the breath I'd been holding for the past week. "Great. How was your trip?"

"It was good. Everyone was so happy to see me."

"I'm sure. You were only gone for a week and I'm going to be thrilled to see you."

She laughed, and my heart ached at the sound. "I should be home in an hour or so. Then I need to shower the smell of airplane off me."

"Can I see you after?"

"Sure. Want to come over at eight?"

"I'll be there at eight."

———

MY STOMACH WAS IN ONE GIANT KNOT AS I ARRIVED AT Charlotte's apartment. I called her to let her know I had arrived.

"Hey, are you here? The door is unlocked."

I cleared my throat. "Uh, I want to show you something first. Can you come for a ride with me?"

"Right now? What is it?"

"I need you to come with me so I can show you."

"Okay. I'll be right down."

I got out of the car when Charlotte walked outside. I wrapped my arms around her, lifting her off the ground in a bear hug. I inhaled her familiar scent, and the knot in my stomach loosened.

"God, I missed you."

"I missed you, too," she croaked. "I can't breathe."

"Sorry." I set her down. "I didn't think I'd get to do that again."

Her nose scrunched. "What are you talking about?"

I shook my head. "Nothing. Come on."

I watched Charlotte out of the corner of my eye as I made my way to our destination. Once we arrived, I parked in front of the brick colonial house.

"Whose house is this?" she asked.

"A very nice couple owns it. Tom and Joan."

"And you're taking me to Tom and Joan's house because ..."

"I'm not taking you to their house. I'm taking you up those stairs to the apartment on the side of their house."

Charlotte's eyes darted around while her brows pressed together. She followed me up the concrete stairs and watched silently as I turned the key to unlock the door. I switched on the lights and stepped back to watch Charlotte's expression as she looked around.

"Tanner, what's going on?"

I closed the door behind her and took her hands in mine. "This is our apartment."

"Our?"

"I'd been saving to get my own place. I wanted an apartment so we could have somewhere to go without our family members being around. I planned on bringing you here the night we got taken by John and Tommy. We were out of commission for a few days after that. Then, you said you were going to Florida. I wanted to tell you sooner."

Charlotte's hands slipped out of mine. I waited for her response as she walked around the living room and into the kitchen.

"I know it's small, but it'd be just us here. We don't need anything big just yet."

"Who bought all this furniture?"

"Tom and Joan's son recently got married. He left everything here."

"Wow. Fully furnished."

I nodded. "What do you think?"

Charlotte turned her blue eyes to me. "I think it's a little soon for us to be moving in together. Now, with the bakery out of commission, I don't have an income anymore."

"The bakery won't be out of commission much longer. TJ, Derek, and I ripped up the floor in the kitchen and put new tile down while you were gone. Your dad was going to pay someone to do it, but they were going to charge him some astronomical amount."

Her eyes widened. "You've been fixing it?"

"I needed something to do after work while you were gone."

Charlotte closed the gap between us and wrapped her arms around my waist, burying her head against my chest. "Thank you. You are incredible. I don't deserve you."

I pulled her away from me to look at her. "Why would you say that? I love you. We deserve each other."

Her arms dropped at her sides. "We should talk."

I sucked in a breath, bracing for her words. "Okay. Let's talk."

Charlotte's eyes were watery, and she wore an expression I couldn't read. "Now that everything is out in the open, I hope you can understand why I tried to keep it from you. A part of me always knew my past would catch up to me. I burned down the bakery—my mom's bakery that she loved—and ran away with the insurance money like a criminal.

"But what was even worse, I left John to die in there. I saw him get knocked out, and I looked the other way to save myself. I've had to live with that guilt for a year. The guilt of killing a man. I was too scared to tell you. I didn't want you to hate me."

"I could never hate you. You did what you had to do to save your and your father's lives. John would've killed you, Charlotte."

She nodded as the tears ran down her cheeks. "I know. I get that. But it was so hard living with that guilt."

I wiped her tears. "It's okay, baby. Everything worked out in the end. We just had to go through some scary shit to get here. But we're here."

"I know it's a big thing to ask, but I need you to be honest with me."

"Of course. What is it?"

"I need to know if you can forgive me for everything I've done. For everything I thought I did in Florida. For everything I've done to put you in danger. All of it. Because I love you more than anything in this world, Tanner, and now that everything is out there for you to see, I need to know. I need to know if you can forgive me. I need to know if you still want to be with me."

My heart swelled. I didn't have to justify such a silly question with an answer. I gripped Charlotte's face and slammed my lips against hers.

She opened her mouth and our tongues found one another. We stripped each other down in the middle of the living room, our hands frantically searching for skin. I picked her up by her ass and carried her into our new bedroom. *It was ours, whether she acknowledged it or not.* Dropping her onto the bed, I climbed on top and pressed myself against her.

"Tell me you forgive me," she breathed. "Tell me you want me to be yours again."

I gazed into her eyes. "I forgive you. I love you more than life itself. You will always be mine because I will always be yours."

Charlotte didn't need me to forgive her. She needed to forgive herself. I could help her with that. The way she had helped me.

From day one, something had drawn me to Charlotte. I was never able to pinpoint exactly what it was. She was beautiful. Caring. Smart. But there was always something more. Something I saw whenever I looked into her eyes.

Now, after everything that had happened, I finally knew what it was. Charlotte wasn't a damsel in distress. I'd had it all wrong. I'd defended her and tried to protect her, but she didn't need my help. My girlfriend, the love of my life, was a *fucking badass*. She was an incredibly strong woman who fought for the people she loved.

Technically, I'm the damsel in distress here.

And that didn't bother me one fucking bit.

Chapter Twenty-Five

CHARLOTTE

"What do you want for dinner?"

"I don't know. Why don't we order in?" I dug my car keys out of my purse and waited for Tanner to lock the garage.

"You've wanted to order in a lot lately. I think you like being at the apartment a lot more than you're letting on."

"I love the apartment. That was never in question."

"You're right." Tanner grinned and wrapped his arms around me. "The question is, why don't you want to live there with me?"

"I already told you, I—"

"Excuse me, Ms. Thompson."

Tanner and I jumped. I clutched my purse out of habit, and Detective Williams smiled. "Sorry. I didn't mean to scare you."

"Says the man lurking in an empty parking lot." Tanner's jaw worked under his skin.

I squeezed his hand and swallowed the dry lump in my throat. "That's okay. We're both still a little jumpy."

"That's understandable after everything you've been through." Detective Williams took a step closer. "I just have a few more questions to ask you. I won't take too much of your time."

"What more could you possibly have left to ask?" Tanner wrapped his arm around my shoulders. "She's answered all your questions."

"I want to make sure I have all the facts straight. I'm sure you double-check a vehicle after you're done working on it, right?"

"It's okay." I stepped forward. "What do you need to know?"

Leafing through his notepad, Detective Williams clicked his pen several times. "Your father admitted to getting involved with John's illegal gambling. When he couldn't pay them, you said John came to your old bakery and broke your arm?"

"Tommy was the one who broke my wrist, but yes. They came to the bakery after we'd closed and threatened us."

"Then you said John came back at the end of that week and tried to burn the bakery down."

"Yes. My father had already gone home for the night. I was in the kitchen when John came in and started dousing it with gasoline."

"And where was Tommy when this happened?"

"I don't know, sir. I didn't see him."

"But you managed to get out without getting hurt."

My chest tightened. "Yes. John slipped on the gasoline, hit his head, and was knocked unconscious. That's how I was able to escape."

The detective nodded as he scribbled on his pad.

I hated lying to the police, but insurance fraud is illegal. Dad and I could both face jail. I couldn't let that happen. We'd been through enough.

"Are these Mafioso pricks going to stay in prison?" Tanner asked. "They tried to kill my girlfriend. Twice."

I shuddered at the thought of John and Tommy walking free. *Would they come for me again? Would they ever give up?*

"We've got them for racketeering and gambling, but they're being charged with attempted murder. If they plead guilty, it will be an open-and-closed case."

"If they don't plead guilty?"

"Ms. Thompson and her father will have to testify against them in court."

"What are the odds they'll be found guilty?" I chewed my lip waiting for his response.

"Pretty high, considering this isn't their first offense." He shoved both the pen and pad into his pocket. "Thank you for your time. Sorry to interrupt your night."

"That's it? What happens next?"

"Ms. Thompson, you have nothing to worry about. Those men won't hurt you anymore." He turned and walked to his car.

Nothing to worry about.

Tanner held my face and kissed my lips softly. "He's right, you know. You have nothing to worry about anymore."

"What if they plead not guilty? What if it goes to court and I have to testify? What if they don't believe me? What if—"

"Easy, baby. Let's take it one day at a time. We'll worry about things when it's time to worry about them. Right now, all I'm worried about is getting you home and getting us something to eat."

I mustered a smile as Tanner took my hand in his. I tried to quell the thoughts swarming my mind, though that was an impossible task knowing there was even the slightest chance John and Tommy could go free.

When will this be over?

TANNER

"MOMMY! THEY'RE HERE!"

I closed the door behind me and braced for the impact of Khloe's tiny body. She flung herself into my arms and wrapped her legs tightly around me. I felt guilty for moving out of the house. In the matter of months, Khloe went from a family of five to living in a house with only Mom. I felt guilty about leaving Mom, too.

"Are we going to make pancakes now? I'm starving!"

"Of course! You're going to help me, right?" Charlotte asked.

Khloe dove from my arms into Charlotte's. "Yes! Let's go!"

Charlotte carried Khloe into the kitchen, grinning over her shoulder at me.

"That kid's got way too much energy in the morning," I said as I walked into the living room.

"You think you were any different when you were her age?" Mom asked, smiling up at me. She was curled under a blanket on Dad's recliner.

I took the recliner next to her and leaned over to kiss her head. "How has she been since I moved out?"

"She's fine. I told you: you don't have to worry about it."

I opened my mouth to respond but the ringing of Mom's phone cut me off. Chase was calling.

"To what do I owe this early-morning call?" She paused and I watched her smile disappear. "What do you mean there was an earthquake?" Mom jumped up to grab the remote off the coffee table. When the TV didn't turn on, she smacked it against the palm of her hand. "This damn thing never works!"

"Give it to me before you break it." I took the remote from her and placed my hand gently on her shoulder.

When the TV turned on, Mom's hand flew to her mouth as she saw the images on the screen. "Oh my God, Chase. Are you all right? Where are you?"

"I'm in the hospital with Merritt. Everything is okay."

"Merritt's with you?" Mom and I asked in unison. *I just saw Merritt yesterday. How is she in California?*

Mom put the phone on speaker so I could hear.

"Merritt arrived last night. She was just in time to get me and a friend out of the bar after the earthquake hit. I was knocked out, and she saved me."

"Jesus Christ! I want you both to come home!"

"We will. I'll call you after the doctor checks me out."

"I love the both of you so much."

"We love you, too."

Mom ended the call and sat down slowly onto the edge of the coffee table, her eyes still glued to the TV.

Charlotte stepped into the living room with Khloe not far behind. "Everything okay?"

I pulled her close to me while Khloe climbed into Mom's lap.

"There was an earthquake in California. Chase just called to say he'll be coming home."

"Oh my God! Is he okay?"

"Yeah. Apparently, Merritt is with him."

Charlotte looked up at me and her face twisted in confusion. "What's she doing in California?"

I shrugged. "I guess we'll find out when they get home."

"You get kidnapped. He gets caught in an earthquake." Mom rubbed her head. "You kids are going to be the death of me."

———

MOM COOKED A FEAST FOR CHASE AND MERRITT'S ARRIVAL. THEY looked bruised and battered, but they were alive. Mom and Khloe were thrilled to have a full house again, and Merritt was equally thrilled to have Chase home. I didn't want any of them to get their hopes up though. *Would Chase stay home for good? Would Merritt want to go back with him?* There was too much uncertainty, and Chase had made his priorities clear when he'd left us all in the dust before.

"Tanner, you got a sec?" Chase motioned for me to follow him into the living room.

"I'm clearing off the table."

Merritt nudged me with her elbow. "Go. I've got the dishes."

I sighed and followed my brother into the other room. Chase sat on the edge of the couch and waited for me to take a seat.

"I need to thank you."

I raised an eyebrow. "For what?"

"For taking care of Merritt when she came back."

"It was no big deal."

"Yes, it was, and you know it. I don't know what I would've done if you hadn't been here to help her."

"I didn't do anything. It's TJ you should be thanking."

Chase shook his head adamantly. "No. You're the one who convinced her to go to TJ in the first place. You're the only one who was able to get through to her." He looked down at his hands. "She trusts you."

For the first time in, well, let's be honest—ever—Chase was being vulnerable. Real. Something was different about him. I guess almost dying in a natural disaster had changed his perspective on life.

"She trusts me because I'm real with her. I don't tiptoe around her feelings."

"Are you saying I tiptoe around her?"

I shrugged. "I don't know about your relationship. But I know Merritt, and I know she needs you. She needs you to be there for her. She needs you to put her first. Everyone she's ever loved has left her. You can't leave her again."

Chase looked straight into my eyes. "I'm not."

"You're not going back to California?"

"No. It's not worth it. Nothing is worth it. You showed me that."

I sat back as if blown back by an explosion. "Me?"

"You remind me of Dad so much. You always have. You worked your ass off and made this family your top priority. You have this certainty about you. You know exactly what you want, exactly where you belong. You always make the right choices."

I laughed once. "I make the right choices? You sure about that? I'm the hotheaded and impulsive one."

Chase smiled. "Yeah, you have a temper ... but it's only because you're so positive in your convictions. You love fiercely and you stand up for what's right. I look up to you for that."

I was absolutely dumbfounded. "You sure the doctor said you didn't have a head injury?"

Chase laughed and I cracked a smile. "Look, you helped Merritt when I couldn't, and I'll never forget that. You took care of this family when I didn't. I just wanted to say thank you. For everything. I owe you."

"Nah. You don't owe me anything. That's what family is for."

Chase stood and I did the same. He stuck his hand out and looked at me. "Brothers?"

I put my hand in his and gave it a firm shake.

"Always."

Chapter Twenty-Six

CHARLOTTE

*I*t was finally summer again.

I'd spent the day basking in the warmth of the sun's rays at Beverly's house celebrating Chase's birthday. Tanner flipped burgers on the barbeque. Khloe splashed in the pool with Chase and Merritt. Everyone was at peace. Everyone was happy.

John and Tommy agreed to take a plea deal. They even ratted out several other men they worked with in exchange for a lesser sentence. I wouldn't have to testify. I wouldn't go to jail. I wouldn't have to see them again. A weight had been lifted from the shoulders I'd no longer have to look over.

They'd forget about me after twenty years in prison, right?

Tonight, I was especially happy because Carla had agreed to visit. I secretly hoped I could convince her to quit her job and move to New York. Part one of my plan was scheduled to unfold. Carla, Tanner, Mallory, and I were on our way to Big Nose Kate's.

"Is TJ meeting us there?" Mallory asked.

"He'll be there."

Mallory turned to Carla beside her in the back seat. "Wait until you see this beef-stick of a man. He is the most gorgeous thing I've ever laid eyes on."

Carla chuckled at Mallory's enthusiasm the same way I did. "Is he single? Why don't you two hook up?"

Mallory shook her head vigorously. "He is way out of my league."

"Ah, come on, girl! Don't say that. You're hot!"

I turned to look at Mallory. "What she said!"

"I think TJ's been a little too preoccupied to notice anyone." Tanner shook his head. "If he couldn't crush me with his bare hands, I'd have killed him."

"Tanner's still mad that TJ fell in love with Merritt," I explained to Carla.

"And Merritt is your brother's girlfriend?" Carla asked.

"Yup. I don't know what he was thinking."

Mallory laughed once. "He spent all his time rolling around in that cage training Merritt. Of course feelings are going to spark. I just can't believe that girl has two of the hottest guys at her feet. No fair!"

Tanner rolled his eyes.

I patted his arm reassuringly. "You're still the hottest guy to me, babe."

"So what's your story, Carla? Are you single?"

"I am." She still had that faraway look about her, and she still wouldn't tell me what had happened between her and Joe. I didn't understand why she didn't want to tell me. We'd always told each other everything.

Well, except that one time I didn't tell her I was moving to New York in the middle of the night after burning down my father's bakery with an evil mobster inside of it.

Once we were in the bar, Mallory ordered shots. Tanner scanned the room for TJ and I watched him intently until he caught me.

"What are you smiling about?"

I wrapped my arms around his neck and pulled him in for a kiss. "I'm smiling about you."

"Oh, yeah? Why is that?"

"Because I love you."

Tanner grinned. "If you love me so much, why don't you move in with me?"

"I told you why. It's too soon."

"Too soon for what?" Mallory nudged me with a shot glass.

Tanner gestured to me with his thumb. "She thinks it's too soon to move in together."

Mallory rolled her eyes. "You guys have been through so much shit already, it's like you've been dating for years." She handed Carla a shot. "Their relationship has been exhausting. Be glad you missed it."

Carla raised her glass in the air. "Time means nothing. You could be with someone for years and not truly know them."

Tanner clinked his water bottle against Carla's glass. "Exactly."

"You guys are supposed to be on my side." I tapped my glass against Carla's before moving to Mallory's. "That's messed up."

We threw our shots back as TJ appeared beside Tanner.

Mallory indiscreetly elbowed Carla in the ribs to get her attention. Carla made no facial expression whatsoever. I could never read her.

Tanner slapped him on the back. "What's up, dick-face?"

TJ nodded. "Shit stain." He turned his attention to me. "How ya doin', champ?"

"I'm great. TJ, you remember Mallory."

He winked at her and she giggled.

"This is my best friend Carla."

He extended his hand. "Nice to meet you, Carla. Glad to see you let your friend come back home."

One of her eyebrows arched. "Florida *was* her home. This is just her new residence."

"It's my new home." I wrapped my arm around her shoulders. "Maybe it will be your new home, too."

"Are you thinking of moving up here?" TJ asked.

Carla shrugged. "It's a possibility."

"If you move here, I'd get an apartment with you," Mallory said. "I'm dying to get out of my house."

"Why didn't you ask me to get an apartment with you?" I asked.

She gestured to Tanner. "You're moving in with him."

"I never said that!"

She rolled her eyes. "You will eventually, and I can't carry the rent on my own."

"You're really looking to move out?" Carla asked.

Mallory's eyes went wide with excitement. "Hell, yes! Let me know. I'll start apartment hunting!"

Tanner snaked his arm around my waist. "See, babe? Your friends are going to live together. We should live together. Everybody wins."

"And when you guys start fighting, I can tell you to come stay at my place." Mallory laughed.

"Hey, who says we're going to fight?" Tanner hugged me tighter.

"Please." Mallory turned to Carla. "They've broken up at least five times since they started dating."

I sunk my hand on my hip. "That's an exaggeration."

"Bullshit," TJ coughed loudly. He and Mallory laughed.

"Whatever. You're together now," Carla said. Then she pointed her finger at Tanner's nose. "But if you break her heart, I'll kill you."

Tanner held up his right hand to swear on the invisible Bible. "I will never hurt her."

TJ's eyes sparkled as he laughed. "She's feisty and beautiful. I like your friend, Charlotte."

"Wish I could say the feeling was mutual." Carla tugged on my elbow. "Come on. Let's dance."

I pulled Mallory with me as we made our way to the dance floor.

"You know TJ was just being nice," I shouted over the music.

"Whatever. I'm not in the mood."

Mallory's eyebrows shot up. "Not in the mood for *that?*"

"I just want to forget about men for tonight and enjoy my time with you girls."

Mallory looked at me and we exchanged shrugs.

I caught TJ watching Carla as she danced throughout the night. I didn't know too much about him, but he seemed like an incredible person. I didn't expect Carla to swoon over him the way Mallory did, but she was sending out major bitch vibes, which was uncharacteristic of her. I had a feeling it had something to do with her breakup with Joe.

Mallory kept the drinks coming and by the end of the night, we were giggling and stumbling over to Tanner.

"Are you ready to go?" He was fighting the smile tugging at his lips.

"Yes. My feet are killing me. Wait. Where's Carla?"

"She said she needed some air," Mallory said. "She's probably waiting for us outside."

"You're slurring," I told her.

She held her middle finger up. "Your ass is slurring."

I burst out laughing.

Tanner held out each of his elbows for us to take. "All right, ladies. Let's go."

We walked out to the parking lot to look for Carla.

"I don't see her."

"I do." Tanner was laughing and shaking his head.

I looked in the direction of his stare and saw the back of Carla's head. Two large tattooed arms were wrapped around her waist.

I squinted in disbelief. "Is that …"

"Holy shit!" Mallory exclaimed. "Carla's making out with TJ!"

"Is she going home with him?"

Tanner shrugged. "Does she do that sort of thing?"

"Not that I know of."

Mallory sighed. "Lucky bitch."

Tanner unlocked his Mustang. "You two get in the car. I'll go ask."

I watched from the passenger seat as Tanner interrupted the make-out session. No matter how attractive women thought TJ was, Tanner would always be it for me. We'd definitely been through our share of ups and downs, but it all proved worth it in the end. Tanner and I loved each other. We were happy together. My heart raced as he jogged back to the car and locked eyes with me, flashing me his heart-stopping grin.

"That boy loves you," Mallory said from the back seat.

"I love that boy."

"You should move in with him."

I sighed and leaned my head against the window. "I think I will."

The End

EPILOGUE

5 Years Later

Tanner

"Happy birthday to you. Happy birthday to you. Happy birthday, dear Khloe. Happy birthday to you!"

Khloe squeezed her eyes shut for several seconds before they popped open again. She blew out her candles and we all cheered.

"Your dad's cake looks great, baby." I squeezed Charlotte to my side.

"Only the best for Khloe."

"I can't believe she's ten." I shook my head. The wide-eyed, outspoken little girl had grown into ... well, a wide-eyed, outspoken ten-year old. "Where did the time go?"

Charlotte smiled up at me, tightening her grip around my waist. "Time does fly."

Merritt waddled over to where we were standing. "You guys having cake?"

"Yes, thank you." Charlotte took our plates from her. "How are you feeling?"

"Like I'm a volcano about to blow!" Merritt smiled, patting her protruding belly.

"Are we talking about her temper?" Chase asked with a wink.

Merritt swatted his arm. "I do not have a temper!"

Mom laughed as she cut another slice of cake. "She just compared herself to a volcano. Are you sure you want to tease her right now?"

Chase stood behind Merritt and wrapped his arms around her, splaying his fingers across her stomach. "Oh, I'm not teasing. I wouldn't be surprised if this baby rolls her eyes at the doctor when he pulls her out."

"Ew! Gross!" Khloe stuck her tongue out as her face twisted.

We all laughed, including Merritt. It felt good to see the two of them so happy. After everything Merritt had been through in her life, she deserved to have a happy family of her own.

I looked down at Charlotte, thinking about how incredible the past five years had been with her by my side. Coming home to her in our apartment at the end of every day was the best feeling. I could see our whole life together so clearly.

"What are you thinking about?"

I kissed Charlotte's temple and smiled. "How much I love you."

"Besides that. You've been acting weird all day. Tell me."

My stomach twisted with anticipation. "I don't know what you're talking about. Eat your cake."

Charlotte gave me the side-eye, and I grinned.

Time crept by. We ate our cake and watched Khloe open her presents. Then, it was finally time to leave. I drove as fast as I could without raising Charlotte's suspicion.

"I can't wait to get our comfy clothes on. Shall we Netflix and chill tonight?" Charlotte asked as we made our way up the stairs to our apartment.

My hand shook as I twisted the key in the lock. "Sure. There's just something I have to do first." I peeked inside before fully opening the door.

Mallory came through.

"What are you doing?" Charlotte nudged me gently.

"Just checking." I opened the door and walked inside.

"Checking for wha—" Charlotte's mouth dropped open as she stepped through the doorway.

I tugged on her arm until she was standing in the middle of the living room. Red and pink stemless Gerbera daisies were scattered all over the floor, LED candles strategically placed amongst them. I took Charlotte's hands in mine and turned her to face me.

"Since the moment you walked into my life, my heart has belonged to you. You've made me a better man. You've made my life better just by being in it. I love you more than words can say."

A tear rolled down Charlotte's cheek. "I love you, Tanner. What is all this?"

I cradled her precious face in my hands and pressed my forehead against hers. For just a moment, I closed my eyes. "I want to spend forever with you." Releasing her face, I dug the box out of my pocket and slowly dropped down on one knee.

Charlotte's hands flew to her mouth as she gasped.

I opened the box before her. "Charlotte, will you wash our clothes according to the instructions on the tag for the rest of our lives?"

More tears spilled as she giggled. "Yes!" She fell to her knees and kissed me sweetly.

"Yes?"

"Yes," she breathed.

Yes.

THE END

Want more of TJ? Read Book 4: Fighting the Odds

MORE FROM KRISTEN

The Collision Series Box Set with Bonus Epilogue
Collision: Book 1
Avoidance: Book 2, Sequel
The Other Brother: Book 3, Standalone
Fighting the Odds: Book 4, Standalone
Hating the Boss: Book 1, Standalone
Inevitable: Contemporary standalone
What's Left of Me: Contemporary standalone
Dear Santa: Holiday novella
Someone You Love: Contemporary standalone

Want to gain access to exclusive news & giveaways?
Sign up for my monthly newsletter!

Visit my website: https://kristengranata.com/
Instagram: https://www.instagram.com/kristen_granata/
Facebook: https://www.facebook.com/kristen.granata.16
Twitter: https://twitter.com/kristen_granata

Want to be part of my KREW?

Join Kristen's Reading Emotional Warriors
A Facebook group where we can discuss my books, books you're
reading, and where friends will remind you what a badass warrior
you are.

Love bookish shirts, mugs, & accessories?
Shop my <u>book merch shop</u>!

ACKNOWLEDGMENTS

First and foremost, I need to thank my wife. Babe, you've endured countless hours of book talk. You've listened to my obsessive rants. You've read every single review, scene, chapter, and book (more than once, because I re-write everything at least twelve times). You've stared at the back of a laptop while I sat on my stool typing for months. You put up with my Instagram obsession. You always have my back. If it weren't for you pushing me and inspiring me every day, I'd never have become an author in the first place. You're the love of my life and I want you next to me on this crazy journey. Also, I'm sorry, but you're going to have to deal with the fact that everyone else agrees that I'm hilarious, and you're going to have to continue listening to *The Greatest Showman* songs. Just love me.

To my editor, Jennifer Sommersby: You were worth the wait! Your edits were not only helpful, educational, and thorough, but they made me laugh. You were a pleasure to work with. Thank you for fitting me into your crazy schedule. I'm so glad you did!

To my cover designer, Taylor Danae Colbert: You tweaked and changed the cover every time I came up with a different idea. I annoyed myself, so I'm sure I annoyed you too. I am so happy with the outcome. It looks exactly like what I pictured in my mind. Thank you so much!

SJ Sylvis, thanks for sharing your cover friend with me & helping me out when I needed you. I love being on this crazy ride of self-publishing with you (and I'm so relieved you're just as clueless as me!) I hope you know I always have your back, and that I will continue to laugh about the fact that your daughter fell into a sewer.

Megan Luker, thank you for making my awesome logo and the gorgeous promo! You're so kind & generous, and you make me look like a professional. I'm so glad you took a chance on my indie books. I also feel I should point out that it's not fair you like my wife better than you like me. She doesn't send you pictures of cute puppies, and I had you first!

Mary Meredith, my country mouse, you have been my person from day one. Wherever I go on this journey, I'm taking you with me (hopefully, this journey will take us to shirtless casting calls for Chase, Tanner, and TJ!) Thank you for your constant guidance, your inspiring ideas, and for supporting my writing. This city mouse cannot wait to learn how you "make hay," because I didn't know that was even a thing until last year.

Becca Giuliano, you are my soul sister & my book dealer! You've introduced me to so many amazing books. My writing has grown a lot since my first book, and I have you and your awesome recommendations to thank for that. Also, thank you for telling me the ending of every book so I know it's safe to read! #tacos4life

Andrea Hopkins, girl, you always know exactly what to say when I need a pep talk. You are inspiring & motivating & I'm so glad to have you on my team. Can't wait to sip champagne on our private jet!

Melanie Smith, I look at you like the big sister of all indie authors. Your support not only helps us grow, but brings us together. I can't thank you enough for that. You gave me a home with the coolest Indies.

Luz Acevedo, thank you so much for your constant support and for always trying to spread the word about my books. You are the most badass warrior I know, and you inspire me every single day with your strength. I'm lucky to call you my friend.

Lastly, I need to thank all my friends out there in the #booksta-gram community. Your support, encouragement, kindness, and amazing reviews are what helped push me to write Tanner's story. Being a self-published author is hard, to put it lightly. There were days writing this when I felt so discouraged, and so full of self-doubt. There were questions I needed answers to (because, let's face it, I just don't know what the hell I'm doing most of the time). And there were times I needed inspiration. The reading and writing communities I've become a part of on this journey have allowed me to meet some of the most inspiring, friendly, awkward, and downright hilarious people. I hope you all know how much I appreciate every single like, comment, message, meme, interview and promotion.

Printed in Great Britain
by Amazon

84449917R00139